RISKING HOPE

CASEY DIAM

Risking Hope
Danger and Attraction, Book 2
Copyright © 2018 by Casey Diam

All rights reserved. No part of this publication may be reproduced, distributed, or transmitted in any form or by any means, including photocopying, recording, or other electronic or mechanical methods, without the prior written permission of the author, except in the case of brief quotations embodied in critical reviews and certain other noncommercial uses permitted by copyright law. For permission requests, please contact diamcasey@gmail.com. Thank you for supporting writers and respecting the hard work of this author.

This is a work of fiction. Names, characters, places, and incidents either are the products of the author's imagination or are used fictitiously. Any resemblance to actual persons, living or dead, businesses, companies, events, or locales is entirely coincidental.

Copyeditor: Jovana Shirley, Unforseenediting
Cover Design: Nalja Qamber Designs
Proofreading: AW Editing, The Passionate Proofreader
Paperback ISBN: 978-1-954715-01-1
www.caseydiam.com

"Hope is being able to see that there is light despite all of the darkness."
Desmond Tutu

ONE

Paige

As Caleb pulled to a stop at the curb, I hurried to his familiar, sleek black two-door car. It still had its brand-new car smell. The familiarity should comfort me, but the car was another accessory provided to him by his father.

That made me wonder what he really did for his father.

I settled into the seat and drew the seatbelt over my chest, stopping short when a quiet anger bled through the calmness of his voice.

"This is where you ended up? I have to wonder sometimes. Are you purposefully putting yourself in these situations? Do you have to work at a bar until three fucking a.m., a gym until midnight, and run off on your own, only to end up in the worst fucking neighborhood in the city? Really, Paige!"

Something was changing. I wasn't used to him reacting this way, but it didn't stop the sarcasm waiting at the tip of my tongue. "Oh, yeah. Please tell your brother and your freaking father how much I looked forward to them coming to my house when I was fifteen and killing everyone I'd ever loved. How thrilled I am that they're *still* threatening my life or trying to kidnap me. That *is* what they wanted to do tonight, wasn't it? They were trying to take me. It was why there was a car waiting. They were planning to kidnap me, weren't they?"

"I don't know what their plan was."

"Well, maybe you should stop worrying what I do and focus on why you don't know anything or why you're so scared of your brother. You were hiding from him tonight, weren't you?" A blob swelled in my throat. "When they attacked me, I saw you; you were coming, and then you were gone."

"Rob was there; you didn't need me."

He was wrong. I had needed him, not anyone else.

I peered through my window and felt a hot tear slide down my cheek. A hand touched my arm, but I shrugged it off, curling into the door.

After a few minutes, Caleb said, "You didn't want me to kill that guy, and it's the same reason I didn't come to you. I can't let them figure out that I know you, Paige. Not yet. If Rob hadn't been there or if it seemed like you needed my help, I would've"—he drew in a breath and sighed—"I would've come to you."

He turned up the alternative music station that'd been playing softly in the background, and I continued to lean against the car door, remembering how a much similar one had almost cracked my skull open a few weeks ago. His brother had been aiming to hurt me that time, yet I was still here. Caleb was still by my side. I turned my head, and as I glanced at him, I caught his eyes on me. He'd been watching me. His eyes moved back to the road, and I folded my salty, wet lips between my teeth.

When I came out of the bathroom in my usual tights and tank top, Caleb was sitting on the couch, his eyes on the screen of his phone. I walked into the kitchen and saw a cup of chamomile tea steeping on top of the wooden kitchen island. The muscles in my stomach tightened. Caleb wasn't a tea person, but he knew I was. The coldness inside me thawed before I touched the cup. This was the Caleb I knew, the one who could read my emotions and react in a way that made me want to tread closer, not further away. After removing the small plastic cap blocking the steam from escaping, I lifted the cup and walked toward the leather couch with caution.

He was right. This studio apartment was too small for the three of us—Caleb, me, and the tension between us.

"Would you prefer the bed or the couch tonight?" he asked.

Most nights, I slept on the couch because I was smaller and this was his place, not mine. I would sleep on the couch every night if he didn't insist otherwise.

"The couch is fine."

"I want to introduce you to the guys tomorrow. You know Calvin, and you saw Rob, but there are two more who have been keeping their eyes on you. I should've told you, but I just figured it would be okay as long as you were safe when you weren't with me."

I reached for the breakfast tray at the center of the large ottoman, pulling it toward me so that I could set the hot cup on top of it before pulling my knees to my chest and hugging my legs. "I want to say I would have been okay with it if you had told me before. Hey, I want to say I'm okay with it now, especially after tonight, but they can't possibly be playing my security guards for free."

"Don't worry about it. It's the least I can do. We'll talk tomorrow. Getting all worked up while you drink your tea will only defeat the purpose of the tea." A smile tugged at the corner of his mouth. "I just didn't want you to go to bed without knowing that I'm looking out for you."

"Thank you." I hadn't done anything to deserve his kindness.

Combing a hand through his tousled black hair, he stood.

I couldn't help but admire his long, lean, and powerful physique, which obscured the previous tension in the air and created an entirely different kind. My skin warmed, and all of a sudden, I was parched. After what'd been discovered tonight with Alex Connor possibly being Caleb's dad, Bailey's confirmation of Caleb being Olivia Sawyer's son, and my knowing Carrie and Peter Wells were my real parents, not Leanne and David Sawyer, our worst fear of being related was far from possible and never to be uttered again. My parents were killed, the real ones and the ones who raised me. The only thing we didn't know was why it happened. How did all these pieces fit together? And why was I taken?

My eyes never drifted from Caleb's as I got lost in my thoughts. I should be mad at him for the way he'd acted earlier and also for leaving me to fight for myself. Instead, I was gazing at him and wondering where we would go from here.

CALEB

The last time I'd checked my phone, it was sometime after four in the morning. I couldn't sleep, and since my usual wake-up time was around six in the morning, I knew I wouldn't be getting any sleep tonight. All I could focus on was how close I'd come to losing Paige and how Alex Connor was potentially my real father, not my adopted father as he'd claimed for my whole life.

As I listened to the quietness in the studio apartment, I could hear a pin drop, but that wasn't what I heard. It was Paige and her breathing growing heavier. I waited a few seconds before switching on the bedside lamp and then another few seconds before getting out of the bed.

I walked over to the edge of the ottoman and sat in front of the sofa, watching her in the dim light, wrapped in a white down comforter, still asleep, still beautiful, but her breathing was labored. I considered waking her, as it could be one of her nightmares, but before I could go through with it, she awoke.

She gasped as she saw me and sat up, the comforter falling to her waist and her hand moving to press against her chest.

"What's wrong?" I asked.

She shook her head and started to get up.

I stopped her. "Hey, what's the matter? Was it a nightmare?"

A sniffle left her. "I'm okay."

She acted so strong and invincible sometimes that I forgot just how delicate she could be.

My hands moved to her shoulders. "Paige, what's going on?"

"My heart."

"What?"

"It's nothing."

"It isn't nothing." One of my hands moved to the left side of her chest, over the soft curve of her breast, and before my mind could register the intimacy of my touch, the hotness of her skin and the rapid pulsation of her heartbeat spread through my palm and radiated into my own chest.

"Shower," she murmured.

Confused, I cocked my head, and then it hit me. For the past two weeks, I'd been wondering why I sometimes woke in the middle of the night to the sound of the shower running. This would explain that. I stood and led her to the bathroom, and then stepped aside so she had room to move around.

She stepped into the tub with her clothes on and turned the knob, flinching as the cold water hit her.

What the fuck is she doing?

Her arms folded across her chest as she shivered. I leaned on the bathroom vanity and watched her for a few minutes, and when she turned her head to me, my heart split in two. Because, right here, at this moment, she was making herself completely vulnerable to me.

Closing my eyes, I scrubbed a hand across my forehead and went to the closet where I grabbed one of my clean T-shirts. I returned in time to see her stepping from the tub to the mat. With her blonde hair knotted on top of her head, only the edges framing her face had gotten wet. My eyes lowered to the now-transparent white tank top sticking to her skin and the taut nipples beneath. I pulled my gaze away before I needed a cold shower myself. Setting the clean T-shirt on the counter, I removed the additional towel folded under the sink since hers was most likely still damp from earlier.

I wrapped it around her and pulled her to me, kissing the spot above her temple that had been injured in my car not long ago. She pressed her head to my bare chest, and something about having her like this centered me.

"Get changed and come lie down with me. We need to talk," I told her.

This was me being strong and in control. She was tough enough by herself, but she'd been doing it alone for too long. So I needed to be impervious to this shit—everything that was unraveling around us—for her. I didn't know how it'd happened so fast, but she was right; she'd become like family, too. Calvin and her, whether related by blood or not, they were my family, and I'd do anything to keep them safe.

When she slid under the covers next to me, I leaned up on my elbow, and she curled onto her side, facing me.

Her eyes lowered to my chest, and after a moment, she muttered, "Anxiety."

That was what I figured it was the first time I'd seen her have an attack on the sidewalk. "How long has it been going on?"

She sighed and looked up at me, blue eyes weary. "A long time. I had it under control for a while, but with everything going on, it reminds me too much of the past, and I-I was stupid."

"What do you mean?"

"I manipulated my therapist into believing I was okay by not really dealing with what had happened back then. Now that I'm being forced to deal with it, all my symptoms are coming back stronger."

"I'm guessing you're not seeing a therapist now, but shouldn't you be on some kind of medication?"

She shook her head and closed her eyes. "I'm not."

"Why not?"

"I can't."

"Why?"

She denied my invitation to talk with a slight jerk of her head again.

"Paige, please."

She chewed on her lip, and I was reminded of how they always tasted like her bubblegum lip balm. My tongue slid over my lips, and I could almost taste her on them.

Her lips moved, and I had to drag my eyes away, refocusing them on the tiny silver hoop piercing the innermost part of her ear.

"I can't afford it, and I hate pills. They made me numb to what I should feel."

I swallowed. She should still be living in a mansion, driving a fancy car, and going to some prestigious college. Instead, she was here with the son of the man who had done this to her because she had nowhere else to go.

"I'll take you. I'll pay for it."

"No—"

"Don't fight this, Paige." I smoothed a thumb over her cheek. "Let me do this for you."

"You've already done so much."

Her eyes found mine, and I watched as her pupils dilated until most of the blue was gone.

I'm mesmerized by it every time it happens.

Blood traveled down my body, infiltrating the thick root of desire I'd buried two weeks ago, and a muscle moved in my jaw. I shouldn't feel like this. Not after what we'd been through. What made it worse was that I could still see the same want burning in the depths of her own eyes. And, though we could both use a distraction, the guilt of last week's experience ... wondering if we'd crossed a line we didn't know existed, leveled my awakening.

I dropped my hand from her cheek. "It doesn't matter. You can't go on like this. I'm surprised your body hasn't shut down from all the lack of sleep and the energy you must expend trying to hide it from everyone alone."

She remained quiet.

"The condo should be ready next week. Move in with Calvin and me. You'll be safe there."

She shook her head, ready to protest, but I hushed her. Resting my hand on her shoulder, I started a slow caress before the invincible Paige could surface.

"Hear me out. If we have any hope of finding out what happened to you and your family, I need you to get better at dealing with what happened. If you feel safe, you're more likely to sleep through the night, right?"

She gave me a barely there nod, so I kept going. "I know you don't want to, but I think you should quit the gym, too." Her perfect lips parted, and I stopped her before she could voice the protest I knew was coming. "Quitting the gym means they'll lose the trail, giving you time to deal. If they can't find you, they'll think you've disappeared again, and by the time they figure out you're still here, we'll have a plan to take them down for good."

"He's your dad."

"I know." I didn't know—*yet*.

A small part of me hoped it wasn't true. But one of Alex Connor's puppets, Tom—also known as Tee—had given me this information in exchange for his life, and since then, a thousand different things had been racing through my mind. Things that didn't add up. Like Alex Connor not giving a shit about me. Still, I would need to confront him about everything, even knowing there could be repercussions, and this time, I had no idea what they would be. That meant I needed to keep Paige out of it. It was the only way to guarantee her safety.

Her eyes closed and her voice softened. "I'll move in with you guys, but I'm not quitting my job . . . I'll talk to my manager about taking a leave of absence. It could be our way of luring them back in when we're ready."

"Sounds good. We'll wait until it's the right time." Too bad I was already thinking of ways to keep her out of it.

I could tell my "father" I knew everything, but that would be like handing him a bullet from my own gun. A bullet that he'd load into his own weapon before aiming the gun in my direction and pulling the trigger. I needed to be smarter, two steps ahead.

"Just so you know, my room will be right across from yours. I'll leave my door unlocked so that if you have a nightmare or need anything, you can come to me."

"Caleb, do you think we'll . . ."

My eyes traveled to her now-flushed cheeks and then to her lower lip being sucked into her mouth as she nibbled on it. The impending question breathed life into my own selfish needs. She was back to her shy, pre-sex allure, and I knew exactly where her mind was. It made my cock twitch in anticipation.

Stopping her before she could finish and we ended up doing something we would both regret, I whispered, "Try to get some sleep. We'll talk more tomorrow."

But I was hoping we wouldn't—at least, not about us. It was still too soon, and not only that, but in the past, she'd slept so much better after sex, which made me think I might have been helping to shadow what she needed to face.

I lay awake until about six in the morning, and while I was in the kitchen making coffee, Paige awoke and went straight to the couch. Turning on the television, she snuggled into the comforter left there from last night.

I smiled when a groggy, "Morning," came from her, but my smile quickly faded when my eyes moved to the television screen and saw *her*.

The brunette I'd buried three weeks ago.

Sophia Cruz.

My chest constricted as I held on to the counter.

I didn't want to know her name, but straightway, I knew I wouldn't forget it.

THREE

Paige

"Twenty-year-old Sophia Cruz has been missing for three weeks. She was last seen at Octave nightclub with two of her friends. Anyone with information, please call..."

"Turn it off," Caleb snapped.

My attention was so drawn to the image of the young girl on the television screen that my thumb pressed the triangular up button for the volume instead of the power. I wanted to hear what could have been my fate last night. A second later, the remote was ripped from my hand, and the television went off.

"What?" I turned to see Caleb tossing the remote onto the ottoman.

"Do me a favor and keep the news off while I'm around."

"I was watching it."

"Yeah, well, don't. You should be searching for doctors online. We're on a timeline."

My eyebrows pinched together, and I frowned as he left and locked himself in the bathroom.

Why is he all pissy this morning?

A soft knock came from the front door, and realizing I was still wearing Caleb's T-shirt, I headed into the closet and changed into a pair of jeans and one of my own shirts. Checking the peephole, I opened the door to a very awake Calvin standing in the hallway, dressed in a T-shirt and jeans, his warm, golden skin glowing like his everlasting smile.

"Well, good morning. I figured you would still be sleeping," he said, walking inside and kicking off his shoes.

"I'm awake now, and I think your best friend is PMSing or something." I gathered the comforter and carried it to the unmade bed.

"Definitely sounds like him." Calvin laughed, plopping down onto the couch. "Did you give him a tampon?"

I grinned. I liked Calvin, and for a big, muscular dude who looked as if he'd be nothing but a mean grump, he was actually kind of silly.

"Are the rest of the guys like you?"

"What do you mean?"

"My other secret bodyguards. Are they like you?"

"I wish I could say yes, but I'm kind of awesome, you see. So, no, sorry. But, look at it this way, you get to like me the most, which is good because guess who's babysitting today?"

I rolled my eyes. "I'm not a baby. I can take care of myself." I brought my phone to the couch and coiled into a ball in the opposite corner of him, leaning my head onto the arm.

"So I heard. I'm sorry that I wasn't there for you last night, by the way. I was with my sister. She's coming of age and all, and I had to make sure she wasn't doing anything she shouldn't. But are you okay?"

"Yeah," I said.

The bathroom door unlocked, and I tried not to move or seem too interested, but it was no use. The scent of Caleb's body wash spread into the rest of the apartment and right up my nose. My throat dried as I imagined a towel wrapped around his slim waist, water trickling down his skin and over the V I used to trace with the tips of my fingers. I nibbled on my bottom lip. That seemed like so long ago.

"Paige?" Calvin said, probably noticing how distracted I was.

"Yeah?"

"What are we doing today?"

"Uh, I have to go talk to my manager at the gym." I frowned. "I usually would work out, too . . ."

Where am I going to work out now?

"Calvin to the rescue because it's what I do." He raised a leg and propped a foot up on the ottoman. "Come work out with me at my gym. I could get you a guest pass for a week. After that, our condo in Quincy will have a gym."

I sucked in a breath through my teeth and stared at him. "That's right. Caleb mentioned that. Are you ready for a female roommate?"

"Depends. Will you judge me if a different female walks in and out of my room every week—or day, if I'm so lucky?"

I scrunched my nose. "You're *that* guy."

"Hmm . . . maybe."

I grinned. I never thought I would be excited about living with Caleb and his best friend, but Calvin made me feel welcome, and it was exactly what I needed. People. Friends. A sense of normalcy. "I won't judge you. I like you, remember?"

"Aw." His mouth pulled into a lopsided grin before his eyes shifted to the side. "Good choice on the roomie, dude. We're already besties."

I rolled back and tried to peer over the back of the couch, but my eyes could only see Caleb from his pelvis up. He was in a three-piece suit, hair still damp, and the look in his eyes would have made the ruler of a kingdom bow before him. This wasn't the Caleb I knew. This was the lethal version of the Caleb I'd only seen glimpses of beneath the surface. Discomfort threw me as he glowered at Calvin a second longer.

Sitting up straight, I frowned. "Don't get pissed off at him, too."

His mood might have been from his lack of sleep last night, but I'd never known him to behave this way after a sleepless night. We'd been creatures of the night since we met.

He stalked toward the door without a glance my way.

"Don't worry about it." Calvin grinned. "He still loves me."

The front door slammed shut, and I looked at Calvin while fighting the smile stretching across my pursed lips.

"Are you sure about that? Because I think he was trying to stab or kill you with his eyes."

Caleb had almost killed someone last night. It made me wonder if he had killed someone before.

My eyes remained on the closed door.

"Hey." Calvin's voice jarred me from my thoughts. "He's okay."

"Is he?" I asked. "Because I suddenly feel like I don't know him at all."

"Do you want my advice?" He didn't wait for my response. "Don't try to figure him out."

I squinted, and he smiled.

"Take for example, what do *you* do when people try to figure you out?"

I pushed them away or led them off course. I chewed on my lip. This mindset was no way to head back into therapy.

"So, you have a point." I got up. "Let's go to the gym."

"I have to tell you that I'm kind of a beast, so plan on being there for a while." He smirked.

The gym was bigger than the one I worked at on the other side of town, and it was filled with morning people. I called this time of the day my morning buzz because this was the motivating crowd, and I could go for hours when I was in the gym with them.

"Jesus, woman, how much longer?" Calvin whined.

"What happened to the beast?" I joked.

"Ha, very funny, but he was busy lifting five times as much as you."

"Oh, sure, that was what you were doing," I badgered, but I was sure that was exactly what he'd been doing.

Calvin's muscle mass screamed, "*I might or might not be on steroids."*

I was totally going to toss his medicine cabinet when we became roommates to make sure it was the latter.

I hooked the bar resting on my shoulder on the stand and stepped away. With all my muscles coiled tight, I felt like I could be one of those blue people in *Avatar*. Strong, renewed, and light on my feet. I loved this feeling.

Calvin's head turned to the side, and I followed his gaze to the redhead sauntering toward us, her gaze locked on me.

Sergeant Bailey.

I swallowed.

"Madelyn," she greeted, a bright smile on her face, and then she realized her mistake. "I mean, Paige. Sorry about that. Photographic memory. I didn't know you worked out here."

"Uh, yeah, just for now, with this guy," I said, pointing my thumb to Calvin.

She looked even more petite out of her uniform, and her freckled skin was glowing from sweat. She looked at Calvin for a second too long, and I frowned.

Do they know each other?

"Hey, I'm Calvin. Nice to meet you." He held out his hand, giving her what I was guessing was his I'm-taking-you-home-tonight smile.

She was hot, so I didn't blame him, but she was also the only cop I trusted to help me put an end to Alex Connor.

My eyes narrowed as Sergeant Bailey flushed, her hand still in Calvin's.

"Um, so . . ." I turned my attention to Calvin, "Hands off. She's taken." More like married to an FBI agent, but I wasn't going to be the one to put that out there with the way she'd been looking at Calvin. "Excuse him. He's kind of full of himself. So, this is your gym spot?"

She cleared her throat, and her head bobbed. "Yes." She wanted to say more but didn't seem too sure of herself. Maybe because she didn't know if Calvin knew about what was going on.

But there was nothing that needed to be said right now, except for what'd been bothering me.

"Do I need to worry about Agent Langley interfering or pushing anything right now?" I didn't trust him even if he was her husband. He'd given me the you-are-crazy eyes, and I wouldn't forget it.

"No. I know you need to go at your own pace, and I told him that. He shouldn't be a problem for you."

"Okay, well, I'll see you around." I turned to go and then I paused. "You shouldn't trust Rodriguez."

Her eyebrows drew together. "My deputy superintendent?"

I nodded.

Bailey's boss had been dabbling with the enemy, and it was better she knew in case things got ugly. Plus, if she was going to help me, she needed to start processing whom she'd be up against because, when I was ready, she needed to be ready, too.

CALEB

My eyes landed on Calvin, who was sitting at our usual corner booth inside the underground bar with Rob, Luke, and Ryan—the three other guys who'd been keeping an eye on Paige. I liked knowing she was protected, but I hated how close she might get to these guys, my best friend included. The image of them flirting on the couch this morning was imprinted in my mind, and I hated him for that. As my best friend, it was a dick move. It didn't matter if Paige and I weren't together. She wasn't some new toy any of them would get to play with if I had anything to do with it.

Giving a solemn nod to the guys, I allowed Paige to sit first, and then I slid in next to her.

"I placed our order," Calvin remarked before his eyes shifted to Paige, and he grinned. "Lemonade, right?"

What the . . .

"Yes. Thank you," Paige replied.

"Everything good, man?" Calvin asked.

I gritted my teeth and stretched my lips into what I hoped wasn't a sneer. "Yeah."

Paige was already talking to Rob, who was sitting next to her. I didn't know as much about the guys as Calvin did. All four of them had a history together in the military, and Calvin trusted them. So, even though I disliked all his flirting with Paige, his trust for these guys was enough for me to trust them to keep her safe.

Since she was moving in with Calvin and me, I might not need all of them.

But who was I kidding? I probably needed a few more guys. This was Paige I was protecting, after all. One minute she was hot, and then the next minute, she was cold. One minute up, and then the next minute down. Her emotions were so intense that it was best to be prepared for anything. Plus, having someone around at all times satisfied me more than the thought of her having to fend for herself ever again.

Calvin dropped a hand on Ryan's shoulder. "Paige, this is Ryan. Don't fall for his pretty-boy act. He's a turd."

Next, he pointed at the fully bearded man, who was sporting a man bun and full sleeves of tattoos down his arms.

Before Calvin made the introduction, Ryan spoke up, "That's Luke. He acts all tough, but he's nothing to be scared of. He's a softy. *Real* softy. Makes me wonder what he's doing here."

Luke narrowed his eyes at Ryan.

Calvin slid his arm around Ryan's shoulders while he pointed at Rob. "Don't expect much out of him."

"He doesn't like people," Ryan divulged. "Dude barely likes us, and we've spent years together, blowing up shit."

"Don't talk about Rob like he isn't here," Calvin goaded. "Just because he's a loner, it doesn't mean we don't still love him."

"Well, this is fun," Paige said without humor.

It might take them some time to get used to her frankness.

I chuckled, and it was a relief after reliving the constant flash of that girl's face from the news in my head all day.

"I thought you said she was nice," Ryan said to Calvin, loud enough for the rest of us to hear.

"She is. Just think of her as another one of our troubled kids," Calvin responded.

"She isn't troubled," Paige said, referring to herself in the third person, which wasn't helping.

I spoke for her, "She'd rather you not talk shit about the guy who saved her life."

She looked at me as if she couldn't believe I understood, but why wouldn't I? I'd seen her. She put on a show for everyone, even tried to do it with me, but when all was said and done, I was the one she'd crumbled on.

Her eyes remained on me, trying to find the guy she had given herself to a few weeks ago, but I couldn't let her find him in my eyes. He was all kinds of fucked up at the moment, thinking about how, in two weeks, he would find out if his adopted father was his real father, if Brad was his real brother, and if his mother—shit. It didn't matter if Alex Connor had killed her himself. I needed to know what had happened to her. So, yeah, that guy Paige was looking for wasn't in there. He was changing—and not for the better. But Paige, she was still good, and if she was going to heal, she needed good. I wasn't good.

A corner of her lips twitched in an attempt to smile, but it didn't quite make it. She looked back to the guys. "Rob's awesome."

"Thank you," Rob said, smirking at Ryan and Calvin.

The waitress arrived, interrupting the guys, who still didn't quite know how to address Paige without pissing me off. I knew they were dying to make a crack, but they seemed to reconsider when they met my serious expression.

Paige left the booth for the restroom after the waitress set down a tray with four plastic baskets, each containing a burger and fries. After handing a basket to each of the four of the guys, she told us she would return with the rest of our meals and refills for our drinks. By the time I looked in the direction Paige had gone, she was almost to the back hallway leading to the restrooms. As she passed the last table, someone stood, blocking her path.

Miller. Right away I wanted to strangle him for approaching her. He hung out with Amber and Lisa at parties I'd once attended on a regular basis, but he fucked any and everything. Paige wasn't one of the girls he could talk into having a quick fuck in the restroom. And it pissed me off that she stood there, talking to him with no idea who this guy was.

"Miller is bad news," I told her when she got back to the table.

"Okay. So?" She shrugged, sliding into the booth.

I broke it down for her. "*So*, he's trying to get into your pants."

"Uh, no, he isn't. He was just asking me about the fall semester." She sucked on the straw leaning against the rim of her glass of lemonade.

"Caleb's right," Calvin advised, and I silently thanked him. "Miller cheated on his girlfriend and has slept with more than half the girls who come here."

She stuck a fry into her mouth, chewed, and swallowed before offering, "I don't care. Why are you two acting like you haven't done the same? Besides, it isn't as if I'm planning on sleeping with him." She shook her index finger. "And, shame, shame, we're at the *no judgment* table."

"I think I like this table. What's this *no judgment* business about?" Ryan asked.

"You can sleep with anyone, no judgment," Paige explained, giving Calvin and me a pointed look like she would fucking dare participate in this *no judgment* shit, but I held my tongue.

"Fuck, I really like this table." Ryan rubbed his palms together. "Count me in."

Paige looked around the table. "Have you guys met Amber and Lisa?"

Luke, Rob, and Ryan nodded, but it was Ryan who felt the need to clarify. "Oh, we've met." With a lopsided grin on his face, his eyebrows jerked. "Soooo met."

"You can shut the fuck up now," Calvin said, defending our other friends' honor, but I had an inkling his outburst was more about Amber.

After a few beers, the tension loosened in my body, and Paige and I took the metro home, leaving the guys behind to mingle with the crowd I was already familiar with.

As I twisted the key in the lock at our apartment, Paige tugged on the hem of my T-shirt and asked, "What's going on with you?"

"Nothing. Why?"

"You seem different."

"Yeah?"

"Yep."

"After you ran off that night, Tom told me that Alex Connor goes to the lab for a cholesterol checkup twice a year, and his next appointment is in a few days. So, I'll have to bribe a nurse to take an extra tube of his blood for a paternity test." Something true but off track to what was really bothering me. If I wanted to talk to her about it, I knew she would understand, but I couldn't talk about it, not yet.

"How are you planning to bribe her?"

I closed the door behind us and removed my shoes at the door. "Honestly, I'm just hoping she likes my smile and takes pity on me."

And a ton of pity, because if she decided to help me with Connor, I would need her to help me with Brad as well. I had to know if he was really my brother. And, at this point, it would be stupid to go to the cops asking for favors without any proof of Alex Connor's wrong doings.

"I would wish you all the luck, but you won't need it. That smile had me taking off my underwear in days."

"If I remember correctly, you weren't the one taking them off," I teased, my eyes meeting the blatant desire in hers, and I knew I shouldn't have done that. I shouldn't have reminded her about the us from before if I wasn't planning to follow through on it, but it was as if I couldn't fucking help it. "You should date someone."

What the fuck? What the fuck did I just say?

"What?"

"Nothing," I said, but it was too late.

"Um . . . okay." She turned and headed to the bedroom.

And fuck me . . . literally because I'm so fucking horny, and I want her. I fucking need her.

"I didn't mean that," I said, following her as she walked into the small closet.

"It's clear you aren't interested in me anymore. It's fine. I've seen it. I've been seeing it for days. You don't need to pretend or console me, Caleb. We're adults, and I knew what I was getting myself into when I slept with you. It's no big deal."

She was lying. It was a big fucking deal.

"I just . . ." I started but stopped, two seconds shy of charming her because I was fucking horny and needed a release, but that was the wrong answer. This was Paige, and she was special to me. "There are things that need to be resolved, and we'll just be a distraction to each other." Even my reasoning sounded like the sorry excuse it was, because I was *so* fucking interested in her.

"As I said, you don't have to console me."

For fuck's sake.

Her defiance only tugged on my willpower, persuading me into the direction I didn't want to go.

The blood drained from my head and settled into the one closer to gravity that required less thinking. Turning around, I marched to the bathroom and flicked on the shower, needing to shock away the constricted heaviness inside my briefs before it ended up deep inside her.

For years, sex had been my go-to. The only thing that kept me sane. It was a hobby—a *fucking* hobby. If Alex Connor had me do some stupid shit I didn't want to do, if he punished me, if I had a bad day, sex was always the answer. And Paige, she didn't know that guy. I looked in the mirror.

And, right now, this guy.

I peeled my shirt off and tossed it on the floor and then unbuckled my pants, throwing it and everything to the side until I was naked from head to toe.

As I walked to the tub, I caught sight of my raging hard-on and paused. Wrapping a fist around it, I squeezed and then glanced at the closed door.

When was the last time I even masturbated?

I worked my palm over my cock in light strokes as I walked to the vanity, where I had a bottle of lotion. Squirting some into my hand, I switched on the shower and stepped under the spray, hoping that, one day, I could get back to a place where I could slide in and out of the girl on the other side of this door.

A few minutes later, I lay on the couch and started to watch the old footage from the surveillance cam I'd placed in Alex Connor's office. Not Dad. Never Dad. My boss's office. It was going to take me some time before I could figure out which of his other men had access to the vault beneath his office. And, since I'd already removed the camera, not wanting to risk it being found, I hoped what I needed to get in there was on these feeds because it might be the answer to all my questions.

When my eyes grew tired, I walked over and stood by the bed where Paige lay. The building lights outside the window cast a subtle beam over her. She was on her stomach, and judging from her soft, steady breaths, she was asleep.

I kept my mind from drifting back to the previous night because I knew the chunk of stone in Brad's chest well enough not to wonder what he would have done to Paige had he succeeded in snatching her from the streets. They'd wanted to kill her, but if he was trying to capture her, something had changed, and that just made everything so much worse. If only I could lock her inside until all this shit got resolved, but I knew what it felt like to be locked inside, to be a prisoner in one's own house, and because of that, I could never make her feel trapped.

As Alex Connor's very own trained predator, I lay next to her without so much as a dip in the bed, and then I persisted to reason what I couldn't before.

"We're both damaged, and for that reason, we can't fix each other. Right now, I can only try to help you get better and hope what I do from here on out will be the right thing. You were right before, by the way, when you said I was scared, but you don't know half the shit I've done, half the shit I've been through, that Connor and his men have put me through, and if you did, I'd bet you wouldn't be able to stand the sight of me. I can barely stand the sight of myself sometimes, and I see the way you look at me now." I bit my lip, picturing her round blue eyes glinting with disappointment the night she'd watched me almost pull the trigger on Tom.

"The way you look at me has already changed because you're starting to see the other side of me. I'm sorry I called you out for talking to Miller when I'm so much worse. I might not be a cheater, but still, I'm worse, and that is why I have to fight everything in me that's pushing me toward you. You deserve much more than Alex Connor's son. You deserve everything, Paige, and I can't give you that."

I wish I could.

I shifted slowly and leaned forward to press a soft kiss on her cheek that wouldn't wake her, and how contradicting because all I wanted was for her to feel every fucking part of me.

Paige

"How are you today?" the psychiatrist asked, her British accent more prominent than it had seemed when I had scheduled my appointment over the phone.

She looked about forty-something, and her chestnut hair was scooped into a clip at the back of her head. Her face held a touch of makeup, but there was a natural glow about her.

Caleb had recommended her to me, and I'd decided it would be simpler than trying to find one for myself. It was even better since she could fit me in on such short notice.

She leaned back in a chair to my right, and her positioning threw me off. My previous therapist always sat behind a desk.

So, even several feet away from me, and it felt like she was in my personal space. "I'm fine," I managed, still shifting and fidgeting.

"Would you prefer I sat behind the desk? I don't want this to be so formal that I sit and write down unnecessary information every few seconds. There isn't a right or wrong way for me to help you, but I do want you to be as comfortable as possible. If anything is bothersome, please tell me. I'm here for you, so if I'm staring at you too long, please say, 'Marian, look away. I can't. I just need a break.' Whatever you need."

"Thank you." I had been planning to force myself to do this because I knew I needed to, but I already liked Marian. "Where you're sitting is fine," I answered. "And I guess I'm feeling okay."

"What do you do for a living?"

It was a nice, non-threatening question. I had expected that, and it put me at ease a little.

"I work in a bar some nights as a barback, and I also work at a gym."

"And you're in college?"

"Yes."

"What are you studying?"

"I've just finished my second year, so I've only been taking the general education requirements. I have *no* idea what I want to major in."

"On a scale of one to ten with one being the least, how satisfied are you with the way you live your life right now?"

Wow, that's a jump.

I paused, thinking her question over. "If you'd asked me that question about a month ago, I would have said three. Now, I think it's a six."

"And what's changed that for you?"

I threaded my fingers together. "A guy. Sad but true."

"What is his name?" Marian asked, crossing her legs and adjusting the way her forearms rested on the armrest.

"Caleb."

"And you've known him for a month?"

"Yes," I confirmed. "But it's different with us. With him."

"How so?"

"He knows things about me. Things that people who've known me for years still don't know. I have basic work connections, but it never goes beyond that. I always feel the need to hide"—*the demons inside*, a voice whispered in my head—"the effects of what happened five years ago. I guess, in a way, I feel like I'm protecting them."

"Protecting them from what?"

"From everything that incapacitates me. From a problem that

isn't theirs to bear."

"But it's different with Caleb?"

I nodded. "He saw right through me from the start. Before him, I hadn't felt comfortable enough to have the kind of friendship I have with him with anyone else. He makes me feel like I'm not alone. Recently, he's been introducing me to his friends, and it's strange, but I feel comfortable with them. I still don't understand why."

"When we keep people out for a while, it makes it harder to let anyone in, but once we let someone in and see they can be trusted, it becomes that much easier to let someone else in, especially if it's someone your friend also deems to be trustworthy."

That made sense. Caleb trusted those guys to look out for me when he couldn't. There was no way I would feel comfortable around them otherwise.

"Five years ago, you were diagnosed with PTSD and anxiety disorder, and you received treatment for three years but stopped when you turned eighteen. Do you believe those treatments helped you?"

I shook my head. "I was still in denial."

"That's understandable. Is that the reason you discontinued treatment?"

"My treatments were being paid for by the parents of the people who'd allegedly kidnapped me. I thought the treatments were the reason they'd removed me from the ward and placed me in a community home, so I went along with it until I was eighteen. After that, I was kind of okay for a while because I'd stopped thinking about the past, and by the time I realized how much worse I was getting, I didn't have the money to get help. I self-treated by staying away from the things that triggered it. Alcohol. Caffeine. My memories. Only everything changed this last month, and I can't control it like I used to."

"This past month? The same time you met Caleb?"

"Yes." I nodded. "Even though we didn't know it at the time, it appears that our lives have been tangled in ways we are still trying to figure out, and this means I've had to think a lot more about the past. I even went back to the mansion, and as brief as it was, I couldn't handle it."

I didn't want to discuss my most recent days; it was complicated and unresolved, but it was all Marian had me talk about in my first session. She also made some other suggestions on how I could naturally improve my psychological state, which I was all for. I hated pharmaceuticals, but when she wrote me a few prescriptions, I slipped them into my jeans pocket just in case I needed them.

"How was that?" Calvin asked as I got into his cigarette smoke–infused car.

"Not too bad, I guess. I just feel raw and disgusted."

"Yeah? Don't like spilling your guts?" he taunted.

Leaning my head on the headrest, I sighed. "Nope."

"How about hanging with new friends and furniture shopping for the new pad?"

"Aren't we moving the stuff from the other apartment there?"

It was move-in day at the new condo, which meant lots of furniture assembly and moving around. It was perfect. I didn't want to think about anything at all.

"Nah. Caleb wants that place to stay like that."

There was no point in wondering why when it came to Caleb, so I conserved the energy.

"By friends, I'm assuming Lisa, Amber, and the guys?"

"Yep, we can grab your stuff from the apartment first and then meet everyone else at the furniture store. Rob's getting a moving truck, so it should be easy-peasy. We'll be done in no time."

Out of curiosity and since I was about to become a constant in these girls' lives, I asked, "How long have you known Lisa?"

"About ten years. Pretty much since the first day she moved here from Costa Rica with her folks."

"Have you guys ever dated?"

"No. Gross." His head turned, and he saw my frown. "It isn't that I don't find her attractive, she's gorgeous, but she's more like a sister to me."

"But Amber isn't?"

"No." He rolled his shoulder and leaned his head in a stretch from one side to the next.

"So, you and Amber have dated?"

He let out a breath, his discomfort with the topic apparent. "No."

"Do you trust her?"

"No. But I'm guessing you're asking because you're looking for a replacement for your shitty bartending pal. If you are, Lisa's your girl."

My thoughts drifted to Caleb because, though I no longer held his interest, he still had mine. Looking through the window as we approached the neighborhood for the last time, I asked, "Has Caleb ever dated Amber or Lisa?"

Calvin quieted for a moment. "He's my best friend, Paige."

"I know. I was just curious, but your lack of an answer answered my question."

"No, it didn't. If it's something you want to know, you should ask Caleb."

"I would," I confessed, "but things are different between us now."

For some reason, I'd thought the condo was a three-bedroom place, but it had four bedrooms with three and a half baths. My room and Caleb's each had a private bathroom, but Calvin's room on the other side of the unit shared a bathroom with the other room, which I assumed would become a guest room.

It took us three and a half hours and four stores to pick out furniture, and getting it from the truck to the thirteen-floor condo was as fast as Calvin had predicted. Then again, there were five strong dudes carrying as much as Amber, Lisa, and I could carry, combined.

The last things to be carried into the apartment were six large pizza boxes and two liters of soda, courtesy of Ryan, who was insanely hot just like the rest of Caleb's friends. So, while the boys were lifting the heavy furniture, Amber and Lisa weren't the only ones drooling at all the muscles flexing around us. I wasn't even boy crazy, but damn, if this was the life I had to look forward to, then I had nothing to complain about. Though, the most important thing of all was that I felt safe with them around.

The guys opened the four new balcony chairs inside and offered them to us while they occupied a space on the floor with the pizza boxes centered in the middle of the circle we'd formed. None of us spoke, only hummed in delight as we stuffed our faces with the first couple of slices of greasy goodness.

"Oh my God, this is so fucking good," Ryan marveled. "Forget that need I was talking about, Amber. I think it's been fulfilled."

"You two at it again?" Calvin asked without looking up.

Ryan jerked his head. "Oh yeah, she can't get enough of my—"

"Got it." Calvin cut him off.

Amber remained quiet, and I stared at her for a moment. It was hard to get a gist of the type of person she was. Lisa was bubbly and friendly, both drunk and sober. Amber, on the other hand, was more reserved when she was sober but loud when she was drunk. I wondered back to Lisa telling me about Amber's crush on Caleb and not only that, but things were always awkward between Amber and Calvin too, like they also had a history beyond friendship. And then with Ryan . . . Was she only sleeping with other guys until she could get Caleb, or was she doing it to try to make him jealous? Did she like him *that* much? Did Caleb like her like that?

Amber was also blonde. Maybe he liked blondes. He used to like me.

At times I felt so welcomed in their group, but I was the outsider. There were secrets among them I wasn't privy to, making me wonder if I could actually trust them.

What if they were only putting up with me because of Caleb? I mean, half of them were being paid to be around me.

Lisa got up from the chair with a slice of pizza in one hand and walked to the breakfast bar. She pulled a long, tightly rolled brown blunt from her bag and waved it as she walked back to us. "Are you sure about that, Ryan? How satisfied are you right now?"

"Ah, damn it." Ryan looked at Caleb, and I turned to him in time to see him shrug.

For hours, I'd avoided looking at him, but with my eyes on him now, I found I couldn't look away. His biceps were bulging from all the lifting today, and a few veins visibly trailed down his arm to his wrist. My eyes drew upward, over what I knew firsthand was a sculpted torso to the tip of his tongue gliding over his lips. Need stirred in the lower part of my abdomen, and as if sensing my want, Caleb's head turned and his eyes locked with mine before they swept over me. It was simple yet so compelling that my muscles tensed, and I found myself leaning back into the lounge chair and squeezing my thighs together.

I wouldn't give in to what my body wanted, not anymore. Especially after he'd pretty much told me to find someone else. Almost his exact words.

SIX

CALEB

The furniture assembly was going to take much longer than I'd anticipated, but I should have known. When everyone got together, things hardly ever went as planned. Turning to the large quartzite breakfast counter separating the living room from the kitchen, I started to remove the most important device from its box—the coffeemaker.

"I'll get my portable speaker," Calvin said, heading to his room. "There's also beer in the fridge—"

"You mean these?" Luke asked, holding up four bottles of beer and pushing the stainless steel fridge door closed with his hip.

It seemed, I was the only one looking to put our new place together right away.

"Thanks, dude." Ryan held up his hand for a bottle of beer as Luke walked by.

"For what?" Luke asked, passing off a beer to Amber and Rob before holding one out to Paige, who shook her head. Instead of giving the remaining bottle to Ryan, Luke held it up. "Caleb, I got you."

I grinned as Ryan complained, "That's fucked up. Caleb can grab his own. He's already in the kitchen."

"Ryan, my lighter's in the car. Could you be a babe and—"

"I swear, if you tell me to 'fetch' your lighter, Lisa," Ryan said, holding up air quotations, "we're going to have problems."

"Fine, be a darling and . . ." Lisa pouted and stomped a foot. "But I like saying fetch."

"You're in college. Come on, you can find another word. Oh, wait, never mind. I forgot you're studying, what, drama?"

"You don't have to be a jerk. Please," Lisa begged, "I'm so tired."

"Fine." Ryan shoved the last of his pizza into his mouth before pushing up from the floor and sucking the tips of his greasy fingers clean. "Now, while I'm downstairs, would you be a dear and fetch me a beer?"

"Of course," she replied.

Over the next hour, Ryan, Calvin, and Amber finished the entire blunt out on the balcony and were high as a bunch of kites—though they swore they weren't. Rob, Luke, Paige, and I had stayed inside, assembling all the beds in the rooms. Sometime later, the less functional group sat around the living room, trying to figure out how to put an end table together. Needless to say, it didn't work out too well for them.

"I got you another one," Amber said as she bent, replacing the empty bottle of beer I'd set next to me with a full one.

Without thinking or choice due to her proximity, I peered down her loose-fitting top to the black lace bra beneath. She stepped away, and I watched her a beat, wondering what that was about before my eyes shifted to Paige. She had been looking at me but then her gaze dropped to the table she and Rob was assembling.

As night touched down, the main purpose of everyone being here was forgotten. More beer was consumed, and the music coming from Calvin's Bluetooth speaker grew louder. Ryan slid across the wood floor in his socks and started doing some ridiculous, hip-thrusting dance in a corner. Even Paige, who'd been quiet most of the evening, laughed. Getting down on all fours, Ryan crawled across the floor like a stripper, tossing his head back like he had a full head of hair and not his crew cut. I shook my head and took another swig of beer. I always controlled the amount of alcohol I drank, but tonight, I hadn't felt like it.

"We should play Truth or Dare," Amber suggested when Ryan's entertaining session ended with him lying flat on the floor on his back.

"No." I scowled.

"Why not? It'll be fun."

"Because it's fucking juvenile," Calvin replied.

If anyone could shut her up, it would be him. No matter how much she wanted to fight Calvin on any given thing, she knew better.

After a while, Luke turned on the television mounted over the fireplace, and everyone leaned against the still-plastic-wrapped white sectional sofa. Everyone but Paige. I looked around, trying to remember the last time I'd stolen a glance of her, but it had been a while.

So, I went in search of her. Her room door was closed.

I knocked, and without hearing an answer, I asked, "Can I come in?"

"Yeah."

I stepped inside what seemed to be her safe haven. "Everything okay?"

She was sitting on the floor, leaning against the bed, knees drawn to her chest. "Yeah."

My phone vibrated in my pocket, and when I pulled it out and saw it was Brad, I hit Ignore and ambled over to sit alongside Paige, stretching out my legs on the floor.

I showed her the phone in my hand before stuffing it into my pocket. "I have two different phones by the way. The one I use with you, and the other I use with Connor, his guys, and people at work."

"That's a good idea," she replied, dropping her eyes to her knees.

I didn't respond, but after a minute, she said, "You went somewhere last night."

"You woke up?" She'd been asleep when I'd left for the hotel.

"Yeah." A finger scratched at the tights covering her knee before she lifted her hand to curl an errant strand behind her ear.

"I went to Luxe."

Her eyes lifted. "Why?"

"I had to see Brad when I knew he would be passed out. It was the only way I could get his blood. The nurse had agreed to come over, and she withdrew what she needed to do the DNA test."

Paige's mouth fell open. "You went to his suite with the nurse? What if he was awake? And how do you know she won't say anything?"

"She won't. That would put her job on the line, and I know Brad. Outside of the suite, he might be unpredictable, but inside, with his drugs, he's a creature of habit."

Her eyes dropped to her knees. "Why didn't you tell me?"

She had the most gorgeous face, so small with big blue eyes and a pink pout I'd left swollen with kisses more than a few times. "Because you deserve a break from all these constant problems. I wanted to wait until I had an answer for you."

"When will you get the results?"

"A few days, a week or so."

I didn't know why I'd told Paige that. Stacy Lenard, the nurse, had told me just three days. I supposed I knew I would need time to process what it would mean after I had proof that Alex Connor was my father and that Brad was my brother.

"Why are you in here instead of out there with everyone else?"

Paige went silent for a moment and then sighed. "I'm so different."

"How so?"

"I don't fit in. I don't like drinking, and I don't smoke. Your friends are fun, and I'm just . . . boring."

"You're not boring. You're not familiar with them as yet, that's all." I lifted an arm to slip around her shoulders, but as my hand brushed her shoulder, she recoiled. A weight pressed down on my chest as I dropped my hand back to the floor between us.

This was what I had wanted, wasn't it? Why I had told her she needed to date someone else? Why I'd been pushing her away even after we found out there was no way we could be related.

It was, but for her benefit. She deserved more than what I could ever offer her.

Still, I lived for those brief moments of connection, no matter how simple they were. As I was about to ask her about her reaction to my touching her, Lisa stuck her head inside the cracked door.

"Good, you're dressed. Thought I was going to walk in on some crazy acrobatic sexcapade shit. You two might be gorgeous, but I'm not ready for that sight." Lisa moved into the room like some belly dancer, her head and body swerving as if the music from earlier was still playing. "What are you two up to?"

"Nothing, just chilling," I said.

"Oh. Well, I was checking to see if Paige was okay. I hadn't seen her in a bit."

I tapped my thumb on the floor, and said, "You guys are overwhelming."

Lisa gasped, putting a hand over her mouth before a smile broke free. "I know we are, but we're kind of okay once you get to know us. Kind of."

Paige glared at me in disapproval.

"Actually, those were Caleb's words, not mine," Paige told her. "And I'm okay. I was about to make my bed and take a shower, that's all."

"So, if I asked you to sneak out with me to check out the pool, it would be out of the question or . . ."

The corners of Paige's mouth drew upward. "Sounds fun."

I wanted to kiss her, and as I imagined water glistening off her creamy skin as she walked out of the pool, I wanted to—

Fuck.

Pushing myself up from the floor, I said, "I'll get my shorts."

"You aren't invited, and don't tell the others." Lisa pointed to the door and then touched her index finger to the center of her lips. "It'll be just Paige and me. We need girl bonding time. You know, because if we are all going to be friends, you and Calvin can't keep her to yourselves." Lisa folded her arms across her chest. "Calvin wouldn't even give me her damn phone number."

I frowned and looked at Paige, needing to know she was okay, but then I remembered how little she actually needed me. She'd been running and fighting on her own long before me. So, I pulled my phone from my pocket, nodded, and walked to my own room to return my missed call.

Brad answered after a few rings. "You haven't been in your suite."

"So?"

"For weeks. Where have you been?"

"How's that your business?"

"It is my business because now, I have to tell Dad," he snapped.

"So loyal, aren't you, little brother? Tell me, how would Connor feel about his favorite son's habitual drug use at his legit business?"

"Think of it as a level of importance, Caleb. A little drug use or a big, suspicious red flag, revealing his least loyal son's recent activities."

Hating that he was right, I ground my molars.

"Yeah, that was what I thought. I thought that little mishap a few weeks back would get you back on track. But I think you're forgetting how much he owns you. How much I own you. By the way, have you been watching the news lately? Pretty little thing, wasn't she?" Brad laughed. "But you know what the best part is, Caleb? You did it. Everything leads back to you. You were the one she came to see that night. Not me."

Blood pumped through my veins, and I chucked the phone across the room and watched it smash against the wall. The cover flew in the opposite direction of the body before it all clattered to the floor. With my heartbeat racing and my fists curled at my sides, I paced, feeling trapped. I needed to get out of here.

Paige

Lisa waved her arms back and forth, treading the water in the deep end of the pool. "I can't believe you only have a one-piece swimsuit with that body. It literally looks like something I wore in the eighth grade. I'm assuming you don't go to pool parties?"

"No, and I'm not much of a socialite. And *you* aren't even in a swimsuit." Liking the way our voices echoed through the room, I closed my eyes and lay backward until I found my buoyancy. It seemed no one else liked to swim after nine on a work night. If this turned out to be the case every night, it would be my favorite pool time. "Do you go to a lot of pool parties?"

"I go to all the parties. But, yeah, the pool ones are great, too."

"In your thong and bra?" I smiled.

Lisa had decided to jump in wearing what was beneath her clothes since we were by ourselves.

"Nah. Sometimes, in a bikini. One or two times, nude."

I opened my eyes and stared at the plain ceiling. I hadn't expected that. "Really?"

"Yeah, it was a dare the first time. The second time, I was wasted."

"Skinny-dipping at a party? Weren't there a lot of people there?"

"Oh, yeah. The second time, Amber and I did it, someone

videoed the whole thing on their phone."

"Oh my God." The fear of that kind of reality caused me to start sinking, so I let my legs drop and rotated to face Lisa.

"It wasn't as bad as it could have been. It happened at night in an outside pool, and the video quality was shitty. Anyway, what do you do for fun?"

"Not much. Mainly go to the gym and read."

"Oh." She frowned. "I don't read anything besides my college books, and by reading, I mean, scanning over words before an exam. And, I don't work out at all. There has to be something we have in common."

"How are you so toned if you don't work out?"

"Maybe all the dancing at clubs," she said with a smile and then added, "and sex. Hmm, I guess I do work out a lot."

My cheeks flamed, having nothing to do with the heated pool.

"Oh gosh, you don't like talking about sex. That's too adorable."

"Is it that obvious?" I asked.

"No, but how is Caleb in bed? I heard he's packing some serious tool."

I held my breath, sank to the bottom of the pool, and stayed for a few seconds before resurfacing to Lisa's laughter.

"I'm just messing with you, but yeah, it's really obvious. So, I'm apologizing from now because I talk about sex. A lot."

I thought about her words. She'd said she heard.

"Does that mean you haven't slept with Caleb?" I whispered, though my voice still echoed.

Lisa shook her head. "I wouldn't try to be your friend without putting that out there first, but no, I haven't, and I don't plan to. I know you like him."

I chewed on my lip, not knowing what to say to that.

"Anyway, I don't know what's going on between you and Caleb since you two threw out the *friend* word, but Miller has been asking about you."

I swallowed, forcing out the words I also needed to hear.

"There's nothing going on between Caleb and me."

She looked at me for a second before she lay back and did a few backstrokes. While she did that, the cocky, brown-haired college football player with green eyes popped in my head; however, it wasn't Miller who'd been occupying my thoughts day and night. It was the black hair, brown-eyed beauty with the sexy five o'clock shadow. The one who Amber had been flirting with tonight.

Caleb was right about one thing, I needed to date someone or at the very least find something or someone to take my mind off him. He wanted me in his life as a friend, and if I wanted him in a way he didn't want me, it would ruin everything. Then I'd have to go back to having no one. Tears welled in my eyes, and I took in a few breaths to regain control.

I swam to the wall, putting me at the opposite end of where Lisa had drifted. When I grabbed on to the edge, I heard her voice.

"We're all going to this pool party on Sunday. And by all, I mean Amber and me. Maybe Calvin, too. Anyway, I think Miller will be there. You should come. It'll be fun."

I hesitated, not wanting to be that awkward girl in the corner with no friends at a party. "I don't know."

"Come on. It'll be fun. We can go shopping tomorrow, and if you absolutely hate hanging out with us, you never have to again. I will forever leave you to your books and the gym. But you know what I think?"

"No, not really."

"I'm thinking that it's time you explore all life has to offer, Paige. Let me be your guide."

A smile tugged at my lips.

"Oh no. Let her *not* be your guide. Lisa, come on, are you trying to become enemies with my best friend?"

I looked over my shoulder to see Calvin running toward the pool. He leaped up into the air, tucked his knees to his chest, and plunged in. Water sprayed everywhere, and I ducked under the surface to avoid the splash.

When the water settled around us, I said, "Caleb won't care if I hang out with Lisa."

"He probably won't, but that isn't the point. You should let *me* be your guide. You like me the best—you said so yourself." Calvin grinned.

"I said that because I'd only spent time with you."

"Exactly," Lisa said from the other side. "Poor girl doesn't even know what she's been missing out on, hanging out with you and your moody best friend."

"Remember when I said Lisa could be a good friend? I take it back. Pick me. I'm better." Calvin turned away from me and swam toward Lisa.

For the next few minutes, it was the three of us, and then Amber showed up. She'd been in shorts all day, so instead of getting in with us, she sat at the edge and let her feet dangle inside the pool.

"How did you guys find us?" Lisa asked. "Did a certain someone I'd sworn to secrecy say something?"

"I hadn't seen you in a while, and then Calvin disappeared, too, so I wandered around," Amber responded, also mentioning how the guys had discovered a beer vending machine down the hall, which was where the rest of them were because, apparently, they'd walked right into the greatest thing ever invented. "I have to tell you, Paige, I'm so jealous. Not only is this place awesome, but also you get to hang out with all of Caleb's gorgeous friends."

"I guess I'm kind of lucky," I said, trying to focus on the positive, not the reason I was moving in with them in the first place.

"So, am I the only one curious about who's staying in the fourth room?" Amber asked.

"Don't worry about it. Just know that it'll never be you," Calvin said before swimming to the edge of the pool and getting out.

I followed him because I'd been in the pool too long, been away from Caleb for too long.

Damn it! Why do I feel this constant need to have Caleb around?

"Calvin!" Lisa exclaimed. "That wasn't necessary. You're being a jerk again. Seriously, what the heck is going on with you two?"

I should've felt bad because he always treated Amber this way, but instead, I was relieved. I didn't want Amber to move in with us because then I'd have to watch whatever was happening between her and Caleb, continue to read into the way she'd been looking at him. I shouldn't think like this. I shouldn't be jealous. But it was the same reason I'd pulled away from his touch tonight. If there was the slightest chance he wanted her, he could have her. I just didn't want his hands on me after. I wanted him too much.

I might have told him what we had done together wasn't a big deal, but it *was* a big deal, and I just hoped he knew that.

CALEB

The next day went by without any run-ins with Brad at Luxe. Any day I didn't see him at the hotel was immediately a better day than it would have been. So, I left work early, and after purchasing a new phone, I stopped by the underground bar to let them know I would be playing tonight. It was the only thing other than sex that made me feel some kind of calm inside. But sex was the last thing I wanted if it wasn't with Paige.

When I got to the condo, there were no signs of her and Calvin.

I hadn't seen her since she went down to the pool with Lisa last night. On my way to my room, I started to strip out of my work clothes so I could get a workout in before I headed out to the bar.

Two hours later, I returned to find Paige on the couch. She had a towel around her shoulders to catch droplets of water from her wet hair as she read a book.

She looked up. "Hey."

"Hi." I bit my bottom lip as the air grew strained between us. "How was your day?"

"Good. How about you?"

I brought my head up in a halfhearted nod. "Good."

"I talked to Bailey today."

I thought we'd agreed to wait. I didn't want her getting further involved in anything that had to do with Alex Connor.

"About what?" I asked, walking to the kitchen to grab a cold bottle of water from the fridge. I could feel the sweat I'd carried from the gym still running down my body.

"Any relatives that I might have. I want to find them. If I was kidnapped from my real parents, I might still have family out there, and I'd like to get to know them."

Shit. Doesn't she know by now that Connor leaves no stones unturned?

"What did she say?"

"She'd let me know."

I gave her a half-nod again before I went to my room. After my shower, I picked up my guitar and headed to my balcony where I played my heart out for the next hour, connecting with my guitar and my love for music. This should have been my life. Music. Singing. It was what I loved, everything I wanted. Instead, the only thing I would be looking at by the time this was all over was serious jail time for all I'd let happen, and for all the things Alex Connor would make me take the fall for, but it didn't matter. I would still be free. Free of Alex Connor. Free of Brad.

When I opened my room door, the smell of steak attacked my senses and left me drooling.

"So, you learned how to cook?" I asked, walking into the kitchen and peering into the pots on the stove. One had vegetables steaming, and the other had a chunk of steak.

Calvin was brushing the steak so delicately with a shrub of herbs, I wanted to laugh at the sight. But the way it smelled, I knew it was going to taste good.

"That was one time, dude, and I only burned it because of Lisa. Anyway, now that you're here, what do you think? Should I tell Paige about Amber? She's been asking me about her since I was apparently a *jerk* to her again last night at the pool."

I looked over at the couch to find Paige still seated in the same spot, staring at us.

His question threw me off, and I shrugged, not knowing why he was asking me. "What does that have to do with me?"

Calvin still had no idea what had really gone down that night, and I would rather keep it that way.

"See, no excuses," Paige said. "Just tell me. Seriously, how bad could it be?"

Calvin turned around, walked to the sink, and deposited a spoon inside. Then he stared at Paige across the room. "It happened years ago. I had a thing for her, and—"

"It was more than a *thing*. He was in love with Amber," I informed Paige, grabbing a much-needed beer from the fridge.

"Yeah, whatever. Anyway, she knew how I felt about her, so I thought it was why she'd slept with me at a party one night. Come to find out, I wasn't the only one she'd slept with that night. I knew this because it was the only fucking thing Ryan could talk about the next day."

"You mean, Ryan—"

"Yep, our friend Ryan, who also ended up dating her for a while, and I don't mean now since they're apparently fucking again."

"Ouch," Paige remarked. "Wait, so why aren't you upset with Ryan, too?"

"It was his first time visiting. He didn't know I had feelings for her."

I took a seat on one of the stools at the breakfast bar and spun around to face Paige. "No one else knew Calvin liked her like that. I only knew because he was so pissed off he told me about it."

"Yeah, well, that's done, and your little input is only pissing me off, bro." Calvin scowled, turning to the stove to attend to the steak.

What he didn't know was that Amber had given me a blow job in the bathroom that same night. It hadn't been the first time. She called those moments her party favors, but it wasn't something I talked about, so Calvin had no idea it had been going on at the time. What was even worse was that I had only been taking advantage of those party favors. Amber wanted a relationship with me, but I never liked her that way. So, after that blow job, I'd been a complete dick to her, and not long after, I'd seen her leaving a room with Calvin, which I didn't give two shits about. My buddy had gotten laid. I'd gotten my dick sucked. Life was good. Until I'd found out how he felt about her. I guessed that was the same reason he never told Ryan he'd slept with Amber that night. Ryan liked her, too.

"So, you hate her now. Got it. Do I have to hate her, too?" Paige asked.

I grinned. "No, you don't. In fact, Calvin is the only one who hates her." I had a feeling it was the wrong thing to say because she went quiet for a moment.

"So, you like her?" she asked.

I bit my lip and watched her, needing to figure out where she was going with this, but she looked back to the pages in her book.

"I don't have a problem with her, and she's been a good friend to Lisa and the others. I'm not saying she didn't do something stupid, but maybe she had her reasons."

"Caleb," Calvin said.

I closed my eyes. *Fuck.* The one thing I didn't want to do was lie to Calvin. So, I prayed he wasn't decrypting my words.

"Can you get some plates ready? I'm fucking tired of hearing about that girl."

I breathed a sigh of relief, but when I lifted my head and got off the stool, Paige was watching me. With a slight shake of her head, she closed her book and looked away.

See? She doesn't know this guy.

I didn't need a blood test to tell me I had come from a bloodline of Connors. It was all over me—how I thought, how I felt, how I found opportunities in the weak and used them to my advantage. Like persuading Stacy Lenard to do an after-hour blood test on my brother or persuading Paige to live with me because, let's face it, what other choice did she have? The last thing I needed to do was persuade Bailey to drop this shit with Paige. I was her guy.

All I needed were those blood test results.

Paige

Lining up my front sights to my rear sights, I steadied my grip on my subcompact 9mm. As I inhaled a breath, my diaphragm rose before slowly falling with my exhale, and then I fired. A shell popped out to the side, and I paused, letting the gun smoke rise through my nostrils, infiltrating my thoughts. Center mass was getting boring. I lifted my sights higher until it was centered on the target's head. I fired. I fired again and again and again. And then I breathed.

Better.

Setting the weapon on the stand, I flipped the switch and watched my paper target return exactly how I'd wanted it.

I felt a tap on my shoulder and turned to see Calvin. He'd been shooting in the lane next to me, but in my mind, I'd been somewhere else entirely. I'd been on the hunt, searching and finding the center of my fucked-up mentality. I shifted my earmuffs down around my neck.

"I knew you carried, but holy shit! How long have you been shooting?"

"Long enough." I smiled and looked over at his target. "You aren't too bad yourself."

He shook his head, and appreciation seeped inside me at his look of admiration.

"Let's do the outdoor range next time. The guys and I go there. You'd like it."

A wide smile passed my lips as I refilled my magazine. "Awesome. I can't wait." I turned back to my target and started to put my earmuffs back in place but stopped and twisted to face Calvin. "I'm going to need your help with something, but you can't say anything to Caleb."

He tilted his head. "I'm intrigued."

I had known he would be.

We'd been living in the condo for a week, and between working out, the bar, and therapy sessions, we'd been bored out of our minds. Not only that, I'd been dying to go back to my job at the gym even knowing I shouldn't. I missed being a trainer, and I missed sparring at night with the fighters; it was what had settled me before. Without it, all I could focus on was Alex Connor. He was out there, still walking the streets, training men to do evil things to people, while probably kicking back and laughing at how easily he was getting away with it. My parents were in a grave. My sisters, Reese and Alaina, were in graves. All because of him.

"I need to know where Alex Connor lives," I said.

Calvin's lips parted to say something, but he didn't.

Even though I was pretty sure he knew this, I added, "I'll find him with or without your help."

With a frown still set on his face, he nodded, and I went back to shooting, not stopping until all seven of my rounds appeared as one on the paper. But I wasn't satisfied. And even more unsatisfying was Caleb's blood test results. Alex Connor was his father. It wouldn't have been a bad thing, but he'd gone even quieter since then. He'd been avoiding me, which showed me his uncertainty. He'd been consistent before.

He wasn't the Caleb I knew anymore.

He was Alex Connor's son, and he was Brad's brother—not by paper, but by blood. It wasn't that I didn't think he cared for me, but he had a real family, and he was in this with them. So, it bothered me, not knowing how far he would go to make sure everyone got what they deserved.

It was simple. I wouldn't be satisfied until I could stop looking over my shoulder, stop wondering if they would find me again, stop wondering if they knew where I was, stop wondering if they were waiting in the elevator for me each time I returned. I would never get better until Alex Connor and his men were out of the picture for good.

I sighed, looking at the empty boxes that had contained three hundred rounds an hour ago. I looked over at Calvin. "Too much gun smoke. I'm starting to feel like I might be a danger to society."

He laughed. "Judging from those targets, you are, girl."

I smiled, wondering how Amber had passed up on Calvin. He was funny, charming, attractive, sincere, and fuzzy... well, that was, as long as Amber wasn't around. Though, remembering the look on Caleb's face, I shouldn't have to wonder why. All it took was one glance to know that he had slept with Amber. That could be a part of the reason why my growing friendship with Lisa was so much easier. Thinking about her warm personality and the silly text messages she'd sent me throughout the day was quieting a deeper longing inside of me. A longing that'd been there since I lost Reese and Alaina.

I gave the man standing at the counter a polite smile as we walked out of the gun range building in town and toward Calvin's old white Camry parked on the street.

"So, what do you know about Red?" Calvin asked.

"Red?"

"The redhead. Sergeant Bailey?"

"Oh, not much. Why?"

"Just wondering. Anyway, I know exactly where Connor lives. If he still lives there. It's about a mile from the house I grew up in."

"Really?"

"Unfortunately, yeah," he said with a hint of remorse. Pulling on the car door handle, he looked over the roof at me. "I can drive by it, but we can't go anywhere near that house, Paige. Caleb would fucking lose it. Promise me you won't."

I nodded, but I wasn't making any promises.

It took an hour's drive for Calvin to reach inside of a suburban neighborhood north of the city. I had been paying attention to everything on our journey here while he talked about his little sister in high school and some boy he was worried about messing with her. He probably thought I was texting, but I was on the map, making a note of the location. I would be back, just probably not with him.

The car slowed.

"Look to your right. It's that first house on the corner."

The five-story brick building I looked at had a custom-made garage built into the first floor of the building. None of the other nearby buildings had a garage, not that it stood out on this one since it even had a concrete driveway.

"House? That looks like an apartment building."

The windows on the entire building were dark, haunted. A sudden chill traveled through my bones as we went by. Like my sisters were here with me, encouraging me. Telling me it might be up to me to let them have peace.

"Trust me, it's a house," Calvin reaffirmed.

But I was already getting lost in my own thoughts with Alaina's or Reese's scream from that night ringing in my ears.

It'd saved me from going back to the rooms. My sisters were the reason I was alive. And, if I was here and I knew the person responsible for doing that to them, to my whole family, why wouldn't I do something about it? The cops, the FBI, or whoever was on the case didn't care enough to put these people away for good. It was in my hands, and I wouldn't stop until Alex Connor suffered. He needed to feel the pain I'd felt, cry the tears I'd cried, feel the way I'd suffered for five years without anyone to turn to because I hadn't been able to trust myself to be normal. I hadn't been able to trust . . . anyone. Until Caleb.

I turned my head and kept staring at the house now behind us.

"Go back around," I told Calvin. "I need to see it again."

I hadn't felt this productive in a while.

I knew where Alex Connor lived. I'd burned out some aggression at the range, though not enough that I didn't still want my predator dead.

My predator.

For years, he'd sought out my family and me.

A plan formed as I thought of the perfect way to start Alex Connor's suffering.

Letters from his victims.

With his address, I could mail a letter to him from each of my family members who he had killed and then a final letter from me. It was going to hurt me to write those letters, but it could be freeing as well. Like the last farewell, only to Alex Connor, and he was going to be so pissed, but it was the perfect beginning to the end for him.

He needed to know that I was no longer the prey. Though that was for another day, because I was about to start my first shift at the underground bar in Quincy. It was close to where we lived, and all it had taken was a little convincing for the manager to take me on as a temporary until the fall semester began in four weeks. He'd even allowed me to start right away.

I still worked some nights at Stilts Bar in downtown Boston, but since I wasn't working at the gym, I wasn't making enough to live on. And I hated depending on Caleb to take care of me. It was wrong in so many ways.

Kari was my friendly go-to person and trainer for the day. The few times I'd seen her working in the bar, I'd been a wee bit intimidated. Probably due to the tattoos all over her body. Skulls, blood, guns, and I could see the head of a snake baring its fangs on her neck. Even with the silver piercings above her eyebrows, a nose ring, a lip ring, and a small gauge in each earlobe, she made it work. Not just anyone could pull that look off.

I'd seen her perform once before on the small stage in the back, and she was incredible. I was starting to think this was why Caleb loved this place. It was filled with people who were as talented as he was. Although, in my opinion, Caleb was the best. I must not have been the only one who thought so because as soon as he was on the stage, it was like a spell had been put on the entire bar, and the whole room went quiet.

Something in his voice when he sang reached so far, so deep, it clung to whoever was listening. Most times, I couldn't shake the feeling for days. The feeling that behind the sexy, sad, raspy voice he sang alternative covers with, there was a boy who was just broken. That might be true, but he fought not to show it. But I knew; I'd seen it in his eyes, heard it in his words, and felt it in the way he'd kissed me before like nothing else mattered.

It was stupid that I still found my eyes blurring with tears, no matter how many times I'd heard him perform.

Though it hurt more than the first time because I knew he sounded like his uncle, David Sawyer. A natural talent from his mom's side of the family. A family he never knew yet still shared something so special with.

"You're crying again," Lisa said.

"What?" I asked, using the back of my hand to wipe my eye. She stood and pulled me into a hug.

"I'm not crying. I just . . ."

"It's fine, but you know"—she placed her hands on my shoulders and looked me square in the eyes—"even though Amber still has the biggest freaking crush on Caleb, I'm rooting for you and him. I'm such a shitty friend for saying it. But he likes you, not her. I've tried to pull her away from him over the years, but she's still stuck on him for some weird reason."

Instead of telling her how I kind of felt that way about Caleb myself without having known him for that long, I smiled. Then I wondered where Amber was. In fact, the more time I'd been spending with Lisa, the less I'd seen of Amber.

"Oh shiznit! Can I have another drink? I know I've had enough, but Kari is kind of staring, and I don't want to get you fired on your first day. So, take my order."

I laughed. "Okay."

As I was walking back to the bar, Miller came out of nowhere and blocked my path. "Are you going to try to pretend you didn't see me this time?"

I'd been making U-turns all night. A failed attempt at avoiding him, I realized. He was everywhere.

"No, and unfortunately, I can't *unsee* you because you're right here, literally standing in front of me, and I need to work. You're preventing that from happening."

He laughed. "I'm only inviting you out this weekend, that's all."

"I'm not going on a date with you."

"It isn't a date. It's a club. Everyone's going. Ask Lisa about it. It's going to be epic." Miller grinned. "And, if you so happen to be there, just save me a dance. That's all I want. One dance."

"One dance?"

"Yep. Promise."

Lisa had been great, and Caleb had been not so much with his not-so-subtle avoidance of me, so I considered what Miller was asking. I was almost twenty, and for the first time in almost five years, I felt like I was normal. Well, as normal as one could call a person who was planning on trolling a killer. But, anyway, this was what normal nineteen-year-olds did, right? They spent time with friends, not hiding inside in fear of attention, in fear of being recognized or being found by predators lurking in the dark.

"You okay there?" Miller asked, bringing his beer bottle to his lips.

"Yeah, I just . . . uh, I'll think about it."

I moved around him and to the bar and kept my eyes off the stage, wishing I could block out the sound of Caleb's consuming voice seeping into my soul from the speakers. But I couldn't, and as I listened to the words he sang, it was as if he were speaking to me, telling me something no one else in the audience would understand.

CASEY DIAM

"You can't save me now, but I can save you.
Fallen angels don't make it through.
This is your chance . . .
Because when you've got nothing to lose.
Baby, that hope,
It will destroy you."

If he was trying to tell me something, I didn't understand. I had hope and I didn't need saving. Alex Connor would get what he deserved.

I would make sure of it.

TEN

CALEB

I stood at the door to my brother's suite, cracking my knuckles.
For a second, I couldn't remember why I was doing this, why I was here. It was a Saturday night, and if he wasn't already high, he was getting there. I hoped he was getting there.

Inhaling, I counted to three, let the air slowly compress out of my lungs, and then knocked.

The door swung open, and for the first time, I really looked at him. Besides the five o'clock shadow I wore all the time and him always being clean-shaven, we had the same black hair, and as of recently, he'd forgone his usual buzz cut, making our similarities even more apparent with his dark eyes and light-beige skin tone. The only real difference was the few inches I had on him in height and build.

"Need something?" Brad asked.

"We need to talk," I said, forcing myself into his suite.

The image of Sophia Cruz's body on the couch a few weeks ago hit me along with guilt. It shouldn't have happened, but Brad had been molded to be this person, as had I. I turned around to face him as he closed the door and leaned against it. His body did a small twitch before he reached up and scratched his neck.

"Make it quick. I got shit to do."

Good, he was getting there. It would be easier to reason with him while he was on edge. Because, in this small window, it meant he was stuck with his true self. The addict desperate for his next fix.

Gauging his mood before I said anything would be even better, but with Brad, there was no baseline. If he was happy, he became impulsive and evil, and if he was gloomy, he was evil. It always led back to being evil. It made no fucking sense. Though it did when Alex Connor was one's main influence in life. Somewhere inside me, I wanted to have hope for Brad and myself, but I couldn't.

His mind was weaker than mine, and if I could reach him in the depths of that darkness, we could stop everything. The kidnapping, the killing, the abusing. I could try to do it by myself, but the truth was, I couldn't. Alex Connor was smart. Only a few of his men knew enough to be of any help to me or the cops. Brad was one of those few. He knew where the bodies were being buried. He knew where anything that could form a case against Connor would be, and if I could get Brad to cooperate, we could uproot enough evidence to have the upper hand against Connor. An upper hand was the only leverage to my freedom, and I planned to get it by any means necessary, but I would rather have cooperation from Brad. It would make everything easier, and easier meant Paige wouldn't have to get involved.

"What if I told you something that would change everything we'd ever believed?"

Brad cocked his head to the side. "Like?"

If he could feel anything inside the stone on the left side of his chest, this would be the time. I hadn't been alone in this for all these years. He'd been right there with me. And knowing we'd been lied to all these years, that the twenty-one-year-old man before me was my real brother, I had to try for him, for us.

"We're related. Not just adopted. You're my brother, and Alex Connor is our biological father. We weren't adopted."

He narrowed his eyes, but not before I saw a flicker of anger in them. "Really?"

"Yeah."

"And how do you know this?"

"I can't tell you that."

"So, it had nothing to do with the nurse you came in here with at three in the morning last week?"

Fuck.

He read the surprise on my face.

"That nurse won't live to see the end of tonight. Hint, the *I got shit to do.*"

He smirked and pushed off the door, but he didn't get very far because I reacted without thinking, shoving my hand around his throat and pushing him back against the door so hard that it vibrated on contact.

With my teeth gritted, I hissed, "Don't you fucking dare."

"I might be a crackhead and younger, but I'm always ahead, Caleb. Now, get the fuck out before I make you."

"She had nothing to do with this. If you touch her, I swear to God, I'll be turning you in. I'm fucking done."

Brad shifted, and we whirled around as he slammed my back against the door. "Did you just say what I think you did? Because, if so, you're fucking done, Caleb."

I pushed him off me and swallowed, shaking my head. "Fuck you."

He fished a small, black flip phone out of his sweatpants, and my heart plunged as he pressed a button and said, "Call A.C."

Visions of the room Connor kept me in when I didn't follow orders overtook my mind. Starting with the taste of blood on my lips from a broken nose, the pain in my chest from a broken rib or a few—I never found out. Then the darkness and silence. That was the worst of it because it was then everything replayed in my head—the rape, the murder.

"Brad, don't."

The phone was on speaker and ringing. He looked up. "What are you most scared of right now? That nurse dying for helping you, or you being locked away in A.C.'s house for a while?"

"Hello?" Alex Connor's voice echoed.

"We need to change the drop-off. Something came up." Brad grinned, and I stopped breathing. The pressure on my chest was more threatening than a close-range gunshot. My throat dried as I shook my head in a silent plea. "It's more like a rat problem. Anyway, call me back when you have a new spot."

He ended the call.

"You're my brother. You'd do this to me even knowing that? Support the man who's lied you, lied to me, all our lives?"

Ignoring me, he walked to the kitchen and pulled a bottle of eye drops from a drawer. His cocaine, I was sure. He unscrewed the cap and tapped a line of white powder onto the counter before him.

"What did you expect, big brother? Hugs and apologies for what I did to you over the years?" He bent, and with one long inhale, the whole line disappeared from the counter. He tossed his head back and sniffed again before using a thumb and index finger to tweak his nose. He looked at me. "The thing is, Caleb, I wasn't lied to. You were. I've known for years. I just never gave a shit. I still don't. Now, if you want me to do a brotherly favor, I think I can forget this whole *turning me in* thing, but only if you do something for me."

I shook my head in disbelief. I'd rather get in a fight with a bear and go to jail for everything they'd set me up to take the fall for than do something for him, but I humored him. "What?"

"Introduce me to your friend."

"What?" I asked, confused.

"The blonde girl the cop saw you with that night in the car and the one you snuck out of this same building. I want to meet her."

"Why?"

"I'm curious, and you don't have to introduce me. But then I can always tell Connor what you've been doing. And I'm going to take a wild guess and say that you've been gathering evidence against him."

My heart pounded in my chest, fighting against the calm I exuded. "I just wanted to know who my family was; that was all," I said, hoping he'd forget about the girl. Because no way in hell would I ever bring Paige straight into the lion's den.

"Right, well, if you were a real Connor, you'd know all we cared about was money, opportunity, cheating whores, and more money. Anyway, the girl."

I could introduce some random girl to him to get him off my case. It wasn't like he'd seen her face or met any of my friends. As far as he knew, I didn't have friends. But as I was about to agree, I thought about Stacy Lenard.

"What are you going to do with the nurse?"

He smiled. "Play with her for a little bit. Can't send her to hell before I fuck her, now can I?"

I inhaled and shook my head. "There's no way in hell I'm introducing you to anyone." I walked to the door. "I'd rather die. I'd rather go back to the fucking room than have you kill another innocent person."

"So sensitive," Brad yelled after me. "Have some coke. It takes the edge off. I'll give you a few days to think about it. Don't take too long, though, because I could always just put a team on you until I find the girl, take her, and then tell Alex what you've been up to. If you love your privacy and freedom of not sleeping here, then give me what I want, and I'll let you have that. That's my offer. Sweet deal if you ask me."

It was a sweet deal. If Brad kept his mouth shut, I'd have time to get some leads on what they were up to. It wasn't like they were going to stop what they were doing in the wake of Paige going missing. I could just try to get new evidence on everything they were doing or planning to do from this point forward.

As the plan became clearer, I sighed for dramatic effect. "If I introduce you to my friend, will you leave her alone?"

"Of course." He chuckled. "What am I going to do? Kill her?"

Biting my lip, I grabbed the doorknob. Trying to be reasonable with him was obviously a mistake.

"I'm joking, idiot. What are you scared of? That she'll like me more than you?"

I turned around. "I'm not introducing you to anyone unless I have your word that you won't do anything to hurt her."

His face grew serious, and I almost felt like I could trust him as he nodded. "You have my word."

With that, I left, desperate to see Paige.

Over the past days, she and I had gotten into a better place. I'd stopped avoiding her as much, and we'd become comfortable around each other again. I'd even started to lean my head on her shoulder the few times I needed to after a long day. Most times were while we were watching a movie. It was a simple connection. It wasn't like her being in my arms, but still, it was enough to keep me centered.

Ever since I'd met her, she'd been the axis to my world. Not having her would be like a spinning top without its pointed tip, an earth without its axis. And, tonight, I needed my axis. I needed to be centered again.

When I got back to the condo, no one was home, which was weird since it was almost midnight.

Switching on the lights, I threw my keys onto the breakfast bar. I knew Calvin would go out some nights, but not Paige. At least, not without my knowing. I wanted to text her or Calvin, but I knew if he wasn't here either, then she was in good hands.

I walked to the cupboard in the kitchen and pulled out a tumbler, then set it under the ice maker until a few cubes fell in. I grabbed the unopened bottle of Jack Daniel's sitting on top of the fridge and poured. And then I poured some more because tonight was a drinking night. Tonight, I didn't want to control how much I drank.

Without my axis to keep me centered, without sex to distract me, without anyone to distract me for that matter, I needed something to take the edge off, and that something was Jack.

When I was four glasses deep into the amber liquor, the elevator came up. Something opened up in my chest that I didn't understand. But only Calvin budged around the corner from the foyer.

I lifted my head as he walked forward.

"Where's Paige?"

"She's with Lisa. Ryan's with them."

"Oh." I frowned, sliding the glass across the counter before lifting it to my lips.

"Lisa mentioned going to a club, so I thought I'd check it out, but I had to meet someone first. What are you doing tonight besides trying to finish a bottle of Jack by yourself? Rob is waiting outside in his car, so I'm sure there's a full moon tonight. Come out with us. You look like you could use it. I just came up to get my—"

"Is that where Paige is—a club with Lisa?"

"Yeah."

I squinted. "Paige is partying?"

"Told you, full moon. But, yeah, I guess so." His lips flattened. "I think she's coming around. I didn't even recognize her tonight."

When we got to the two-story club, the line was stretched along the building for almost a block, but Luke had a part-time security position at the club, so he came to the front and got us inside.

With the music beating in my chest and the crowd screaming and dancing around, I tried to seek out Paige, and then my heart stopped. The girl I saw on the dance floor in a tight red dress wasn't Paige. Well, she was Paige, just not my Paige. My Paige wore gym clothes all day, every day if she wasn't in jeans. She didn't wear red lipstick, and she didn't curl her hair so that it bounced about her shoulders and collarbone as she danced. My eyes moved to the drink she brought to her lips and then to Lisa and Amber. All three of them were attracting attention from the men all around, lurking on the sidelines, but they paid no attention to anyone else besides each other, the drinks, and the music.

Calvin clapped me on the shoulder and yelled over the music. "Told you. Let's hit the bar unless you want to go say hi."

Seeing her like this forced me to wonder if this were the girl she would have been if Alex Connor hadn't infiltrated her life.

Happy. Free.

It's all I want for her.

"Nah, let's go to the bar."

For the next hour, I stayed by the bar and away from Paige, though I let my eyes wander over to her from time to time while trying my best not to seem like one of the creepers on the sidelines. I'd had too much to drink, and each time I looked over to her, all I saw was us together. I couldn't stop the memories. My hands roaming over her body the first night she had been in my bed, my fingers curling inside her warmth, her perfect breasts in my face and my mouth, and her coming apart beneath me for the first time.

I looked over to the spot where she was still dancing. Miller approached her from behind, and the hair at the back of my neck bristled as he wrapped an arm around her waist. This time, when I saw red, it wasn't her dress. She started moving, looking like some seductress as she rubbed herself against him. Was she drunk? Did she even know who she was dancing with?

His hands slid down low on her hips as he ground against her.

"What the fuck?"

"Don't do it," Calvin said.

I shook my head. "He's fucking dead."

He seduced girls and tossed them to the side without a second thought, and I would be damned if he even got the chance to do the same to Paige. The next thing I knew, I was standing in front of Paige, grabbing her arm and yanking her toward me. Miller stepped forward, and I released Paige, shifting her behind me. The next second, I was in his face.

Low and menacing, I warned, "Stay away from her. If you hurt one piece of hair on her head, I will personally break every fucking bone in your body."

He made a show of smirking and rolling his eyes the same time he was about to shove me, but I saw it coming. I caught his arms and shoved him back into the crowd behind him.

"Caleb, what are you doing?" Paige shrieked.

Ryan stepped between Miller and me, but I was ready for Miller to come back at me. I needed a reason to unleash everything boiling inside me, so I pushed Ryan to the side. Before I could reach Miller, Calvin's larger frame blocked me, but I still moved forward, trying to force him out of my way with my body.

"Caleb," Calvin said.

I was too heated and ready to do anything to punch that fucker in the face. Paige wasn't just any woman he could screw over. She was—

I cursed as Luke joined Calvin.

"Dude, you can't do this here, or I'll have to kick you out."

Turning around, my eyes zeroed in on Paige. "What the fuck are you doing with him?"

"Dancing."

"Is that what it was? Because from where I was, it looked like you were practically having sex on the dance floor," I snapped. "I didn't take your virginity for you to start fucking assholes like him."

Her eyes widened, and somewhere in the back of my mind, I heard Calvin's voice filtering through the thoughts racing through my head.

"Caleb, stop."

"Really? And how much better are you?" She shook her head.

I looked away from her for the first time to the crowd gathered around us.

What did I do? What did I just say? Fuck. I don't even recognize myself right now.

My friends and anyone within hearing range had just found out something that should have been special between Paige and me, and I would never be able to take that back.

I looked back to Paige, but she was already leaving, making her way through the crowd with Lisa, and the douche bag Miller was right on their heels, but I let her go. I had to. Even if I didn't want anyone else to have her. And, fuck, it hurt, more than everything else going on in my life. I'd never felt pain like this. Like my fucking chest was crushing my organs. I didn't even fucking understand it. All I knew was that I needed to drink more.

"Hey, where'd everyone go?"

I looked to my left and saw Amber looking confused with two red cocktails in hand.

I reached for one and plucked out the straw before I chugged it. "Your friends are gone."

Paige

"Are you sure you're okay here?" Lisa asked. Looking over my shoulder into Caleb's studio apartment, I nodded. "Yeah. I can't see him tonight."

I knew he would come looking for me after the club, and I couldn't deal with him, not with the way he'd acted tonight and not with all the memories he'd triggered with his words.

"Okay, but if you need anything, call me."

She wrapped her arms around me, and I relaxed into her embrace, not realizing how much I'd needed it. My gaze went over her shoulder to Rob, who'd come back from walking around the apartment. Lisa didn't know what he had been doing, but I did. He was checking to make sure it was safe for me, and I was so grateful in this moment that my heart couldn't decide if it wanted to remain upset over what Caleb had done or be happy that he'd brought these people into my life.

Forcing a smile to my lips, I pulled away from Lisa. "You really didn't have to leave with me, but thank you. Rob, can you make sure she gets home safe?"

He nodded, and after I closed the door behind them, I slipped off the pair of heels I'd borrowed from Lisa and padded around the apartment. Rob had checked it, but I had to see for myself that no one else was here. So, I opened all the closets and kitchen cupboards because no place was too small for someone to hide. I knew it was stupid every time I did it, but I had to. It was the only way I could ease the tension enough to feel safe inside.

After taking a hot shower, I wrapped myself in a towel and went to the closet. Since I'd taken the few clothes I had to the condo, I found one of Caleb's white T-shirts in the duffel bag he'd left inside the closet.

I tugged it over my head and then laid out a towel on the pillow to keep my damp hair from soaking into it. After that was done, I walked into the kitchen, opened the drawer holding all the knives, and took the biggest one out. Setting it on the floor next to the bed, I lay down, taking a few long, deep breaths.

I hadn't slept a night without Caleb or Calvin around in a while, and I could feel my body tensing, knowing I'd be alone tonight.

Before my mind started to play out different scenarios that would have me up and pacing the apartment and checking the closets and cupboards again, I clicked on my phone and pulled up YouTube. Then I watched back-to-back episodes of *Kim Possible* until I was falling asleep.

Or I had been asleep.

The sound of a lock rattling amplified my senses. It must be what had woken me up. At the sound of the apartment door opening, my heart skipped a beat, and I jumped out of the bed. Grabbing the knife, I ran to the wall and plastered myself against it. I'd played out a scenario like this in my mind a thousand times before. I couldn't be seen from the front in this position. There was no way I was going to run into the closet or bathroom where I could be trapped.

Taking in some measured breaths to calm my heart rate, I watched as the light from the hallway drifted inside the apartment and the shadow of two people moved inside. I clutched the shaking knife to my chest. And, with the deafening blood rushing to my ears, I kept my eyes open wide, scared I might miss something if I blinked.

One of the shadows stumbled against the much taller one, and then a loud, girlish giggle echoed.

"Oh my God, turn on the lights!"

"Wait, I'm trying," a male voice slurred.

Caleb?

I peeked around the corner as the lights came on.

Caleb and Amber were standing in the living room.

Feeling a sudden rush of nausea and a deep-slicing pain throughout my chest, I pressed myself back against the wall, unsure of what to do with myself as I lowered the knife to my side.

"Amber, come on."

She giggled. "What? You used to like it."

"I know, but—"

"I want you on my tongue, in my mouth. A party favor for old time's sake? You know you want to."

"You're already doing me a favor."

I couldn't breathe.

I couldn't think.

All I felt was pain. I looked down to make sure I hadn't stabbed myself. Because it was like the knife I was holding was digging into my chest. I opened my mouth to draw in a trembling breath, but the air clogged in my throat and sent another cutting pain through me.

Hurrying to the bed, I set the knife on the nightstand and grabbed my phone from the sheets. When I looked up, Caleb was looking at me over Amber's head. She was pressed against him, her hands somewhere between them.

Oh my God. Oh my God. I can't—

Why does it hurt? Why does it hurt?

"Paige?" Caleb asked.

I realized I was frozen in place, just staring.

"Paige?" Amber turned around. "What are you doing here?"

The casualness of her voice, like this was normal for them, speared me. Was this why he'd kept the apartment? Had he been coming here with her since we moved? Was this why he didn't want me anymore?

"Paige," Caleb said again, pushing Amber away.

She stumbled back with her mouth agape.

I shook my head, hurrying to the door. He intercepted me, and the strong scent of liquor radiated from him as he grabbed my arm for the second time that night. It was a tight grip. I didn't think he realized he was even doing it. But I'd become used to aggression with the fighters over the years, so I didn't care, because the small pain it inflicted grounded me. If not, I would have freaked out. And if I freaked out, I would have done something stupid. And stupid was not for me to do, not when he wasn't . . . he wasn't mine.

"Don't, Paige. It isn't what it looks like." Caleb said. "She's only doing me a favor."

"I . . . yeah, it doesn't matter." I chanced a look at him and found his eyes were dark and haunted like the first time he'd let me see this side of him, the day we'd met inside that café.

I couldn't think about that.

This was something else entirely.

Staring down at me and making no attempt to put his walls back up, he jerked his head. "Don't say that."

"Well, it doesn't matter. Why would it?" *It does matter. God, it matters.* "I'm leaving. I need to go."

"No, it's three in the morning."

"Well, I'm not staying here." I yanked my hand away.

He grabbed me from behind, and I flinched, not wanting him to touch me. Amber was here, and things were about to happen between them, things I couldn't let myself think about.

"Don't touch me."

He released me. "Paige, you can't go."

"I'm going." I pursed my lips, grabbing the doorknob.

"You're only in a T-shirt, and you have no shoes."

I looked down as my grip tightened around the lock. He was right. I was only in his *stupid* T-shirt. I stuffed my feet into the black pumps I'd had on earlier and pulled the door open. I didn't care what I was wearing. I just needed to get away from here and these emotions. I shouldn't feel like this. We hadn't even been together that long.

But damn it . . . it freaking hurts.

"Paige, don't. It isn't safe." I heard the pain in his voice, but I ignored it. "Stay here. I'll leave, okay? Just stay here. I'll leave."

"I can't."

"Fuck," he sounded desperate. "Just call one of the guys. Please."

"Paige, I'm sorry. I didn't know," Amber said for the first time, and I couldn't even look at her. "I thought you guys . . ."

It wasn't that I was upset with her because I didn't have a claim on him, but I was jealous because she had what I wanted.

I started down the hallway to the elevator, and Caleb followed. "Don't follow me."

"I'm sorry."

"No, you aren't, Caleb. You've been pushing me away. Then you threatened someone who was actually interested in me. Yet, now you're here with her." I pointed down the hall behind him, shaking my head as I repeatedly pressed the elevator button.

"I'm not with her. Paige, baby—"

"Don't call me that, and I don't wanna—I can't see you right now. Just go away." I stared at the button as I pressed it. "Please, just go back to her. She's waiting for you."

He stood there behind me, and I could feel all his energy seeping into me. Anger. Confusion. Torment. The elevator doors slid open, and I stepped inside, keeping my eyes glued to the floor.

"Just take this." He pushed a hand inside his jeans pocket and handed me his wallet.

"What—"

"In case you need a cab, or I don't know."

The small purse I'd carried earlier with my ID and cash was still inside the room.

Shit.

I reached out and took his wallet. When my eyes met his, my heart split in two. Caleb was hurting, and there was nothing I could

CASEY DIAM

do about it but watch him walk back down the hall to Amber. The elevator doors closed, and I let the tears fall.

Caleb

Tapping my fingers on the table in the coffee shop to some unknown beat in my head, I worried my lip between my teeth. Amber sat in front of me, a cappuccino in one hand and her phone in the other.

"He's too late." Amber grimaced. "I'm sorry. I can't stay. I have to be at work in thirty minutes."

I nodded and looked up at her. "It's fine. Thank you."

She gave me a closed-lip smile and stood. "And last night was fun until, uh . . . I'm sorry again."

"Stop apologizing. It wasn't your fault."

"Yeah, but now, she'll never forgive me, and I wanted to be her friend."

"You will be if you really want to. Just be honest with her. She doesn't blame you," I told her because, knowing Paige, I was sure Amber was more on her good side than I was.

She smiled. "Okay. See you around."

I stayed at the table for a few minutes after Amber left and clicked on my phone.

Nothing from Brad.

Ryan was keeping his eyes on Amber in case she was being

followed after leaving here, and he hadn't confirmed if she was. But I had a weird sensation crawling up my spine, as if I were being watched.

Why would Brad want to meet any of my friends?

The answer was that he wouldn't.

Which only brought me to, he wanted to see if I would do it, if I actually had a friend like the officer described. That meant this was a test, and he was here. Just not in person. I did a quick scan of the various faces inside the café, not recognizing any as my father's men or anyone who might even look suspicious.

Since he wasn't here and Amber was already gone, there was little point in staying, so I pushed to my feet and tossed the rest of my coffee in a garbage container outside. Then I walked into the shop next door and bought a burner phone.

I kept a phone for my father and Brad, separate from the phone I used to communicate with Paige and the guys, but if I was going to try to get in contact with Stacy Lenard, who may or may not be missing, I couldn't have it being tracked back to any of my phones.

After fifteen minutes of walking in no particular direction, I stopped at a store selling musical instruments. Removing the new phone from my pocket, I dialed the number I'd used to get in contact with the nurse that night, but it went straight to voice mail.

Fuck.

I sent a text to Calvin, who was posted outside her apartment building.

Me: Anything?

Calvin: Nah.

Then, I messaged Ryan.

Me: Anything?

Ryan: Besides Amber's sexy ass in those jeans, nope.

I messaged Calvin again.

Me: I'm going to check the hospital.

Calvin: Not the smartest one here, but that's a bad idea.

I knew that. But I couldn't face Paige, knowing that I was responsible for this happening. That I shouldn't have risked going to my brother's room that night. How would I even tell her someone else might die and that it was all my fault?

I messaged Luke.

Me: Hey, can you go to the hospital and see what you can find out without being too direct? Maybe find an assistant or volunteer to help.

Luke: Yeah. I can be there in thirty.

Calvin: Go talk to my new bestie. That was a dick move, dude.

I didn't know if he was talking about the dick move of telling everyone I had taken Paige's virginity or Paige finding me in the arms of his frenemy. Though something told me he had no idea about the Amber part.

Me: I will.

I left the music store and retraced my steps to a bookstore I'd walked by a few minutes ago. When I opened the door, a bell jingled overhead, and I saw a woman by the counter, dressed casually and speaking on the phone. As I neared, I realized she wasn't that old. In fact, she was around my age, black hair wrapped in a huge knot on top of her head.

She hung up the phone and turned to me.

"Good morning. I'm sorry to bother you, but I need your help."

She gave me a broad smile. "It's no bother at all. What can I do for you?"

I observed her for a moment. She looked so familiar. She was slightly overweight, and the plumpness of her cheeks pinked as I stared. I smiled, wishing she had a nametag I could use to identify her as I searched my memory bank.

"I'm looking for suggestions. Your best romantic comedy novels."

I continued to discreetly watch her as I picked five of the ten books she'd suggested. Stripping a bill from the few I had left in my pocket, I paid for the books.

When she placed the books in a bag and handed them to me, I said, "Thanks, uh . . ."

"Mackenzie."

"Mackenzie, thank you."

It was her. Paige's best friend from high school. Did Paige know that she worked here in the city?

"You have to tell her," Calvin said when I got back to the condo a few hours later.

"She's mad at me." I hung the bag of books on Paige's doorknob since Calvin said she was out with Lisa.

And, fuck, I missed her.

I missed touching her, holding her, and seeing her. She was the only one who could soothe this ache in my chest. The axis of my world. Even though we lived in the same unit, I felt millions of miles away from her if I wasn't touching her to form some kind of connection.

"But it's one of her best friends from high school. That's like how you and I reunited."

I frowned at the memory. Calvin and I had only known each other for a year when Alex Connor enrolled me in public school. He'd sent me there as a test to see how I'd do if I wasn't constrained to the house, but I had failed that test. So, I hadn't gotten to see Calvin again until I was seventeen when I had the freedom to find him. This was nothing like that.

"She ran away from all of it. You didn't see her when she went back to that house, dude. She was—"The sound of the elevator being called to our floor had my heart racing. I missed her, but with this guilt festering inside me, I wasn't ready to confront her. "I'll be in my room."

I listened at my door as Paige came inside, her voice drawing closer.

"Calvin?"

"Yeah?"

"Did you put these here?"

"Yeah, I, uh . . . yeah. Hope you like them," Calvin answered.

He was the worst person to tell anything I didn't want Paige to know.

"You're such a liar," she said, her voice a caress to the tension in my core.

I shouldn't like that she had the power to do this to me, but I couldn't hate it either.

I grabbed my guitar from its faithful corner in my room, and sitting on the balcony overlooking the Quincy Bay, I played for hours. Only this time, as I played, I thought about Olivia Sawyer, my mother. I didn't know anything about her, and I still didn't know if she was alive. But, as my thumb idled over the guitar strings, I felt this strong connection to her, to my uncle, to everything I never had, to everything that had been taken away from me.

Normalcy. Affection.

I craved it, but I didn't deserve it.

I paused, and my thoughts wandered to Tom. He'd given me information the night they almost got to Paige. But if he knew Connor was my real father, I wondered if he also knew what had happened to my mother? Because, if Bailey's facts were straight when she told Paige that Olivia had disappeared the same time I had, it meant Alex Connor had taken me away from her. I didn't care if he'd done what I feared. I just needed to know what had happened.

THIRTEEN

PAIGE

Lisa was in my room, trying on the new outfit she'd purchased at the mall—a sleeveless orange cotton summer dress reaching her mid-thigh. With her long black hair and olive skin tone, she was practically glowing in that dress. She had a date tonight—well, not a date. *A casual affair.* She was much like Amber when it came to how casual they each were about sex. And, with my lack of experience in that department, it was starting to become an educational experience and less and less embarrassing when she said things like what she said next.

"You don't know what it's like to get your hopes up. That you're finally going to have the best sex of your life, only for it to end as the worst sex of your life. All I want is good sex. Why is that so hard to find?"

"At least you're having sex." The words from my thoughts fell from my lips before I could stop them.

But the more she talked about sex, the more my body craved it, and even though I was mad at Caleb for sleeping with Amber—or not sleeping with Amber—I wanted to go to his room so he could have his way with me.

Damn, I disgust myself.

"Let me be the first to tell you that bad sex is worse than no sex. It's kind of like getting your eyebrows done. You go to someone you think is an expert, only for them to fuck your shit up—not in a good way. So, you go home, thinking, *Well, golly, what the hell? I could have done a better job than this. Holy moly, never doing that again.* And, by *that*, I mean the douche bag who'd claimed he was a nymphomaniac sexpert in bed. Basically, it would be better if you had stayed home and done your eyebrows yourself. Make sense?"

I laughed. "Oh my God."

I couldn't relate. Well, maybe I could because the first few guys I'd struggled to date would make me so uncomfortable when they tried to touch me, that even thinking back on it made my skin crawl.

Caleb was the first guy to make me feel . . .

God. I bit my lip as heat flooded my body.

I needed him to touch me again. I needed him to do more than that again. It was so wrong.

How could I feel this way after what he did?

Last night, when I had gotten back to the condo, I'd texted Lisa about Amber and Caleb. Seeing them together had hurt so much that I'd had to tell someone, and Lisa was the only one I could tell. She'd even promised not to say anything to anyone. Though she'd told me Amber would have told her if there was anything going on with her and Caleb, it still didn't explain them being alone together last night.

That brought me back to the guy who was interested in me.

"What about Miller?" I asked, distracting myself before I looked over to the bag of books I'd set on the floor next to my closet. "You've known him a while. How come you guys have never . . . you know?"

"I've slept with two of Miller's friends. There's a fine line to cross when sleeping with guys and their friends. You sleep with two guys who know each other, and it's like, okay, shit happens. But, when you sleep with three"—she turned, viewing the back of the dress in the mirror—"they stop respecting you." She sounded so pensive that I paused and looked at her.

Lisa liked having her fun with guys, but she still cared what people thought of her. Little by little, I was starting to see what separated her from Amber.

Lying on my back with my feet up on the cushions and my earphones in, I rocked my head to the beat. The only time I ever wore earphones was at the gym, so this showed how much I trusted these guys to keep me safe. At that thought, I removed one of them because the whole safety thing was in my head, and I had to be sure.

I looked around and spotted Rob on his laptop in the den. Calvin had disappeared after Lisa and I arrived, but I hadn't seen Caleb. In fact, I was dying to know if he was here. It was almost four, and I hadn't seen or heard from him all day besides the books he'd left for me, which I wouldn't read until I wasn't mad at him anymore . . . or maybe I would hide in my room and read them. One of them, I'd already read, but still, Caleb getting me books was thoughtful and kind, but I didn't want to think about that. Because not only had he been a jerk last night, but he'd also gotten these books from somewhere in my past. The specific store I used to visit at least once a week with Mackenzie when I lived at the mansion. After what had happened that night almost five years ago, I had stopped going there, along with anywhere else I used to visit.

I hadn't even visited the cemetery where the only family I knew was buried, where Caleb's real family was buried. It was how I'd managed to stay off his father's radar for this long. But another reason I'd left everything behind was to protect the people who'd been in my life. So, if he stumbled upon that bookstore by accident, I needed to know more. It was important to me.

Letting out a breath, I set the book I had been attempting to read and picked up my phone. I sent him a text.

Me: Why that bookstore?

His response came in seconds.

Caleb: Why not?

I wanted to be petty and not tell him why, but I needed to put my feelings aside for this.

Me: I used to go there.

He didn't reply, so I set my phone down and picked up *my* book—not one of his gifted ones—while I tried not to overthink it. It could have just been a coincidence.

A few minutes later, an all-masculine and powerful Caleb stood over me, staring down at me on the couch. I hated how my breath caught and how my nipples tightened.

I'm still mad at him, yet all I can think about is how gorgeous and sexy he looks right now.

As he sat by my head, I sat up, fighting my body's need to be closer to him.

"I'm not talking to you," I said out of nowhere, staring at the television on the wall.

His presence even confused the way my body knew how to conduct the simple task of breathing. From what I could see in my peripheral vision, he positioned his phone on his lap and typed right before my phone vibrated.

Caleb: When was the last time you went to that bookstore?

Me: Five years ago. Why were you there?

Caleb: To buy you something.

Another text came in.

Caleb: If I knew where one of your high school friends was, would you want to talk to her?

I looked at him, taking in the solemn expression on his face as I pulled out the other earphone from my ear.

"Mackenzie," he said before I could ask the question.

I swallowed, and I knew he was watching to see if it bothered me. "Where did you see her?" I asked.

"The bookstore. She works there."

"Why would she work in a bookstore? Her parents are, like, stupid rich." Pulling my bottom lip between my teeth, I chewed on it in thought.

Caleb shrugged, and at the same time, guilt came over me for running away. I would know what was going on in Mackenzie's life if I had been there. If I'd stayed.

"Hey, it's okay. You don't have to see her if you don't want to. I just wanted you to know."

"How did she . . . did she seem happy?"

"She seemed okay. She looks different from the girl in the picture you showed me. I don't even know how I noticed it was her. I think it was her smile."

"Different how?"

"She's gained weight. You want to see her," he said knowingly, "but you're unsure."

"With everything going on, I wouldn't want to put her life in danger."

"No, it's more than that."

I swallowed, trying to push down the dryness in my throat, and looked away. "I left her. She probably hates me for leaving."

"I doubt that. But, if you're up to it, I can go back there and leave my number or yours, you two can talk, and if you want to meet somewhere, you can bring her here. Or just be careful about meeting her in the city."

The heaviness inside dissipated, and my chest swelled. "Really?"

His lips twitched, a small smile appearing. "Really."

I frowned. He wasn't supposed to make me happy.

"Damn it, Caleb." I pouted, folding my arms over my chest. "I'm mad at you."

"But I'm sorry—"

"I don't want to hear it." I plugged the earphones back in my ears, not caring if I was being immature.

He shouldn't get off this easy for embarrassing me in public and hooking up with Amber. That was not okay.

Caleb moved over and removed my earphones before I could press play on my phone while I sat there, immobile, as his hand went around the back of my head. He held the side of my face to his, and everything inside wound tight from the contact.

His lips moved over my ear, but as the words came out, I could hear the bite in his tone. "I didn't sleep with her." He released me and stood, looking at me like it was my fault or that I should be fucking grateful.

That, that right there, set blaze to the fire I'd been stomping out since last night. "Wow! You're such a dick. Should I be thankful that you claim to have not slept with her after inviting her over to spend the whole fucking night alone with you?" I stood. "You know, maybe I should just invite Miller over to spend the night in my room, so I can *not* sleep with him. Would that be okay with you?"

He frowned, biting his lip and shaking his head. "If it's what you want."

"*God, Caleb!* Are you kidding me? So, you freaked out at the club just to, what? Embarrass me? Let everyone know how you got there first?"

His eyes moved over my shoulder. "Not now, Paige."

"No, fuck you." I stomped around the couch toward my room, and he came from the other side to block my path. "Caleb, if you touch me right now, I'm going to lose it. Don't—"

"Paige."

I held up my hands away from him.

"God, fuck, damn it!" He huffed, walking away from me as he ran his hand through his hair.

I hurried into my room and locked the door.

Damn it.

I paced, trying to shake the anger, the pain.

He shouldn't have brought Amber to our old apartment, and he shouldn't have told everyone about what had happened between us. That should have been ours alone. And, it was pissing me off that he was making it out to be ... *nothing*. He hadn't brought Amber back to the apartment for nothing. He hadn't pulled me out of Miller's arms because he wanted me for himself. He hadn't done it because he wanted me back. He'd just done it because—I stopped in the middle of the room—why had he done it? Why was he acting like this, and hurting me?

He'd started to change since he found out Alex Connor was possibly his dad. That was when he'd begun to push me away. Then he found out Connor was *actually* his dad. Freaking Alex Connor. Why did everything lead back to him?

I drew in a breath and glanced at the small desk in my room. Walking over to it, I grabbed a pen and my notebook from it and sat on the floor, my back against the bed. There was a better way to release this aggression. My letters to the one and only. I had written the first one when I came back here after seeing Caleb with Amber last night. Inhaling, I set the notebook on my knees. It was time to write the second.

Alex Connor,

My name is Reese Sawyer. You might not remember me, but no worries. I'll paint the perfect picture ...

FOURTEEN

CALEB

The next day, I didn't talk to Paige. She needed space. The worst part was that I had known it from the start. I had known it was bad timing when I attempted my apologies, but I had to try because I hated her being mad at me, hated that she was hurting because of me, another Connor. So today, I wanted to do something for her, which was talk to Mackenzie.

When I went back to the bookstore, the clerk informed me that Mackenzie only volunteered there once a week and wouldn't be back until the following Sunday. I'd left my number there and asked her to pass it along.

After that stop, I called Tom, and he claimed he didn't know anything else about my past and Alex Connor. I had no choice but to believe the sick fuck. So, that was a dead end.

With nothing much going on at Luxe when I returned, I decided to go home earlier than usual.

Home. I smiled at that.

After living at my father's mercy for years and then in a suite for another few years, the places I considered home were the first apartment I'd rented because of Paige and this condo I hadn't even been living in for three weeks. Yet it felt like home.

It was home.

I keyed in the digit to our floor, swiped my key card, and then entered the six-digit code specific to our unit. It was then that the elevator doors closed. When I got out in the foyer and walked toward my bedroom, I heard giggling. Paige was working at the bar, so it couldn't have been her.

A loud moan reverberated through the walls, and I paused.

Another moan.

I looked behind me at the closed door, shaking my head.

Calvin.

A grin tugged at my lips because this was the most normal I'd ever felt. My best friend was screwing some girl in the other room, and the girl I liked was my roommate. As the sounds grew more pornographic, my balls tightened.

Shit.

Continuing to my room, I locked the door behind me. All fun and games until I was the one listening, not doing the screwing.

This is what having no sex is like.

Fucking hell.

Changing out of my work clothes, I headed down to the gym with my gym bag hanging from my shoulder. Only a few people were here, and no one was currently using the small space in the corner for kickboxing or other groundwork. I dropped my bag on the floor in front of the area covered by black tumbling mats and removed my shoes. Then I took out my white wrist wrap and walked to the single suspended kickboxing bag. Most days, I omitted the gloves because I liked the impact. I liked feeling the way my hits vibrated back into my body with a hint of pain. I used to like it so much that, by the time I was done, blood would be seeping through the white material around my knuckles. But that'd had to stop after discovering how much I also liked playing my guitar. Although with some practice, I'd figured out the exact number of times I could hit before the discomfort in my hands would carry over to the days I settled for just my guitar.

There was always a limit to the amount of pain the body could withstand before breaking. Anyone who'd ever been through real pain knew that limit. That limit was called the breaking point. I'd been there. The point where all I could focus on was the pain. The fear of dying. Then, actually wanting to die because anything would be better than that pain. It was how I'd become obedient. Why I kept my nose out of Alex Connor's business. Breaking had pushed me to look the other way. It was what kept me calm when all I wanted was to do something, tell someone. That would be when someone else would get hurt. Not just me.

See, Alex Connor didn't break me through physical pain. I didn't care about what happened to me, and he knew that.

He knew my weakness was watching someone else get hurt, and with that, he'd ripped out every ounce of willpower I ever had to do anything but serve him. So, even though I wanted answers and him and his men to be in jail, I found myself questioning my choice to go against him. Because how many others would get hurt before he could be stopped?

I feared taking that risk to find out.

I took a risk with Stacy Lenard, and she was missing because of it.

Was it worth it?

No.

About an hour into kickboxing, I was drenched in sweat and my pulse was racing when Calvin appeared at the edge of the black mat. "You got off work early."

My precise hits to the bag stopped, and I brought my arm up to wipe the sweat from my forehead. "Yeah."

He looked stressed for someone who had just been fucking less than an hour ago. His eyes moved to the suspended bag. "Up for a real challenge with me instead of this helpless piece of crap?" he asked, pointing a finger at the bag.

I chuckled. "You're joking, right?"

"Nah. I just need to get my gloves."

He walked away without making eye contact, and I folded my

lips, tasting the salt from my sweat on them.

"Weren't you just up there with someone?" I asked, curious about the way he was acting and hopeful that I wouldn't have to tell him whoever it was couldn't remain up there without supervision.

"Uh . . ." Calvin paused and scratched the back of his head before looking at me. "You heard that?"

"A little bit."

"Yeah, she's gone. It was just some girl," he said. "I'll be back."

Hadn't sounded like just some girl, but I nodded.

Late that night, I was lying in bed, staring at the ceiling, trying to figure out the best way to get more information about what had happened to my mother. I didn't want to do anything that would involve anyone else getting hurt. Like the wrong call I'd made with the nurse, whom I still couldn't get in contact with.

My door cracked open, and I looked over.

With my eyes adjusted to the dark, I could see exactly who it was. Couldn't see her face, but I could make out that perfect physique from anywhere. Paige.

As she closed the door, a shaky whisper came from her, "Caleb?" She sounded so afraid.

Sitting up on the bed, ready to go to her, I grabbed the sheet I was covered with from the waist down to throw it off but stopped.

I was naked.

I was naked, and Paige was coming to me. In my bed. And judging from the sound of her voice, she wasn't here to—

"Caleb."

Oh fuck. Fuck.

"Yeah?" I cleared my throat as she drew closer. "Uh . . . you okay?" I asked, my voice sounding rusty and choked.

"I had a nightmare," she said, her voice weak, still shaken. "Can I stay in here with you? Please."

I cleared my throat again. "Yeah, of course. Come here."

Deep breath. Fuck, fuck. Fuck. I need to tell her I'm not dressed. Should I tell her? I don't want her to leave.

I pressed a hand to the tent rising between my thighs in a silent command to stay down. Probably wouldn't listen, but I had to try.

Paige's eyes wouldn't be adjusted to the dark yet. I could get off the bed and—

She climbed onto my bed, crawled over to me, and wrapped her arms around my neck. I'd waited so long for her to hold me like this again that I fucking melted. I wrapped my arms around her and squeezed, feeling my world as it shifted back on its axis.

This girl.

She fucking owns me.

For a few minutes, we stayed like that, her arms around my neck and my arms around her waist. A small part of me knew she would regret this tomorrow, but for the moment, I wanted to live in the present, wrapped in her softness and breathing her in. God, she smelled so good. Like rose petals, lavender, and sugar.

"Let's lie down," I said, moving with her, but she stayed put. "Paige?"

She held me tighter. "No. I can't lose you. Promise me."

"Take my pain, and I'll take yours," she'd once told me.

The funny thing was, she was the only one who could take my pain, but I didn't want her to. I'd much rather take hers.

So, I told her, "You won't. I'm not going anywhere." It was a lie. A path I couldn't walk away from had been carved for me. "Let's lie down. It's okay. I'm here."

She obliged, settling into my arms after I swiftly stuffed as much sheet as possible between her butt and my front, leaving my ass completely bare, but that was way better than her bolting when she realized how turned on I was.

"I'm still mad at you."

My lips curved against the silky strands on her head, which smelled like rose petals, too. "I know."

"Are you and Amber—"

"No," I answered before she finished. "There's nothing between Amber and me, Paige, and there never will be." I rubbed my nose on the back of her head and smoothed my hand down her chilled arm. "I know what else is going through this pretty little head, and I'll give you some of the answers tonight, but the heavier stuff, I'll leave that for another day. I honestly don't know what happened at the club, but I know I hurt you. I'm sorry for that. I really am, but you're safe now. I'll be your dream catcher for tonight. So, I want you to free your mind. Whatever you were dreaming about earlier is gone, and you know what's even better? One day, those dreams won't come back. One day, they'll just be memories. One day, you'll dream about rainbows and ponies—"

"I don't want to dream about rainbows and ponies."

"What do you want to dream about?"

She never answered, but I wanted her to say me. The thought made me smile. Then I really thought about it, and it scared the hell out of me. She was giving me something I never wanted. She was giving me something I was too scared to have. Paige was giving me hope.

FIFTEEN

Paige

The comfy warmth that had been wrapped around me disappeared, and I shifted, seeking that strength and security around me again. When I didn't feel it, I pulled the sheets tighter around me. Everything felt so nice and soft.

My bed didn't feel like this. My bed was cold and—

This wasn't my bed.

My brain scrabbled and threw out random snapshots of the night. Nightmare. Freaked out. Caleb's room. Caleb's bed. I opened my eyes.

Oh no. This is so embarrassing. Especially after how I was yelling at him, like, two days ago. Now, I'm in his bed. God, he must think I'm loony.

And why was his bed so cozy? I was pretty sure we had the same bed and sheets.

"Hello," came Caleb's husky voice from somewhere behind me. He cleared his throat. "No, it's okay. I'm usually up by now."

My chest burned. This jealousy wasn't even subtle.

I turned around and saw he was sitting at the edge of the bed, his back to me. "Yeah, I was hoping you'd call."

Oh my gosh, if that's Amber, I swear, I'm going to hurt him.

A saner voice calmed me as I gazed at all the dips and rises of the muscles across his back. God, I'd almost forgotten how good he looked without clothes. My eyes traveled down to the waistband of his boxers, my mouth almost watering by that point. I licked my lips and swallowed. Instead of wanting to be mad at him, I wanted to caress any tension in his body, lure him off that phone. My body heated, and want spread from my lower belly down to a much needier place.

Taking a ragged breath, I tapped him on his back. He twisted around, smiled, and then turned around all the way to face me. He lay on his stomach, propping himself up on his elbows and keeping the phone elevated between us. Then he put it on speaker.

"I've been working there, hoping that, one day, I'd run into her again."

Mackenzie. My Mickey.

Oh my God, I mouthed as the sound of my best friend's voice filled the room.

She sounded the same . . .

"I'm sorry I called so early, but when can I see her? Is she available for breakfast, lunch, anything? I'm available whenever, just . . ."

My mouth opened, but I couldn't get the words out. I couldn't think, period.

"I think she can do breakfast," Caleb said.

I inhaled, my heart freaking ready to explode.

"Oh my gosh, yes, that would be perfect. Where and what time?"

Caleb raised his eyebrows, and I grabbed his wrist, squeezing. Finally, my brain decided to function again. I peered down at his phone. The time on it read a few minutes after seven.

"Nine would be fine," I told her.

"Oh my gosh! Paige. You're there. Oh my gosh, it's you. It's really you."

Overwhelmed by emotion, I covered my mouth for a second before I responded. "Hi, Mickey. It's me, and it's you."

"Oh my gosh, I can't wait to see you."

"I know. I'll text you the address, okay?" I said, trying to catch my breath.

"Okay."

Caleb ended the call, licked his lips, and grinned at me while doing this little flirty thing with his eyebrows. "That went well."

Trying to suppress a delightful tingle in my heart, I smiled. "I can't believe you did that, even after I yelled at you."

"I deserved it, and you deserve this." He showed his phone where the call had ended. "And so much more."

"You could ride with me to the city if you want, and Ryan could pick you up, or I could have him drive you there."

"Caleb"—I threw the sheets off and moved over, tackling him to the bed when I jumped onto his back, my arms circling beneath his chest—"thank you. I'm almost *not* mad at you anymore. Almost."

I settled the side of my face between his shoulder blades, and the heat from his skin warmed my cheek. Having the strongest urge to turn my face and lick and bite into his smooth skin, I bit on my lip.

What is wrong with me? He doesn't want me like this.

I hurried off him. "I'm sorry. I didn't mean to tackle you like that." I scrambled off the bed. "I'm going to go shower. Um . . . I can leave with, uh, Ryan."

Driving for a half hour, alone, in Caleb's car to the city was not a good idea, not when all I wanted to do was sink my teeth into him.

God, I'm such a creep.

Slipping out of his room, I let out a breath. I was in the clear. Only I wasn't. Calvin stared at me from the living room with a cup halfway to his mouth.

A deer caught in headlights? Yeah, I was pretty sure that was exactly what I looked like.

Everyone had been aware of Caleb and me fighting, yet here I was, looking like I was sneaking out of his room.

Okay, I was sneaking.

Ignoring Calvin, I hurried into my room and flopped onto my unmade bed.

This was going to be a thing between Caleb and me that no

one would understand. Except for Calvin. He was the only person who knew that Caleb was my rock. He had become my rock the first time he saw my weakness and tried to take it away, the first time he kissed me and took it away, even though temporarily. But, one of my weaknesses dwelled inside of him.

I thought back on his words.

"I honestly don't know what happened at the club, but I know I hurt you."

He didn't have to explain what had happened at the club because I knew exactly what had happened.

He didn't have to explain why he'd held a gun to that guy's head the night I was attacked, because I knew why.

Caleb had blacked out. It explained everything about the way he'd been acting, and from what I'd gathered from Calvin, this wasn't like Caleb. Caleb was calm. Always thinking things through.

Even yesterday, when Calvin had driven me to my therapy session, he'd confided, "Caleb's never lost it like that."

And all I could think at the time was, *Why would he now?*

So, I hadn't said anything back to Calvin because I didn't understand then what I understood now.

"I honestly don't know what happened at the club."

My rock was breaking.

And that wasn't good for either of us.

This restaurant was Caleb's idea. He'd recommended it because it was hidden in the midst of the city, and it was also where a majority of law enforcement officers had their meals. So, I wasn't surprised to see two officers heading into the restaurant at the same time I was, one holding the door open for me.

The tables were all made of dark wood and had the same shade of the flooring. The incandescent lighting brightened the area along with all the windows stretching down the walls, giving the place a less depressing look and feel, though not by much.

No better way to bring an old friend into my much gloomier world.

It only took me a second to spot her. Her long black hair hung on either side of rounder cheeks, but it was my Mickey, my sometimes Mac and Cheesy. I smiled, a wave of nervous energy coming over me. Mackenzie stood, dressed in jeans with a pink-and-blue blouse.

"Oh my God, KP." Mackenzie smiled, calling me by the nickname she'd given me once upon a time. Her arms opened up to me for a hug. "I thought I'd never see you again."

"Mickey," I returned, reaching my arms around her, this moment seemingly surreal. I'd never planned to go back until two days ago when the opportunity had presented itself.

Mackenzie did most of the talking, which was a lifesaver. Even though I had been excited to see her, I hadn't thought about what I would say that didn't involve the things going on in my life. Things I didn't want her to know. Caleb's father was still looking for me, and I had no doubt that eyes could be on Mackenzie. But I couldn't tell her today. Today shouldn't bring that much baggage.

And it didn't.

Mackenzie was studying medicine, which I knew she'd hated in the past, but she'd done what her parents wanted after all.

Life had gone on, yet it seemed nothing had changed.

In fact, it felt like it was just yesterday when we'd last seen each other.

"I can't believe you chose this place. It's kind of dead. I would have chosen a more awesome spot for us to hang out."

"You would have?"

"Oh, definitely. I know where all the cool kids hang out. Not that I'm cool anymore, but . . . yeah." Mackenzie smiled, taking a sip of her water.

"Well, I'm not cool anymore either," I offered, looking at the half-eaten scrambled eggs on my plate. "Caleb chose this place. Sorry. He's, uh . . . protective."

"Aw, that's so cute. Now, it makes sense why there're so many cops here." She threw a glance around, playing with the long tresses of black hair hanging over her chest. She looked so adorable, her plumper cheeks adding to her natural beauty. "I recommended your awesome new books, by the way. He was all handsome and clueless when he came into the store. He seems like a really good guy."

"Yeah, but we aren't, um ... oh, wow, I can't even explain us. We aren't together like that. I mean, boyfriend-girlfriend." I scratched at a spot on my forearm that wasn't itching, unsure of why I was even trying to explain it.

"Oh." A smile formed on her lips. "Well, I think he likes you—a lot. I mean, he buys you books. No one else knew how much you loved books besides me."

"Yeah, it's funny, too, because he calls me KP—" I stopped before I let the *as a codename* slipped out.

"What? No way. So, you still love watching *Kim Possible*, huh?"

I scrunched my face. She had no idea. "Embarrassing really."

Mackenzie laughed. "But that's even better. He knows the real you."

Again, she had no idea.

"How about you, Mickey? Is there any lover boy I should know about?"

She played with her fingers on the table. "No."

"Hmm, I don't know if this is good or bad because you were legit boy crazy." I smiled.

"Yeah, I was." She giggled, though I still saw the wistful look in her ice-blue eyes. "Do you remember my parents' mansion about an hour and a half north of here? The one on the lake?"

"Barely, but I think so."

"There are parties. I don't usually go, a bunch of frats pay for the place and throws them up there, and they're starting up again next weekend. They call it The Four Weekends of Summer Party. It's pretty much an end-of-summer event, and it goes on for four weekends until the semester begins. Anyway, you should ... we should go. I mean, if you want to. I know it'll be your birthday and you probably have something planned and this is the first we've seen each other in years but—"

I'd forgotten it would be my birthday this weekend.

"I'll go with you."

The last time my birthday was celebrated had been with my sisters at one of our ultimate pajama parties. Ultimate because we'd had them with nothing less than about thirty girls from school. Boys hadn't been allowed in the mansion.

But, going with Mackenzie wasn't about my birthday. This was about the reason she hadn't been attending these parties, and from the way her face lit up, I knew I was doing the right thing.

"Are you serious?"

I nodded. "Positive."

"Oh my God!" Mackenzie clapped her hands together and wiggled in her seat. "I'm so excited. We'll even have our own room. So, everyone drives up on Friday, and then on Sunday, everyone drives back down."

I was scheduled to work both nights, but as of late, I didn't look forward to my shifts alongside Chelsey at Stilts. She had stopped bothering me about what had gone down with me and her boyfriend, Ian, but there was still this negative energy when I was around her, and I hated it. So, I didn't care about giving up those shifts to go this weekend.

Oh, right. I think I have a crew now.

Biting my lip, I smiled. "How many extra invitations and rooms are available?"

My eyes went up to the two men walking by our table. I couldn't see the faces, but I remembered that baseball cap and that voice.

"Charles said he would have that done by tomorrow, so we shouldn't have any other delays."

Agent Langley.

"Uh, did you drive here, Mickey?"

"Yeah."

I dug out the forty dollars stuffed into the tiny pocket of my leggings and stood, unfolding it on the table. "Let's go. This place is dead. Show me one of those cool spots you know about."

SIXTEEN

CALEB

Brad leaned against the doorframe to my office as he said, "I saw your girlfriend. She was pretty hot."

I usually had the door to my office closed, but I'd been in and out all day, dealing with maintenance for a pipe leak in one of the suites.

Inhaling a long breath, I continued staring at my computer screen as I typed, though my fingers were jamming down on the keys harder, judging by the echoes filling the tension in the air.

"Dad wants you over this weekend."

"I'm busy."

"What, with your new girlfriend?"

Sinking the line I'd tossed him when I waited for him with Amber at the café, I asked, "Yeah, so?"

"Shit, maybe I shouldn't have kept my distance. I'll be sure to introduce myself next time. Anyway, you know what's priority. Make it happen. Thanks for that new toy, by the way." He sucked a breath through his teeth. "She's a frisky little thing."

I stopped typing when Brad left. There was no word on the missing nurse from any of the guys, and Brad had just confirmed she was still alive. And, since Alex Connor wanted to see me this weekend, this couldn't be good.

I texted Calvin.

Me: Get me Bailey's number, but don't let Paige know about it.

The number came in a few seconds later. Like it had already been stored on his phone. I should have thought something about it, but shit, I should have had Bailey's number a long time ago. She was the key person in helping us.

However, Paige didn't tell Bailey about me, so she would still think I was missing, which meant I couldn't exactly summon her.

I sent another message to Calvin.

Me: Send a text from Paige's phone to Bailey. Write this: Meet me in the parking lot outside of the café where we've met before in exactly two hours. Please come alone this time.

My phone lit up.

Calvin: I'll text you when it's done.

A silver Honda turned into the parking lot from the main road on my right. The one I'd been waiting for. It was the same car she'd driven to meet with Paige. Since it was almost five and the coffee shop closed at four p.m., the parking lot was empty, except for the unoccupied white car parked a few spaces behind me. I'd been sitting here, waiting for twenty minutes, and no one had approached the car, so I assumed someone had left it there and taken the metro to work. Either that or the car wouldn't start. But I didn't like that it was here, and it was causing my spine to tingle. But I couldn't change the plan.

Praying we weren't being watched, I scanned the parking lot again for anyone wandering about. Then I sent a message to the phone number Calvin had given me for Bailey.

Me: I know Paige. I've been helping her. She didn't tell you about me. My name is Caleb Sawyer. I need your help.

I watched as she pulled into a parking space, and I could see the orange glow of her hair through the windows of her car. She was alone, and she hadn't seen the message yet. Leaving the car running, I pulled the hoodie over my head and pushed my door open. In a few quick strides, I reached the passenger side of her car.

She was still dressed in a navy-blue uniform and staring at the phone in her hand. The small knob that should have been down on the door was sticking out, which was good for me. Bending, I stared through the window at her, knowing I would scare the crap out of her, but that was the least of any of our problems at the moment. She looked up and jumped in her seat, and I pulled the door open and sat. Even though I would obviously look nothing like that missing baby twenty-four years ago, I was guessing she wouldn't shoot me either.

With one hand, I swiped the hoodie off my head and looked at her. "I'm Caleb Sawyer."

Her mouth opened, but I didn't wait for her to find the words. I slipped into business mode.

"Don't tell Paige we've met. You're working with me now. Whatever she was planning with you a few weeks ago, to use herself as bait, forget it. I'm your guy, and by the time I give you all you need, I'll even put my hands behind my back, so you can arrest me."

"But you . . . how do I know it's you? And does this mean that you weren't missing?" Bailey asked.

"It's me. You're going to have to trust me. I would show you my ID, but I was given a different identity. My Social Security number will only be traced to the person my father adopted and raised—Caleb Connor. And my ID leads to a Caleb Sheppard."

I stared at the café before us. "Paige seems to trust you, and she doesn't give that freely. So, I'm going to trust her instincts about you. The first thing you need to know is that my father is the man you want. He has businesses both here and in New York. I work at Luxe in downtown Boston, but I also oversee four condominiums in New York. He is smart. His men are smart. You go after him, and you will find nothing."

I looked at her. "You see where this is going. He's the man who put the hit on Paige's family. He views Paige as a loose end and he won't let it go because she keeps getting away. If he gets his hands on her, she isn't going to be so lucky again. She has been on his radar for too long. That is why you can't involve her. It's too dangerous for her. But you have me now. The only thing I'm asking for in return besides keeping Paige out of this is my birth certificate. I already know who my father is, but I know nothing about my mother."

"I told Paige your grandparents still call—"

"She told me. She also told me my mother's name is Olivia Sawyer. But I need proof. After everything I've discovered over the past few weeks, mere words don't do it for me anymore. I need solid proof, and I don't want my grandparents involved." Enough of my family had died. I would be an idiot to show up on their doorstep just so I could add them to that list.

"Okay, I can get that for you."

"Thank you. Now, let's talk about the reason I'm here," I said, getting back on track as to why I'd sought her out today. "There's a nurse who's gone missing. Her name is Stacy Lenard. I don't know where they have her, but if my instincts are right, she could be in trouble."

"What makes you think this nurse is missing or in trouble?"

"Because of my father and what he's capable of making disappear. My brother also made it obvious when he came into my office today and told me that they have her. My fault really. I asked her to do something she shouldn't have done to help me. But it's possible I could find out what is happening to her since my brother said my father wants to see me this weekend."

"Your brother?"

"Yes. I'll explain everything later because I'm sure you have a lot of questions and doubts. But right now, you need to think of colleagues who can help. You won't be able to do this alone. Your boss works for my father, so that's already a no-go."

"You mean, the deputy superintendent? Rodriguez?"

I nodded.

"Paige mentioned it, and I do have another way."

Taking her mindfulness as a good sign, I continued, "He's meticulous about what he does, and the only way you'll be able to find any of his locations is by putting a tracking device in me." I didn't need to spell out the definition of locations. That would come later.

"If what you're telling me is true about your father, are you willing to put him in jail?"

"His name is Alex Connor, and I'm willing to put all of us in jail. Weren't you listening?"

SEVENTEEN

Paige

It was ten at night, and I was watching a show in the living room when I heard the elevator's arrival. Calvin was in his room, and the only light in the open space was the flashes of blue coming from the television mounted on the wall above the fireplace. Caleb stepped around the corner, still dressed in his three-piece black suit.

He stopped as our eyes met in the dim lighting. "Hey."

"Hi."

He kicked off his dress shoes right where he stood, and then his jacket went next, falling to and hitting the floor without a sound. This was the fourth time he'd done this since we moved to this condo, and it was so hot. Like he was undressing for me. As he walked to me, he tugged on his tie to loosen it. The few times he'd done this before was right before he rested his head on my shoulder. So, the thought that we were back on solid ground had my heart racing because I loved when he leaned on me. We weren't dating, hooking up, or anything for that matter, but I loved being there for him. I wanted him to lean on me.

Tonight though, I wanted him to do more. I missed his touch so much that, as he approached, I imagined him walking to me, undoing his buckle, and standing before me as my hands went up and reached inside his briefs. I longed for the hard, velvety feel of him in my hands and the taste of him in my mouth. The first few times hadn't been enough. So tonight, I wanted him to do more.

"Are you still *almost* not mad at me anymore?" He sat in the middle of the couch, a few feet away from me.

I inhaled and swallowed, pushing my thoughts aside so that I could act unaffected by him because it was what he wanted.

"No." The single word I managed came out breathy.

He frowned, and I realized he must have thought I was still upset with him.

"I'm not mad at you anymore."

A small smile lifted the corners of his lips. "Good."

He moved closer to me, and I wasn't as upright as the few times he'd rested his head on my shoulder. I was propped in the corner of the couch on my side, an oversize pillow beneath my head and my feet curled behind me. So, my heart thumped as I tried to anticipate the way he was planning to connect with me. A connection was the only way to explain it because, since I'd forced him to stop touching me, I realized it was all I wanted.

Even if the touch wasn't sexual in any way, I needed to feel that connection with him.

He pressed the side of his face to my hip and dropped his large arms on either side of my figure. Warmth and desire coursed through my body from the contact. Him in his white dress shirt, tie loose around his neck, his attention on the television, Caleb was everything I'd never dreamed of. Yet this moment was too perfect to be real.

One of my hands lifted to comb through the silky texture of his disheveled hair. It was like the hair on a cat, so soft and smooth that I couldn't help but caress it, allowing it to glide through my fingers over and over again.

Caleb sighed. "I should probably get changed."

"Long day?"

"Way too long."

My hand moved down to the back of his head, and my

fingernails scratched his nape before moving back up. He groaned, and my sex clenched from the memory of that sound.

"How was your day with Mackenzie?"

"It was good. Kind of like it hadn't even been five years," I told him.

"Makes sense. Calvin was right then. It was the same way with him and me when we saw each other again," Caleb explained.

This made me curious. Neither of them had talked about their friendship in the past, but each had thrown hints that there was something more to their bond.

"How old were you when you guys separated? And I don't know why I'm making it sound like a marriage."

"Yeah. Don't say that too loud; he'll probably propose."

I chuckled. "He probably would."

You're kind of a catch, Caleb Sawyer.

"Anyway, I was eleven, but I got to see him again when I moved into the suite at seventeen."

"How did you lose contact with him?" I tried to sound nonchalant, but I was dying for answers.

"I was homeschooled." Before I could ask more questions, he said, "There's something I have to tell you."

Preparing for the worst, the dark well where I let all the bad things fester opened up in my chest. Even my hand stopped moving in his hair as I waited. I wasn't sure what I was waiting for—for him to confide that he'd slept with Amber or that Alex Connor was making him do something horrible. One of those should be much worse than the other, but right now, they carried the same weight.

"Brad knows about the nurse who drew a sample of his blood."

Way, way worse.

"What?"

"I should have known. I don't know why I thought it could have really been that simple.

"Anyway, that's the reason Amber was at the apartment. Brad said he wanted to meet the blonde the cop had seen me with that night we were on the highway. He said, if I showed him who I was with, he'd get off my back, but he didn't even show.

"And, now, the nurse, Stacy Lenard, is missing. The hospital said she took a month's vacation. But Connor could have forced her to do that, so it wouldn't seem strange when she went missing. I don't know where she is, and I think they're going to hurt her." He let out a loud exhale. "They already are . . . hurting her."

I tried not to think about what *hurting* entailed, but I made a mental note to search for Stacy online later.

Shifting until Caleb eased his weight from my hip, I stretched my legs out at the shorter end of the sectional and tapped him to move, so his head could rest on my lap. This was more comfortable, and with his head still turned to the television, I could play in his hair with both hands.

"How did Brad find out about the nurse if he was asleep?" I asked. He sighed. "I don't know."

"How do you know they have her?"

"Brad told me."

A sick feeling twisted my gut, and I could tell this was bothering him, too. "Well, he could be lying to get under your skin," I suggested. "Or, what if the nurse is working with Connor and his men? I mean, if he has a high-ranking cop working with him, it's possible he could have that nurse too. How did you get her to do it in the first place? She must have known the risk." That last part was vile. I knew the risk of messing with Alex Connor, yet here I was, mailing him letters from the dead.

"I paid her sixty thousand dollars."

My eyebrows flew up.

"Well," I said, pushing aside another important question about all that money, "maybe she took the money and left town. You don't know what happened."

"Don't do that."

"Do what?"

"Give me hope."

I frowned, staring down at him. I wanted to give him much more than that. I didn't understand why he didn't want hope, me, or anything.

What is he not telling me?

Guilt seeped out of that dark, unlocked well.

What am I not telling him?

He didn't want hope, and I couldn't take my anxiety pills, knowing what was waiting for me every time I stepped outside of these walls.

Shaking my head, I continued to pass my hand through his hair, twirling strands of it around my fingers. It was probably due for a trim, but I liked it like this.

He fell asleep not long after, and as my sadness settled inside that dark well, I closed it, pushing it down until next time.

Smiling down at him, I traced a finger over his always-perfect five o'clock shadow.

He was the most handsome man I'd ever seen.

My mind journeyed to what his life must have been like, growing up and getting homeschooled.

Did he have someone to hug or lean on when he was down? Did he have a nanny to take care of him the way a mother would have, the way Olivia would have? More questions I would have to ask him another day.

For the moment, I liked doing this. Liked being this person for him. And, judging by the way he slept, touching his hair was as therapeutic for him as it was for me.

A gush of wind hit me, and I peeked under heavy eyelids to see a heavy blanket being folded across my chest.

Calvin.

Closing my eyes, I drifted off again.

I felt weightless, like a feather wafting through the air. No. That wasn't possible. Something was wrong. My heart skipped a beat and almost lurched through my chest before I opened my eyes. It was dark, and I was being carried. A familiar scent floated around me, and I sniffed. Cool, fresh, and . . . Caleb.

"Go back to sleep. It's okay," came a soothing whisper.

As I snuggled closer to his chest, my worries faded, and I was out again.

EIGHTEEN

Caleb

I was wrong.
 I was wrong about everything.

Tapping my fingers on the metal rods framing the glass-surrounded balcony, I peered at the sun gradually rising over the bay. Paige was asleep in her room where I'd placed her last night because if I woke up next to her again, I would want things with her I shouldn't want. I would want a life I wasn't meant to have.

A life I would never have. Not after what I'd set in motion with Bailey last night.

The reason I was wrong was not for doing what needed to be done to stop Connor, but for believing that Paige and I were too broken for each other. We were perfect for each other. In fact, I was sure she and I were the only ones who could fix each other. Which was also why I should do better at staying away. She deserved forever, and I could only give her right now.

I gripped the bar, fighting every bone in my body that was insisting I go to her room.

Sighting movement to my right on the balcony extending out from the living room, I looked over.

Calvin cocked his head back and opened his hands in a

questioning motion, as in, *What the fuck are you doing on the balcony when a beautiful girl should be lying in your bed?*

Only she wasn't. I shook my head. Calvin pointed at my room, and the small shake of his head was another question.

I jerked my head in a quick, *Nope, Paige is absolutely not in my bed.*

He threw his hands up in a dramatic, *Really, motherfucker? You are so dumb.*

I showed him my middle finger.

"Calvin, what are you doing?" Paige asked.

Shit, she's awake.

"Uh..." Calvin raised both arms again and then drew his hands down to clasp them at his chest. "I'm praying."

Paige sounded incredulous as she asked, "You're praying?"

"Yeah, the sun's rising. I'm awake. Alive." He turned to face the sun as he lifted both arms, welcoming the world around him. "It's a good day to be alive." He cleared his throat. "A good day to be alive and ask God, *Why didn't Paige and Caleb sleep together last night? And why is Caleb also on the balcony, praying to the morning sun?*" He sighed and turned to me. "Sorry, bro. I can't lie to this girl. But it's going to be a good day. Anyone else feel this energy?"

I'm going to ruin his day.

After getting dressed for work, I left my room to find Paige sitting at the breakfast bar, moving so that the black barstool jerked from left and right, though not by much. She was dressed in workout shorts and a loose-fitting T-shirt with her hair gathered at the top of her head.

I walked up to her, ready to apologize for Calvin, when she said, "So, are you done praying to the morning sun?"

I chuckled. "So, everyone has jokes this morning." I moved closer to the edge of the counter and seized the glass of orange juice sitting on the counter in front of her. I brought the glass to my lips.

"Hey," Paige protested as I drank.

"*You* don't get to make fun of me," I said, setting the half-empty glass back where it had been and resting one hand on the back of her chair.

"Why not? It was funny."

"Oh, yeah? I didn't think it was funny. You should be glad I was praying."

"So, you were praying?" She grinned, and I bit my lip.

This girl.

Giving her a pointed look, I leaned in, placing my elbow on the counter so that I was closer to her height. "No, Paige. I was fighting a very sinful urge. You have no idea."

"Did it work? Did you fight it?" she asked, her baby-blue eyes pulling me into a daze.

"No." My eyes lowered to her lips. Somehow pinker than I remembered them.

Did she paint them with her favorite lip balm? Did they taste like bubblegum right now?

"Then, I don't understand why you're fighting—"

I leaned forward, capturing her lips with mine. When I felt no reaction from her, I pressed my lips to hers again, slower this time, before slightly pulling back, but her lips followed mine, wanting...

My hand left the stool and skimmed up her back to cup the nape of her neck, and then I delved in, coaxing her lips apart so that I could taste her. Hunger stirred from a completely famished root, and I took, drowning in her soft, sweet lips that didn't taste like bubblegum but something equally sweet, equally addictive. My tongue tangled hers before I retrieved it so I could nibble on her bottom lip.

So damn delicious.

"I'm guessing this is the answer to that prayer. Huh, interesting."

Leaning my forehead against hers, I broke the kiss, shaking my head.

Fucking Calvin.

"Shit, Mom was right, I do need to pray more."

Tightening my grip at the back of her neck, I pulled back, and hoping she could pick up on my nonverbal cues, I stared into her eyes with a look that said, *We need to talk.*

She gave me a slight nod, and I wanted to lose myself in the depths of those gorgeous eyes, but instead, I stowed this moment as something to hold on to. I would need it one day.

As I straightened, my thumb slid over a rosy cheek before I dropped my hand and turned to Calvin, who was now joined by Luke. "I should ruin your day for that."

As luck would have it, it wasn't a good day. For Calvin.

I wasn't even the one to ruin his day. It was about three in the afternoon, and the sun was sending a searing heat wave across the city, but with all my windows fully tinted and my AC on high, it didn't bother me too much. As my phone rang and blocked out the music in my car, I pressed the little green button with the phone icon on my steering wheel.

"Caleb, I need you," Calvin said.

Air caught inside my chest. The first person I thought about was Paige. "What's going on?"

"I don't know. I just know I'm about to murder this kid." Calvin seethed.

"What? Calvin, what are you talking about?"

"I can't even fucking say it. My sister."

It was then that I heard a girl crying in the background. "Calvin, what did you do? I hate you!"

"Just come to my house, man. You have to talk to her."

"I'm on my way."

The small apartment on the outskirts of Boston was stuffy and smelled of stale cigarette smoke. Although, after doing a quick scan of the apartment, I could see that it was spotless, except for the stained carpeting and a worn-out fabric couch.

"This way," Calvin said, ushering me to what was his sister's room from what I remembered the few times I'd stopped by in the past.

It'd been a while since I'd been back here.

The room we entered reeked of weed, and Calvin's fifteen-year-old sister, Sasha, was kneeling on the floor, practically naked in the getup she had on. She was tending to a dude, who I was sure my best friend had just laid the fuck out. Not only that, but his fly was undone, exposing red boxers. Treading closer to where she knelt, I stared down. This had to be the same dude Calvin had suspected Sasha had been texting over the past few weeks. Blood trickled down the guy's jaw from his busted lip that was already swelling. This was no high school kid.

I was the wrong fucking person to call.

I used my shoe to nudge his side, and he groaned. "How old are you?"

Sasha stared up, noticing someone besides her brother was here. "I love him," she pleaded, her eyes brimming with tears.

Fuck.

"How old is he, Sasha?"

She shook her head, and I could see it in her eyes. She was scared to tell me the truth.

"Come." I extended my hand to her. "Let's go for a walk."

She violently shook her head, glancing at Calvin.

"He isn't going to touch him," I promised, trying to keep her eyes focused on mine.

She nodded and stood, giving me a full view of her shorts that looked like underwear and a see-through top, exposing her midriff.

My jaw tightened. "Get your coat or something."

As soon as we stepped outside, Sasha threw her arms around me. "Please, don't make me stop seeing him."

I wrapped my arms around her and said, "Tell me the truth. How old is that guy? He's nowhere near your age, and I need you to be honest with me."

"You'll hate me."

"No. Why would I hate you?"

"Because what I did was stupid, but I love him."

My forearms held her to me as my hands curled into fists. "What did you do, and how old is he?"

"Twenty-one," she whispered.

"Jesus, what were you thinking? Does Calvin know?"

She shook her head.

"Does this guy ... does he know you're only fifteen?"

"He does now. Calvin—" She hiccuped and started crying again.

Sasha was bigger in size compared to even Lisa or Paige and looked older, which could make it easy for guys to mistake her age—and even worse, if she lied about it.

"Did he force you into—"

"It was me. He didn't know. He thought I was a senior."

"You can't ...." Fuck, I didn't want to be the first one to break her heart, but it was necessary. This was why Calvin had called. It was better she hated me for it than him. He was the only male figure she could look up to. "He's too old."

"No." She held me tighter and stomped a foot. "He loves me."

"So do your mom and brother. And, if that guy loves you, he'll let you go. He'll stop seeing you, so you can enjoy your teen years. He'll wait for you until you're older, much older, or he'll find someone else. But, right now, you and him, it isn't going to work, Sasha."

Removing her arms from around me, she stepped back and raised her voice, alerting a few passersby. "You can't do this. You can't make me stop seeing him."

"But I will," I said without a hint of remorse.

NINETEEN

Paige

It was four a.m., and I was staring at the wall in front of my desk, stuck. I wanted to get at least one letter done, so I could mail it before leaving for the weekend, but apparently, that wasn't going to happen. I had three more letters to write to Alex Connor. One from my biological mom, one from my biological dad, and the last one from me. I didn't have proof that Alex Connor had killed my real parents, but everything leading up to now told me he had before abducting me. So, he'd get a letter from them, too. Only I was stuck because I didn't know what to write. I never knew them. I didn't know what they'd wanted in life or who they had been as a person. And I hadn't been able to find anything online or through Bailey that could lead me back to any relatives I might still have.

Lifting the spiral notebook, I closed it and sighed.

Three slow knocks came from my room door, and my heart leaped.

Caleb.

I'd been so anxious to see him since he left this morning. I'd even thought he would pick me up when my last shift ended sometime after three a.m. at the bar downtown, but Rob had picked me up instead.

"Come in," I said, elation tingling across my skin.

I wanted to rush to him, but desperation was never a good look. Not that I could move when the door opened, and I saw Caleb in nothing but black gym shorts. From there, all thoughts left me as I stared at his chiseled chest and abs so tight that I wanted my fingers to glide over them like clothes on a washboard. My gaze dropped. I should stop, but knowing what was coming was the same reason my eyes continued to lower. It was impossible for him to hide an always-there bulge when he was in gym shorts or sweatpants or—

Oh God.

My throat dried, and my mouth watered.

Great job trying not to act desperate.

I cleared my throat, lifted my hand to my hair, and turned away from him as I rose from the chair at my desk. "What's up?" My voice sounded high-pitched and stupid.

"Happy birthday."

"What? Oh." It *was* my birthday. I turned to look at him.

"You're acting weird," he said, scrutinizing my face before his eyes dropped to my chest.

"More than usual?"

"Yeah." A mischievous smile flitted across his lips, but it disappeared with a quick swipe of his tongue. Stretching out a hand, he opened his palm, revealing a hair tie. "I got you a birthday present."

"What?" A laugh burst out from me as I peered at the multicolored hair tie. I took it out of his palm. "Are you messing with me?"

"No. You don't like it?" he asked, frowning.

He was serious.

"No, I love it. It's"—I stretched it between my fingers—"pretty, and the first birthday gift I've gotten in five years," I said honestly.

"Since you're so casual and never wear jewelry or anything like that, I didn't know what else to get you. I figured this was my best chance to get you something you'd wear. But, if this is your first birthday gift in five years, this is fucking horrible. I'll get you—"

"No. I love it. Really. Thank you." Stepping forward, I closed the gap between us and wrapped my arms around him. "It's thoughtful. You're thoughtful."

We stayed in each other's arms for what felt like minutes until my breathing grew uneven, my body beginning to take note of his strong physique flush against mine. He didn't have an erection, but I could still feel him.

"I'm sorry," he said, smoothing a hand over my hair.

"About what?" I asked.

"For taking what wasn't mine to have."

A sudden ache flared inside my chest. "What?" Loosening my arms around him, I tilted my head.

He closed his eyes for a second, but as he opened them, I could see the darkness. Like there was a war he was fighting inside, alone. I had no idea what else was going on inside of him besides the few bits and pieces he'd told me about the nurse. But this wasn't about that. This was about us.

"Caleb, talk to me."

"It's nothing. You just . . ." His hand brushed the hair back from my face, and warmth flowed through me. "You deserve everything, and nothing should be taken. I shouldn't have . . . it was wrong."

Tears stung the backs of my eyes because, what I'd feared he was saying, he was actually saying. This was about him being my first.

I pulled away from him and folded my arms across my chest. "You're hurting me."

"What?" He seemed puzzled, like this was news to him.

"I've only been trying to stay away from you because it's what you want, Caleb. It isn't what I want. And when you say things like that, it hurts. It makes me feel like crap."

"What? Jesus, Paige. I-I don't . . ." He sighed. "It's not you, okay? It isn't right, what I did. That's all I'm saying. It shouldn't have been me."

"But it was, and I'm sorry if you regret it, but I don't." Turning, I walked the short distance to my bed and crawled into it, keeping my back to him as I lay on my side. "You can see yourself out. I'm going to bed."

"I don't regret it. I regret what it's doing to us now."

"My virginity wasn't a *thing*, Caleb. It isn't doing anything to us. You are. And, if you didn't have sex with me then, you would have by now. You, Miller, or even one of your friends—what difference does it make?"

Words were weapons.

I knew how powerful they could be, which was why I used them. I wanted him to hurt like he was hurting me, and it worked because, the next second, my door slammed shut.

I didn't understand why we kept hurting each other.

Why couldn't it work between us? Why did it always seem to end like this now?

Rolling onto my back and then onto my other side, I faced the door he'd just gone through. I tugged on the hair tie I'd slid around my wrist. It was pretty and super girlie with all the bright green, pink, and orange colors.

My door cracked open, and Caleb walked back in. Combing a hand through his hair and then leaving it to settle at the back of his neck, he looked like how I felt. Defeated.

"We have to stop doing this to each other."

"I was thinking the same thing." My gaze dropped. "You first."

"I'm sorry, I didn't mean to hurt you."

I let my eyes trail from the gift around my wrist up to him. "I'm sorry, too." I swallowed. "For what I said."

I watched as he shoved his hands into the pockets of his gym shorts.

My feelings for him were so intense, so forceful sometimes that I didn't know how to handle them. I'd never felt anything like them before, and I was almost positive I'd fallen in love with Caleb.

That couldn't be right though because, thinking about it, I wanted to panic. People in love were . . . floating on cloud nine or something.

He walked toward the bed, and I met his gaze.

"Is it okay if I sleep in here tonight?"

"You sound like you're scared I might strangle you in your sleep or something."

"Jesus, Paige," he said, and we both chuckled.

I squinted. "Just don't try to kiss me again because you're in the friend zone now."

He crawled under the sheets, inching closer to me, and my breathing stopped. He held so much sex appeal, my lips and throat suddenly felt dry as his half-naked body neared.

"The friend zone? Really?"

The smoothness of his voice sent a tremor through me, and it didn't help that he was tossing me one of his flirtatious gazes. My eyes zoomed in on the flex of his biceps as he pulled the duvet up to cover himself.

"Yep," I said before that same strong arm circled around my back and pulled me close. "Friend zone," I breathed.

"I've missed you." The stubble on his jaw brushed against my cheek and neck as his lips touched a sensitive spot beneath my ear.

Damn it.

"I think a cheek kiss is okay in the friend zone." His breath trailed a fiery path down my neck, and I slanted my head to elongate my neck, waiting for the touch of his lips, but it never came.

"Ugh," I complained.

He laid his head on the pillow nearby with a glint of mischief in his eyes. "Is something wrong?"

Stubbornly, I shook my head, resting my hand on my pillow, but as we stared at each other, I groaned. "Fine. Why don't you want to sleep with me? Are you not into me anymore?" I stared over his shoulder as I continued, "Do you still think we're related? Is that why? I know we don't have your birth certificate, but I have mine, and you know Alex Connor is your father now and the way you play music and—"

Caleb took my hand from the pillow and dragged it beneath

the sheet to the hardness bulging from the soft material of his shorts. I gasped before instinct took over, and I gripped him in my hand. His eyes closed, and my thighs squeezed together with the wetness already pooling between them. It was crazy how I had been embarrassed about my body's reaction before I had sex, but since then, all I could think about was how much he loved when I got this way for him, and how good it felt when his cock was buried inside of me.

"I got my birth certificate today."

I swallowed, my hand still holding his heated shaft, worried he might not let me touch him again if I let go.

"Olivia is or was . . . I don't know what happened to her, but she's my mother." He leaned in and kissed me, caressing and tugging my lips between his, before he spoke against my mouth, his breath adding fuel to the flames inside of me. "A part of me was concerned about the possibility, but now that I have this proof . . ." He thrust his hips, and his length filled my hand so immensely that, for the briefest second, I wondered if he could still fit inside me. "We can talk later. I need you, right now," he whispered, capturing my mouth again.

Large hands yanked at the waist of my leggings, and I released him for a second to help get rid of them while he pulled at his own shorts. Before I could ogle his body, his lips pressed against my collarbone and then kindled a path up my neck and over my cheek to my waiting lips. Squirming beneath his passionate kisses, I sucked on his lip, giving it a gentle nip.

I needed more.

His lips left mine, brushing over my cheek and down my neck as his hand slid down my spine. He grabbed my ass and gave it a slap before kneading it in his palm. As he sucked on the skin at the base of my neck, I moaned and wrapped a leg around his thigh. The heated length of his cock glided over my sex as I writhed, and a desperate pant escaped my lips.

"Fuck, I can feel how wet you are."

He rolled his hip, massaging my sex with his cock, and we both moaned, wanting so much more. His fingers slipped between my folds from behind, circling before dipping inside. I inhaled and my head lolled back.

"Fuck, condom. Please tell me you have a—"

"No," I gasped.

He grunted. "Come here."

He rolled me beneath him and then on top at the same time his feet swung around to the floor. He was so hard beneath me that he could be inside me with one simple movement. His lips found mine, and strong arms pulled me closer as he stood. My legs tightened around his waist as my hands curled around his neck. Not even a second later, we were in his room.

CALEB

My knees hit the edge of my bed next to my nightstand when I stopped the hottest make-out session of my life. I was being selfish, but fuck it. It was my life's mission to be selfish with her at this second.

"Let go and fall back," I said as I leaned forward.

I bit my lip as she did what I told her without hesitation. She still had on her tank top, but it had ridden up beneath her breasts. I would play with them later. I needed to fuck. It'd been too long.

With my eyes still on her, I pulled open the drawer and removed a foil packet as her hands caught the bottom of her tank, pulling it over her head. Beautiful tits stared back at me, begging to be sucked and caressed.

"You thought I wasn't into you anymore?" I shook my head, breaking the wrapper and sliding the latex over myself. "Are you crazy? There wasn't a day that went by I didn't think about fucking you."

"Then why have you been pushing me away?" Propping up on her elbows, she used her feet to push herself back to the middle of the bed.

I crawled to her, separating her legs as I did so, and lowered my head between her thighs. As my mouth became flush with her pussy,

I let my tongue slide over her in a gentle caress. She relaxed beneath me, and I might have given her the wrong idea. This wasn't going to be soft and sweet, but I'd forgotten what she tasted like, and I just had to remember, had to have a taste. I slid my tongue between the lips of her pussy and sucked on her clit.

Lifting my head, I moved until I was hovering above her on my elbows. My hand circled and squeezed a supple mound before I sucked the taut nipple into my mouth.

Oh, she asked me a question.

"I'll tell you after I fuck you."

Grasping my cock, I nudged it against her warmth, my muscles tensing in anticipation because I knew just how fucking fantastic she would feel.

As the head plunged in, she gasped, and I warned, "This is going to be rough. It's been too long."

Looking at me through lowered lashes, she released the lip she had been biting with a breathy, "I don't care how you take me, Caleb. Just take."

My cock throbbed. She might regret saying that later, but she didn't have to tell me twice. I pushed deeper and she winced. Images of when I had taken her for the first time came to mind, and fuck, it made me want to possess every inch of her all over again.

"You okay?" I asked, kissing her chin and then her lips.

Every fucking part of her was adorable. She nodded, shifting her hips to get me to move. Withdrawing, I thrust, and she drew in a sharp breath.

I kissed her succulent lips and rocked into her again. "Tell me how it feels."

"So full of you. I—"

Before she could finish, I plunged inside again, feeling as her muscles relaxed, stretching around me and letting me in deeper.

"That's it. Just keep relaxing and I'll fuck you, really good," I murmured, feeling her wetness spread, making the dive smoother, sweeter. "Oh, fuck."

Her legs curled around my hips, and I sank into her, going deeper with each thrust. I could feel the sharp edges of her fingernails over my back. She never used to have nails, but the bite of them in my skin was encouraging. So, I fucked harder, faster, feeling as her nails dug deeper and hearing as her moans grew louder. Her teeth bit into my shoulder, and I groaned, continuing to ride the wave of tightening muscles around me, fucking her like I'd wanted to for weeks. Fucking her like she was mine.

"Caleb," she whimpered, eyes closing as she threw her head back and contracted around me.

Her body stiffened and quaked, and I let go, indulging in the pleasure of our bodies mending. I was the only one who could fix her, and she was the only one who could make me feel like this. I collapsed onto her, burying my face into her neck.

What is this feeling? Happiness, wholeness?

I didn't know what it was, but I wanted more of it. I was not done being selfish. I wanted her, and I didn't care how long I would get to be with her before I was thrown in jail. Because, until then, she was fucking mine.

Easing off her pliable body currently melted into my sheets, I kissed her cheek. "You're done talking shit about sleeping with other people. Got it?"

She nodded.

Moving to the edge of the bed, I was about to stand when Paige said, "Caleb, your back."

I twisted around and saw her peering at her fingernails.

"Oh my God, I . . ." She looked up, eyes wide before staring back at her nails. "I never grew them when I used to spar with the athletes, but now, I don't do much kickboxing, so I haven't thought about cutting them or filing them or something. I'm sorry. I didn't know they would do that."

Her enthusiasm for sex made it so easy to forget how much she really knew.

A salacious grin formed on my lips. "I liked it."

"But you're bleeding," she said, her innocence blinding.

"I know, and you should do it again. Tonight even." My eyes wandered over her body.

I'd never experimented with anything besides what was considered normal sex, but with Paige, something more forbidden had been pulling at my insides ever since she held that knife to my throat.

As I rose from the bed, her eyes scanned my body, and I let her curious eyes watch as I removed the condom. When she saw me watching her, she blushed, averted her eyes, and curled a finger over the smile stretching across her lips.

Mine.

After we were both cleaned up and I settled behind her, Paige said, "I need to know, Caleb."

I knew what was coming, but I asked, "What do you need to know?"

"Why you pushed me away. It bothers me, being with you like this now, not knowing if tomorrow, you'll push me away again."

I thought about calling on our long-established TTM rule of the things we didn't want to talk about, but she deserved to know what was coming.

"Alex Connor is my father. And, depending on what the FBI finds, I could be in jail for a long time."

She stiffened in my arms, and I bit my lip, squeezing my eyes shut in the darkness. She was going to be the one to pull away this time.

"What did you do?" Her voice was a whisper, almost like she didn't know if she could ask, or she didn't know if she wanted to know the answer.

"It's more like what I didn't do." I sighed. "The bottom line is that I won't push you away again if you want to be with me. I did it before so you could heal, so you could be happy even if it meant you were with someone else. Because, at the end of the day, I know you and me—we're heading in two different directions, Paige. And what I just told you has everything to do with any decisions I make when it comes to us. Because, before I even met you, I knew where I was heading. That path has been carved out for me a long time ago." I thought about the evidence Alex Connor had against me beyond what I was already guilty of.

We remained quiet for a while, her back still pressed to my front, each of us lost to our own thoughts.

Then, she said, "TTM."

She didn't want to talk about it, which made me curious. This wasn't her issue to flag as things that matter. It was mine. I had all the facts, and it would be my tarnished future, not hers. She finally would be free to do whatever she wanted.

I turned my face to the shadowed ceiling.

What is she not telling me?

"I want to be with you."

Her whisper seized the tension gathering inside me, and for a moment, it felt like things were really that simple.

Paige was in the fetal position facing me, loose curls obscuring her face. Reaching over, I swooped a hand beneath the light waves, picked them up, and gently tossed them back. My cock was awakened, ready to be inside her, but she was wrapped in my sheets and sleeping so soundly that I couldn't wake her.

By the time she'd fallen asleep, it had been close to six in the morning, and I knew firsthand that she didn't get much sleep on her own between her nightmares and anxiety attacks.

I traced the tips of my fingers over an exposed shoulder, needing to connect with her. I didn't know how she could be this close, yet it still wasn't enough. She stirred, and I pulled my hand away, but she kept moving until her eyes fluttered open. For a brief moment, I feared she would remember our conversation last night, come to her senses, and run for the hills.

"Good morning. I didn't mean to wake you. I forgot how calloused the tips of my fingers are."

"My dad—" She smiled and closed her eyes as she corrected herself, "Your uncle's fingers were like that. But my fingers were always bruised. He had to get me those little rubber caps for my fingers when I began to play. They were so frustrating at first. They felt like little rubber duckies on my fingertips."

I laughed. She'd never openly spoken about her past before unless it was tied to something we were trying to figure out. Her talking about something I was so passionate about made me want to grab my guitar and shove it into her hands. But there had to be a reason she hadn't picked it up. It'd been lying around the apartment most days where she had easy access to it, but she hadn't touched it.

"The Sawyers might not have been your biological parents, but you can still call them Mom and Dad, Paige. They raised you. They are your parents."

She looked away. I knew this topic was a sore spot for her.

Leaning over, I kissed her cheek. "Happy birthday." I feathered more kisses across her cheek. "Do you know how beautiful you are when you're sleeping?" Lifting my head, I found her softer, less troubled eyes. "Are we okay?" I asked.

She nodded.

"Good, because you'd have a hard time explaining a hickey on your neck this weekend."

"What?" Her hands flew to her neck.

I grinned, lowering my head. "It isn't there yet."

"No," she shrieked, drawing her shoulders up to her neck while trying to push me away. She giggled as I brought my lips to her shoulder and sucked on the skin there. "Caleb, no."

The buzzer sounded from the living room, jerking me out of the mind of this person I wanted to hold on to when I was with her.

But reality awaited, even when all I wanted to do was lay in this bed with her and forget about everything outside these walls. I couldn't believe she'd agreed to go to this end-of-summer-party thing. It was the worst timing, and I was going to be on edge for the time I wasn't there. Calvin wouldn't be there either. It wasn't that I didn't trust the other guys to have Paige's back should anything go wrong, but Calvin was the only one besides Paige who knew what Brad looked like. He was also the only other person besides myself who knew Paige, especially if it had to do with an anxiety attack, which she barely even wanted him to know about, much less anyone else.

I pressed my lips to hers and brushed a hand down the side of her face as I pulled back. "I won't be at the lake house for the whole time this weekend, and Calvin won't be able to make it at all."

Her lips turned down, forming a small pout. "What? Where will you be?"

"With Alex Connor."

TWENTY-ONE

Paige

Extending one of my arms out of the passenger window, I leaned my head back against the headrest. The sun warmed the hand I had outside the window, and I could feel and hear the rapid wind swishing against my face and chest. I turned my palm to the onslaught of the wind, but at the same time, the thought of something popping up and snapping my arm caused me to yank my hand back inside. Heat spread through my body, and suddenly, I wasn't getting any oxygen into my lungs.

I counted in my head, willing myself to stay calm, and fumbled for the buttons on the door. I pressed down until the window wound all the way up. My eyes caught the hair tie on my wrist, and I focused on it until my chest expanded with a rush of air. As soon as it happened, the loud music in the car rang in my ears. I peered at Mackenzie, but she was focused on the narrow road she was turning onto from the main street. Relief washed over me. She hadn't noticed, and since Amber and Lisa were in the backseat, they wouldn't have seen when *it* happened either.

"It's a bit windier up here," Mickey said, her head turning to me. "You should see your hair now." She giggled. "It's too late to put up your window."

I gave her a half-smile before rotating my head to the woodland surrounding us.

I looked down at the hair tie again, the one Caleb had given me, and I hoped I wouldn't lose it with the way these things tended to disappear.

A foggy image of Alex Connor came to mind.

I didn't even know what he looked like, and not from a lack of trying. Even his own luxury hotel downtown didn't have pictures of him or his sons on the company website. But I supposed he would look like Caleb and Brad. Dark hair, tanned.

I had found that Stacy nurse without any difficulty. She was an older brunette who was all over social media. Well, until recently, at least.

Shit, I shouldn't think about this now.

When I looked up and saw what Mickey referred to as her parents' lake house, my mouth dropped. A tall, luxurious four-story property made of cream-colored stones was ahead of us with two wide staircases on either end of the building, leading up into a second-floor balcony. A giant statue stood front and center of the building and the same stones on the building covered the grounds around the property. It was bigger than the mansion Mackenzie had lived in back home. Bigger than the mansion I'd once lived in.

A few college-aged students were hanging around outside, some running around the lawn as a bright orange Frisbee soared between them.

"Mickey!" I exclaimed.

"I told you," Lisa said from the backseat as Mickey turned down the music.

When I'd mentioned the party to Lisa, it had come as a surprise that she and Amber had already been invited. Apparently, Calvin and his friends had also partied here two summers ago.

"It's still a lake house, sort of. It was renovated three years ago, and it's more of a retreat now," Mickey explained, pulling onto a paved area where at least ten other cars were parked. "But, each year since then, a fraternity from St. Andrews pools money to rent the property for the four weekends. And so was born the—"

"FWS Party," Amber, Mickey, and Lisa said.

Grabbing my backpack from my feet, I placed it in my lap, and I could feel the hard metal of my 9mm at the bottom pressing into my thigh. It was comforting. It used to be all I needed.

Swiping the unlock code on my phone, I typed a text to Caleb.

Me: I feel naked.

Mickey put the car in park, and we got out into the beautiful weather. There was a breeze but it wasn't too bad, it was the perfect balance to the sun gleaming down on us. Shoving the straps of my backpack over my shoulders, I walked to the trunk and grabbed two bags of groceries. As I strolled with the girls to the property's main entrance, I felt like I was on some exclusive compound hidden on the lake.

The main foyer was as majestic as I'd expected. Italian tiles overlaid the expanse of the entire flooring, and two large columns mounted from the first floor to the ceiling of the second. As my phone vibrated, I looked down to the text message I received.

Caleb: Have you started drinking already?

Me: No.

I grinned as I hit Send. These days, I couldn't even say *I* recognized myself. Partying, drinking, taking the weekend off work to hang out.

Caleb: Mmm, are you all the way naked?

My cheeks burned.

Me: No.

Caleb: Are you getting naked?

Me: What?

Caleb: Wait, we're not sexting?

Me: NO.

"Oh my God." I laughed, covering my face with one hand, and as it slipped down, I realized my friends were looking at me.

I had friends. Yes, things were kind of awkward with Amber, but still, I had friends. I grinned even wider as Amber's and Lisa's eyebrows crinkled. Mickey was smiling, but I was guessing she knew why there was a stupid grin on my face. She was the only one I'd told about what had happened between Caleb and me last night—well, excluding the dirty details. It was still so weird how natural it felt to confide in her.

"Are you gonna be okay there?" Lisa asked.

"Uh, yeah. Caleb—" I covered my mouth to suppress a laugh as I thought about his text. "He's being funny."

"In what universe is Caleb funny?" Amber asked. It came off as sarcasm, but her eyes held genuine interest.

"Um, I don't know. He makes me laugh," I said, watching as Lisa peered over my shoulder.

I followed her gaze to find Rob and Luke approaching, definitely not fitting in with their over-six-foot, all-muscular physique, commanding the attention of students wandering in and out.

"Holy shit," Mickey muttered. "Are they in college?"

"No. That's Rob and Luke. Two of the friends I was telling you about." I looked at the text Caleb had sent while I was distracted.

Caleb: Then why do you feel naked?

Because you aren't here.

Me: I sort of miss you already.

Caleb: Sort of?

I grinned and sent him a smiley face.

Me: I do. And why are two of your most intimidating guys here? They kind of stand out in a we-don't-bullshit-or-party kind of way.

Rob and Luke surrounded us like wild beasts out of a cave as they took all the grocery bags from our hands.

"Where do you want them?" Luke asked, his voice rough and his attention on Mickey.

I watched her mouth form a little O, and then words like *ah, um, uh, ah* followed. I pursed my lips, wishing I could help her, but I didn't know where the bags went either. Also, this was too entertaining. I'd never seen her like this. I was starting to think these were the moments I might have missed out on over the years.

"I think I know where they go," Lisa offered, but Luke didn't even bat an eyelash.

"Mickey," I said.

Her gaze dropped to the tight-fitting black T-shirt stretching across Luke's chest to the colorful sleeves of tattoos down his arms before she looked over at me.

Taking a few short steps to stand next to her, I gave her a devilish smile and looped an arm around her elbow before pulling her in a random direction.

"Are we putting these in the main kitchen?" I asked.

"Yes," she replied and then whispered, "Oh my God!"

"Mickey," I whispered, "I'm pretty sure he heard that."

"Shit," she muttered.

"He heard that, too."

She groaned. "I need a drink. What do *you* like to drink?"

It was my turn to curse, but only in my head because I wanted to drink, even knowing the consequences. I had friends, and it was my birthday. Besides, I had been fine after that one drink I had at the club with Lisa and Amber.

As we turned the corner into a large, open kitchen, I saw Miller tilting a red cup to his mouth, downing whatever was inside of it.

He lowered the cup and slapped a hand over his chest. "Lisa, you brought my girl! See, that's why I love you."

Uh-oh.

I stopped in my tracks, causing Amber to bump into me. I

turned my head. "Sorry. Hi, Miller."

"No one's here for you, Miller. Get over yourself," Amber said, shocking the heck out of me. For some reason, I thought she would have wanted me out of the way so she could have Caleb to herself.

"Sorry, babe, it's her birthday, and she's ours," Lisa added and then cursed under her breath as Miller's interest was piqued. "Crap, I'm not helping, am I? Heeyyyy, cool! It's just like the last time." Lisa started forward. "Luke, there's tape somewhere to label our own cabinet if one's still available, or we can share one with someone else. That's where we keep the groceries. All the alcohol goes in the fridge."

Trying to make a quick exit while this was being sorted out, I said, "Lisa, I'm going to go check out where I'm sleeping. I know you and Amber have to meet with the girls you're staying with—"

"Come on over here, birthday girl," Miller coaxed, pulling a red cup from one of the few stacks on the counter and then reaching into the cabinet space over the fridge. "I'll make you your first drink. On the house." He turned around and winked, displaying a bottle of Grey Goose. "Only the good stuff for you."

"And that's why I love you, Miller." Lisa grabbed a cup for herself from the stack. "You always bring the good stuff."

"What can I say? You bring the girls, and I bring the drinks," Miller bantered, letting his eyes suggestively roam over Lisa.

Her tight-fitting crop tank showed off her cleavage, and Miller made no attempt to hide that he was checking it out. When she looked at him, even I could feel the heat between them, and I was clear across the room.

Clearly, her rule about not sleeping with the third friend wasn't going to last the weekend.

In a low voice, Mickey said, "We can bring drinks upstairs so we can drink while we get ready. We have our own kitchenette if you don't want to leave your stuff down here, but shh, don't tell anyone. We're staying in the private area."

"That's awesome." I grimaced. "But knowing Miller, he isn't going to let us go before we have a drink here first."

"We'll get them later."

My gaze flitted around the kitchen, noticing Amber had disappeared, but then it stopped on Miller pouring vodka into my cup. He poured more and more and then some more.

Oh shit.

"Miller, that's too much alcohol," Lisa scolded, pushing him aside and sharing the alcohol into another cup. "Are you trying to have her pass out after her first drink?"

The twinge of doubt that had been hovering finally settled onto my chest. This couldn't be good.

Nudging Mickey, I forced an encouraging smile. "Are you ready to party?"

It was an hour or two after sunset, and Mickey and I were reclined on a pair of fancy chaise lounges on the second-floor tiled patio facing the pool in the back. We were staring into the night sky while the music blared around us.

I didn't have my phone anymore. I'd left it in the room while I changed into my birthday outfit. A burgundy-colored tulle skirt that reached mid-thigh and a black camisole tucked into the waist.

At first, I hadn't known why I let the girls talk me into it, but the chic outfit was comfy and made me feel girlish and pretty. My hair was curled and pinned away from my face, courtesy of Lisa, who'd also ensured Mickey's long black hair was done, too.

Mickey was dressed in a knee-length skater dress, and oftentimes, I couldn't tell if Luke was watching me or her.

I sighed.

Seriously, if alcohol can have me this relaxed, why am I worried? I should have been drinking like this a long time ago. On a daily basis.

Turning to Mackenzie, I picked up my drink and leaned forward so I could take a sip without spilling it all over myself. "Are you planning to talk to Luke?"

"No. Why would I do that?"

"Because you think he's hot."

"I know. I do, but it doesn't mean he reciprocates." She looked over to where Rob and Luke were leaning on the stone balustrade surrounding the patio. "I've never seen anything like him. The tattoos, that man-bun thing, and the muscles—oh my God." She fanned herself even though it was starting to get chilly out here.

"Well, you won't know if he likes you unless you talk to him. Wait, I don't even know if he's single. Calvin or Caleb would know. Ugh, why are they not here? You'd like Calvin, too. He's so funny." Thinking about Caleb made me frown. I knew he wouldn't be able to be here for the whole weekend, but I hoped he would make it here tonight so he could see me while I was dressed up and pretty. He'd never seen me like this, and I wanted him to.

"Darn it," Mickey sighed. "We forgot to separate our groceries and bring them to our room."

"We could get them now."

"No way. I am not moving. I like this spot."

"Because you get to spy on Luke," I teased.

"Shh." She grinned. "Didn't you say Caleb might come? How will he find you if he makes it?" She looked around the patio where at least twenty people stood, not counting what had to be hundreds all over the house.

"He'll find me." I stood, taking my cup with me. "Come on, let's go say hi to the boys. Maybe find out if Luke is single."

"No."

"Yes." Mackenzie looked like she might throw up, and my shoulders dropped. "Fine, I won't ask him if he's single, but you know you want to get close to him."

We waltzed over to the guys. Well, I waltzed. Mickey walked.

Rob and Luke were gazing down into the pool on the ground level.

"Hey guys! How's it going?" I chirped.

Expressions passive, they both stared for a few seconds before

Luke answered. "Good."

Rob nodded.

"Yeah?" I said, mimicking Rob's nod.

Silence.

"Are you having fun?" I asked.

Another nod. *All righty then* . . .

So after Rob and Luke's horrible, actually nonexistent conversational skills, Mickey and I stumbled upon Amber and Lisa inside, hanging out with a few guys and girls on a couch.

"Paige! You're still not drunk," Lisa shouted over all the loud chatter and music.

"Um, well, I don't think I'm sober either," I confessed.

Her mouth dropped. "It's your twentieth birthday. Drink. Finish that thing already." She chanted, "Drink, drink, drink, drink."

Then everyone joined in on the chant, looking at me, expecting me . . .

Am I supposed to chug this, now? I'd been taking sips, trying not to overdo it. *But everyone is watching, waiting.*

Bringing the cup to my lips, I closed my eyes and swallowed the sweet pineapple flavor that masked the vodka inside.

Mickey took my hand and twisted it, so the cup faced down, showing the chanters it was empty. As a thunderous shout echoed around me, I grinned, feeling a rush.

More chugging. More. I want to chug more.

"Lisa." I curled my index finger and called her to me. Then I remembered I needed to tell her about Caleb in case he made it here tonight or tomorrow. When she hopped in front of me in her jean shorts and a tank top, I wrapped an arm around her shoulders and told her, "I need to tell you something. Caleb and I—"

A pair of strong, warm muscular hands settled on either side of my waist. I jerked back from Lisa, tilting my head behind me to look up.

Caleb.

My body instantly relaxed. He smiled down at me, the heat in his eyes making me forget that I needed to breathe.

"Are you two . . ." Lisa trailed off as Caleb tugged me closer to his body that my back became flush with his front.

I turned my head to Lisa. "That's what I was about to tell you."

"Oh! I like it." She looked at Caleb. "You should totally have birthday sex with her."

"Oh my gosh." I rotated my body and pressed a hot cheek into Caleb's chest, holding up my empty cup for him to take, and as he did, I wrapped both my arms around him.

His fresh, cool scent filled my nose, and the pure heat radiating off his body made me want to forget this party and go curl up with him in the room Mickey had graciously provided.

TWENTY-TWO

Caleb

"You should find Rob and Luke. They're looking for you," I told Lisa. "You, too, Mackenzie."

Both girls looked at me, frowning. Regrettably, I removed my only free hand from Paige's back to pull my phone from my pocket.

I typed out a quick message and turned my phone screen to them.

Me: I got her a cake.

As their mouths fell open, Paige stepped back and inclined her head. Lisa gave me a thumbs-up and dragged Mackenzie behind her.

"I was going to get another drink," Paige said, her pupils pushing the brilliant blue to the perimeter as they expanded.

I stared at her, my breathing strangled as I fought the urge to ravage her right here. Inhaling, I lifted a hand, pulled on one of her curls, and watched as it sprang back up before I saw the pulse on her neck, ticking.

"Lead the way," I told her.

Her chest rose and fell, and her face appeared indecisive. My eyebrows twitched in a question to her, and she bit her lip and smiled, so I did it again.

She clutched the front of my T-shirt, cheeks tinting to the

same pink hue of her lips. "Stop that."

"What?" I simpered. Cupping her cheek, I let my fingers slide into the loose curls at the side of her head. I needed to get her alone. "Where should I put this cup?"

Paige turned. "Where did they go?"

"I'm not sure. You were doing that thing with your eyes."

"Me?" she screeched. "Give me the cup."

I gave it to her and followed her to the kitchen area.

A few college students sat on top of the counters. Some were making out while others were laughing and carrying on. This environment was too familiar. This was the kind of party where I could have easily slept with two different girls in one night. One to start the night and one to finish it. Those days seemed like ages ago, and so did sleeping with random girls. This beauty who was reaching into the fridge with her tulle-covered butt had become my sole focus.

Damn, she was so fucking cute tonight.

As she turned to face me, I said, "I need to get my overnight bag from the car."

"So, you're staying then?" she asked. Still so hopeful after all she'd been through.

"I don't know, but I brought a change of clothes in case. It's kind of a wait-till-you-get-a-call thing. So, I'm waiting here with you."

"Good."

She handed me a beer, and after she refilled her cup with vodka and juice, we headed through the living room and out the front doors. Vehicles overflowed the driveway and expanded onto the surrounding grass and down the sides of the short road leading to the property.

As we got closer to my car, I took her drink and set it on the top with mine.

"Come here." Taking her hand, I leaned on the car and pulled her against me.

My hands moved down to her waist to splay out at her hips, and since we were in a dark area, I let them lower until they cupped her ass and squeezed. Soft and firm in the right places, and all mine.

Her hands circled around my neck, and her fingers combed through the hair at my nape. Fuck, I loved when she did that—or fucking anything to me.

"You're wearing a skirt. Do you have any idea how tempting you're going to be all night?"

"That's a good thing."

I chuckled. So easy to get lost in her.

Leaning down, I closed my lips over her sweet, tempting ones. And, as I prodded her lips apart, I started to forget everyone along with the music thumping in the distance. In a desperate need, her tongue touched and toyed with mine, stimulating my already-hard cock. I braced the aching bulge in my pants against her, and she bit my lip and moaned.

Lifting her, I spun her around and pressed her into the car as she wrapped her legs around my hips, and it was the worst fucking idea. I needed to be inside her, and all I could think about was fucking her against my car like this, forgetting about anyone who might walk by just so I could indulge.

Detaching my eager lips from hers, I ground my hips against her center. "Let's go back inside before I fuck you right here."

"No one's looking."

I groaned, entangling my hands in her hair. I kissed her again and continued to grind the thick ridge of my cock against her. I'd made her come from this once before, and with the way she was almost panting against my mouth, I knew it was still possible—or it had been before I heard a few girls giggling from somewhere nearby.

As I stopped and set her to her feet, she protested. But I didn't trust these college kids and their cameras. My own phone buzzed in my pocket and I grunted, hoping it wasn't who I thought it was.

Luke: Cake's in the kitchen. We're ready.

After retrieving her drink from the roof of the car, I handed it to her. "Come on. I'll grab my bag and have more of you later. There's something we need to do first."

She took a long drink and then laced her fingers through mine. "Okay."

It was amazing how her quirky, carefree personality spilled through the pain I knew she felt from time to time. If Alex Connor had never happened, this would be her a lot more.

By the time we reached the kitchen, Paige was tipping back the rest of her drink, still holding on to my hand. The few partygoers who remained in the kitchen began to sing "Happy Birthday" when she lowered her cup. A mixture of awe and a hint of sadness only I could see filled her eyes. As I looked up, my eyes landed on Miller, and my jaw tightened.

Fuck.

I didn't give a shit about him, but if he tried anything, I wouldn't think twice about finishing what I'd started.

I guided Paige farther into the room, toward the cake, which had a few candles twinkling on top. Shit, I'd forgotten candles. I looked around and caught Mackenzie's eyes. She must have had them here. I mouthed, *Thank you*, and stood back as Paige blew out the candles.

She got hugs from a few people, including Miller, but I looked the other way. When I looked back, she was hugging Amber, and it seemed as if they were talking about something. But, with the smiles on both their faces, I was guessing it was good, especially when she looked over at me with a glimmer in her eyes.

It was becoming harder to acknowledge that I wouldn't be around to share her happiness, but this was the foundation I wanted for her. A life where I knew she would be safe and happy. And I knew she would be with Calvin and his friends.

For the rest of the night, I hung with Luke and Rob while Paige hung out with the girls. Paige had been right about Rob and Luke standing out, but that didn't stop the girls from approaching them or me. That was why I'd sent them instead of Ryan, who would have been easily distracted. I watched the entrance and walked around most of the night, looking out for any signs of Brad because parties were kind of his thing, too. But Paige didn't need to know that. She was too happy, and this place was too far a journey if Brad wanted to party anyway, although it was almost perfect when I thought about it.

I stopped walking and peered around the darkened lake and fields of forest I knew were out there. Forest that could have bodies that had gone missing over the years.

"Hey, you good?"

I turned to see Luke approaching with a few beers in hand. The night had grown cooler, and most of the crowd had been trickling inside. The few people I spotted were lying down on the grass a few yards away, either making out or smoking pot. Closer to the lake, a bonfire was still going, and most of the lawn chairs surrounding the flames were empty.

"Yeah. Just checking out the place. Sorry you have to be here. I know you hate these things, but I really appreciate it."

"Nah. It's cool. It's like security at the club but better because I'm outside, too." He handed me a beer. "Paige was looking for you, but it's better if she comes out here. Everyone in there is drunk as fuck."

"I'll text Rob that we're out here. We could grab the seats by the fire before anyone else claims them."

The chairs were positioned outside of the landscaped lawn in the dirt. I popped open one of the icy-cold cans and drank until I heard the telltale sign of a drunken Paige.

My drunken woman.

I smiled, twisting in my seat. She was hanging on to Mackenzie, who looked just as drunk, while Rob walked close enough to catch one should either fall. I set the can on the ground, more than ready to take her into my arms. It was like she could sense when I was losing my equilibrium, sense when my mind started to wander, sense when I needed to get lost in her.

"Caleb, you're here!" she crooned, falling into my lap.

Circling my arms around her, I pulled her into my body as I leaned back.

"You're here," I said, as warmth swept over my body.

"I was looking for you," she slurred, her face pressing into my collar.

It was funny because, earlier, she'd told me she wanted to spend time with Mackenzie. I kissed the top of her forehead and tried to run my hand through her curls, but my fingers got caught in them. Squinting, I pried through the curls until they came loose.

"Did you guys have fun?" I asked both her and Mackenzie, who had taken the chair next to Luke.

"Oh, yeah! I don't remember some of it already," Mackenzie said.

My hand ran up and down Paige's thigh a few times before I picked up my beer. "Don't worry; no one was really watching when you two re-created some high school cheer from ninth grade."

"Oh no," Mackenzie groaned.

Luke grinned.

"I can't believe I remember how that went," Paige said, a sigh leaving her lips at the end.

I smiled. She was starting to feel how hard I was getting beneath her. I rubbed a hand over her naked shoulder, and she shivered.

"Are you cold?"

"No, the fire's warm." In a whisper, she added, "But we should go to bed."

Rob picked up one of the beers Luke had brought down and sat in the chair next to Mackenzie.

As my fingers lazily caressed the back of Paige's neck, I asked Mackenzie, "Where does everyone sleep?"

"Sleeping bags, cots. There are about five people to a room."

"Caleb," Paige said in what I was starting to recognize as her I-want-you-to-fuck-me voice.

Damn, I fucking love that voice.

After a few more minutes, I left with Paige, and it didn't take long for us to reach the fourth floor. A key code was needed to enter the stairs for this level, and it had its own kitchenette and living area. Without a sign of any of the other partygoers, I knew this level was prohibited. Safe.

Paige bent and drunkenly fought with the sandals on her feet before she kicked them off in the living room. I grinned. Never a dull moment with her. She opened the door to the room she was staying in, and I went straight for the bed.

"I need to use the bathroom," she said, leaving me before I could even get my hands on her.

A few minutes later, my eyes lifted to Paige bending over, and her hips moved from left to right in a stiff, awkward movement.

What is she doing?

The music barely made it through the walls up here, so it couldn't be dancing. I continued to watch, enjoying it too much to stop the show, but I couldn't stop the laugh that burst out of me as her head took on the same ridiculous motion. But, even with my laughter, she continued.

"Paige, what are you doing?"

"Twerking for you."

"Uh, really?" Laughing, I covered my face with my hand before pinching my chin.

She did a little move like she was having a seizure with her hands twitching at her sides. I liked that I got to see both the worst and the best sides of this girl, and this was the fucking best, but I needed her cute ass in this bed. She peeled her shirt over her head, tossed it to the side, and then the strapless bra she had on went next.

My eyebrows rose. This I could definitely watch.

Her hands went to the back of her skirt, and she fidgeted for the longest time, even stumbling forward in the process.

I would rip it off her if I had to.

"Come to me." Licking my lips, I watched her walk toward the bed.

Damn, I love her boobs.

"Can I tell you something?" she asked, crawling onto the bed and lying flat on her stomach. Her arms collapsed onto the bed above her head. "I'm really tired. I wasn't tired, but I'm so tired now."

"It's okay."

Getting up from the bed, I unbuckled my jeans, stripped out of my shirt, and threw it on a chair close by along with my jeans, leaving only my boxers on. Then I knelt on the bed, found the tiny zipper on the back of her skirt, and unzipped it. That dance might have been a bit too tiring for her because she was fucking done. She didn't even move as I tried to remove her skirt.

"That wasn't my sexy dance, by the way," she mumbled. "Just in case you were wondering."

It seemed she didn't realize I'd been watching her the night I saw her at the club with Lisa and Amber. I knew very well that hadn't been her sexy dance. But I would never forget it.

Pulling the sheets from the bed, I covered her, and left to turn off the lights.

TWENTY-THREE

PAIGE

It was late when I woke up. Or early. I propped myself up on an elbow to peer over Caleb's body to the darkness outside through the window. Then I dropped my head back down onto the pillow. My head was so heavy and my throat dry. Every organ in my body felt shriveled up, as if I hadn't had water in days. I didn't even know where my phone was or Mickey.

Did she come up last night?

Careful not to wake Caleb, I rolled out of the bed and used the moon's soft glow to guide me to the chair where I'd placed my backpack. After slipping into a pair of joggers and a tank top, I walked out of the room, squinting at the bright lights left on in the living area even though no one was in here. The door to Mickey's room was cracked, and when I pushed it open, the light from the living room spilled inside and onto an empty bed.

Where is she, and what time is it?

The sandals I'd had on earlier were smack dab in the living room.

What the hell? When did those get there?

Slipping them on, I hurried down the stairs to the door separating this level from the others. There was still music playing, though at a much lower volume than when the party had been in full swing. I didn't hear any talking either, and when I reached the first floor, I realized it was because no one else was awake. Three people were passed out on the couch, and that was all. Feeling the dryness in my throat again, I remembered our groceries were still down here. I walked over to the kitchen cabinet and rummaged through a bag for my bottle of water.

As I pushed the cupboard door closed and before I could turn around, a deep voice said, "It looks like someone else is still up."

Startled, I turned to see a tall guy with low-cut, dark hair, his eyes glazed over, leaning against a counter a few feet away.

"Yeah, I was thirsty and looking for a friend," I said, holding the large bottle to my chest and unscrewing it.

Giving me a lopsided grin, he folded his hands across his chest. "I could be your friend."

"No, I meant, I'm looking for *my* friend. Not anyone." *Creep.*

"Oh, yeah, that's right. You know, your friends are kind of slutty. What are you doing hanging with them if you aren't looking to hop on the same train?"

"You're a douche bag, and my friends aren't sluts." Feeling myself starting to get worked up, I began to walk away. I still needed to find Mickey.

"So, your precious friend who was licking my buddy's balls earlier in the woods isn't a slut?"

"No, and I'm pretty sure they wouldn't be sluts if they were over here, offering to lick your balls."

"Bitch," he muttered.

I rolled my eyes. "Your participation wasn't necessary, but thanks for proving my point."

As I turned to head out of the kitchen, Mickey budged around the corner from the hallway, and relief flooded me.

"Whatever. You and that bitch can get lost. The only reason she isn't whoring is because nobody wants her," Douche Bag said from behind me.

I watched as Mickey's face fell before looking to the side, as if someone else was with her.

I spun around. "You're an asshole."

"I just tell the truth, and she doesn't belong."

"So fucking disrespectful. Are you so desperate that all you can do is degrade women who want nothing to do with you? This is her house, and you should leave."

"Yeah, well, I pooled money like everyone else. Just because it's her house, it doesn't mean she's invited."

"What?" Dropping my bottle, I was in front of him in less than a second. I didn't care if he was twice my size. I grabbed his wrist, sinking my fingers into the pressure points there. He hissed, bending into the source of the pain. "What the fuck is the matter with you?"

I lifted my other hand to wrap around his throat since he was at my mercy, but before it could happen, I was yanked away and lifted into the air from behind. Then Luke was in front of me, blocking my view, but my heartbeat had kicked up a notch, and there was no stopping me.

I tried to fight off the person holding on to me, but strong arms wrapped even tighter around me, pulling me into a solid chest. "Let me go."

"You can't," Caleb said in my ear.

"I don't care. Because it's assholes like him"—I pointed my finger—"who take advantage of people who've done fricking nothing to them. And it's people like him who make this whole fucking world so cruel," I raged. "And he needs to be sorry. He isn't sorry, Caleb." Suddenly, I wasn't only talking about this douche. "He isn't sorry."

"Shh." Caleb's lips brushed my ear. "Did he touch you?"

He lowered me so my feet touched the floor but kept his hands on my hips, securing me to his front. I shook my head, frustrated as hell as I watched Luke ushering the asshole to the front of the house and through the doors.

My therapist's voice spilled from my subconscious amid the chaos in my head.

"Thoughts. Feelings. Behaviors. Your thoughts create feelings.

Feelings influence how we act . . ."

What have I done? Would a normal person have reacted this way? Everyone probably thinks I am crazy now.

Caleb kissed my temple, and I sucked in a breath.

With shame churning in my gut, I looked at Mickey. "I'm sorry. He was a dick. You shouldn't have people like that in your house."

"I know. But it's okay. I never come here," Mickey said.

And, with that, I remembered how sweet she could be, even to people who didn't deserve it.

"Still, he's a douche. A scum douche-hole. God, I wanted to hurt him." I scowled. "I should have snapped his wrist when I had the chance."

Mickey pursed her lips as she tried to hide her smile. "You always did have a temper."

"I did?" This was news.

"Yeah."

"Really?"

Maybe I'm not that far gone?

But I knew better. It was different. There was a darkness in me that shouldn't be this near to Mickey, but I smiled at the innocent radiance in her.

"All this time, I thought the craziness was only recent."

Mickey and I laughed.

I slipped out of Caleb's hold to hug her. "I missed you."

"I missed you, too." She stepped back and considered my face. "Just so you know, it was never that you looked for trouble when we were young, but whenever it came, you were always ready." She grinned. "I can't believe you don't remember. I think the most memorable was when you confronted your sister's boyfriend in school."

A gasp erupted from my throat, followed by an instant well of tears in my eyes.

"I'm sorry. I didn't—"

"No, no. It's okay." I hushed her, knowing exactly what I'd done. For years, I'd forced myself to forget. There was so much I'd refused to think about, but it was time I started to remember. "Thank you," I told her.

"What? I should be thanking you."

I shook my head. "I left, Mickey. I left everyone behind, and I'm so sorry." I wrapped my arms around her neck, hugging her until I saw Luke.

"I locked him outside. He can get his shit and leave when he sobers up," he grunted.

"Okay, thank you. I'll see you in the morning, Micks."

I turned to see Caleb with my bottle of water in his hand. A sheepish grin passed my lips.

All of that just happened.

I lifted a hand and scratched my head as I stared at him, but he just smiled and threw an arm around my shoulders. It was fair to say, he was used to my crazy.

When we got to the room, I switched on the light, but as Caleb closed the door, I switched it off again. Walking to the window, I peered outside. The walking paths were lit, and the wind was blowing the dark, limber branches on a few trees near the property. The view from our room was from the side of the house, but I could see a glimpse of the parking lot in front. I didn't know what I was looking for at first, but then I realized it was the douche bag from earlier and maybe, just maybe, one of Alex Connor's men.

Caleb came up from behind, jolting me out of my head.

"You okay? He didn't touch you, did he?" he asked for the second time tonight.

One of his hands settled on my hip, and I wanted to lean into him, but I couldn't yet. I would become distracted before I could tell him what I needed to.

"No." I stared into the darkness for a few more seconds and then said, "I'm ready, Caleb."

"Ready for what?"

"I'm going to see Bailey when I get back. Tomorrow, I'll text Graham about getting me back on the schedule at the gym. Then I want to go back to the mansion to see if I can find anything that might give us some answers."

"Paige"—he turned my body to face him and then curled his fingers into my hair—"that's a lot to think about right now. You've only slept for three hours, and you still have alcohol in your system."

"It doesn't matter how much sleep I've gotten or what I've drank. This has always been the plan."

I moved away from him, but only because I felt exposed standing in the open window. No one could see inside with the lights off, but still, it made my spine tingle with awareness. Like Alex Connor had some long-range shooters on standby, ready to take me out. I hated this. I hated thinking like this, but it wouldn't go away. Not while he was still out there.

"It's only been three weeks, and I don't want you to put yourself in danger. You can talk to Bailey, and I'll even take you back to that house, but don't go to the gym, Paige. It isn't necessary."

I made my way to the other side of the room and switched on the light. I turned to Caleb. "It is necessary. I've been working there since I was sixteen, and I love working there." I thought about the Dungeon I'd trained in and the fighters I'd trained with and Andy with his stupid Popeye the Sailor Man tattoo on his bicep. "I miss them."

"Okay, I know, but can we wait? There are some things I need to figure out first."

He was still standing by the window, and it was freaking me out. I looked away, feeling the onset of a headache.

"What things?"

"Well, first, I need to figure out why Connor wants to see me this weekend, and then I'll go from there."

He finally stepped away from the window, and a breath of relief passed my lips.

Peeling off his shirt, he threw it on a nearby chair and sauntered toward me. My eyes lowered to the hard ridges of his stomach and down to the two distended veins snaking out of his jeans. I swallowed, longing to trace those veins with my tongue.

My gaze flicked up to his dark eyes as he rested his hands on my shoulders and squeezed.

"There's something I haven't told you."

With him this close, all I wanted to do—and what I found myself doing, was smoothing my hand up and down the hard ridges of his chest and abs, feeling as it contracted beneath my touch. I reached farther down to the rough material of his jeans and then over the powerful erection beneath. He let out a sigh, and I saw the yearning in his heavy-lidded eyes as they flitted between my lips and eyes. My own vision hazed as his hand went up under my tank and covered my breast.

We stared at each other, feeding off the all-consuming need burning between our bodies. My fingers undid his zipper, moved up to his buckle, and then went to the small metal button on his jeans. As his fingers manipulated my nipples, a sigh escaped my lips. His mouth descended on mine, hard and possessive as he backed me into a wall. My hand dipped into his boxers to grip the immense package waiting there. It was warm and smooth, and I wanted it.

Oh God, I want it so bad.

His groan sent a sweet ache to my sex, and I leaned my head against the wall, my eyelids heavy as heat and want took over my body.

"Caleb," I purred.

A loud breath left him, the heat of it tingling my lips.

He moved back enough to pull my tank over my head. "Fuck, I . . . you have no idea what you do to me."

He bent and took one of my nipples into his mouth. I bit my lip, closing my eyes as my body liquefied.

"I-I need you now. Please," I begged.

He stepped back, taking me with him, and then spun around and pushed me down onto the bed. He tugged off my pants, throwing them to the side. Watching him, I bent my knees and dragged my feet up to my butt. As he got his eyeful of me, I let my gaze sweep down his body, stopping at the throbbing length hanging outside of his zipper. I placed my index finger in my mouth, licking and biting, desperate for him as he rid himself of his jeans and boxers. He lifted the jeans, feeling into the pockets.

"Fuck," he cursed, throwing them on a corner of the bed, pain in his eyes as he looked down at me.

I removed the tip of my finger from my mouth. "What is it?"

"Condom. I . . . it's in my wallet in the car."

He fisted the thick girth of his cock as his eyes drank in my body. Moving forward, he slid his arms beneath my thighs, his head dipping in between them. The stubble on his jaw scratched the sensitive skin on my inner thighs before a warm tongue pressed to my center. I sighed, my pelvis rising off the bed to meet his continuous lapping, sucking, and that thing he just did with his tongue, like it was dancing about as it slipped between my folds. He was so skilled, so passionate, but my fingers curled into his hair, and I pulled, wanting more.

Licking my lips, I moaned, "Caleb."

He groaned, and my eyelids lowered, watching as he stuck his tongue inside me.

Oh my God.

I wanted his cock inside me.

Screw the condom.

I wanted to feel *him*. I *needed* to feel him.

"Caleb."

His eyes opened, and he stared up at me.

"Come to me." I tugged on his hair. "Come now."

I sensed his struggle as he lifted his head. But he came. Crawling over me, his body visibly shaking.

"Paige." As his cock slid over my center, his body jerked, and he closed his eyes. "This isn't a good idea," he rasped.

His eyes found mine, and I reached between us, guiding the

head of his cock inside me.

He tipped his head back, his jaw and body tensing. "Fuck."

All I could hear from this point was his and my breathing and then a loud gasp as he thrust into me. The raw heat of him slid in and out, and I moaned, the pleasure too much, too intense. I moved my hands over his shoulders as his lips crushed against mine, my body buzzing as he filled me over and over. I bit on his lip as a carnal need mounted, and he gripped my hips, gyrating and plunging. Fucking me as if this were our last time, as if he would never get to fuck me like this again.

My muscles expanded and contracted around him as he pounded into me, unraveling everything inside and sending me up so high that I nosedived back down, clenching and scratching and biting into anything I could as my body stiffened and trembled. My legs coiled around him, and I cried out, arching and pulling him deeper.

"Fuck. I have to—" The stubble on his jaw scraped across my cheek, and with panic in his voice, he groaned, "Fuck, Paige."

His hand found a way between our tightly knit bodies, and then I was empty yet still squirming from the aftershock as he gave in to his own release.

He cursed again, and as my breathing evened, I felt a wetness settling at the side of my hip.

Caleb rolled off me and swore as he ran a hand over his face and through his hair.

Feeling self-conscious amid satiation, I asked, "What did I do?"

He shook his head, both hands gripping his hair. "You're not on the pill." He sighed. "That was too fucking risky. We can't have sex without a condom. We shouldn't have done that."

I frowned, moving away from the wet spot in the sheets. Turning away from him, I dragged the rumpled sheets over my body.

Even though my skin still tingled with warmth and what he'd said made sense, the way he'd said it made me feel so naive.

"I'm sorry." His hand came over and gripped my waist, turning my insides into jelly again.

"It's fine. *I just . . .*"

What? What do I want? Things to be normal? Different?

They would never be. Not when Alex Connor was still out there.

His soft lips pressed a kiss onto my shoulder, and a shiver ran through me. He pulled my shoulder down to the bed, and I tried not to look into his eyes. Anger was stirring inside of me because of his father, and I didn't want him to think it was because of him.

"I've never had sex without a condom. And the thought of getting you, especially *you*, pregnant and not being able to be there . . ." He shook his head. "It just can't happen, okay?"

My chest tightened, but I nodded. "I know."

"There's one more thing." He laid his arm across my waist, and my eyes searched his gorgeous face, lingering on the jet-black tousled hair falling over his forehead. "Calvin already knows this, but after what happened the last time with you looking for me at the suite, you should know, too. If I don't come back, don't look for me. It doesn't matter how long I'm gone. Don't. You'll only be putting your life in danger, and it isn't worth it."

As tears sprang behind my eyes, I swallowed and looked away.

What does he mean, it isn't worth it?

Fixing my eyes on the dresser across the room, I shook my head. "No."

"Paige," he pleaded.

But I continued to shake my head because there was no damn way.

"If Alex Connor does anything to you, he's fucking dead."

"Paige." His thumb moved to my chin and held it, twisting my head so that I would look at him, but when he saw the determination in my eyes, he backed off.

We didn't speak for the rest of the night. Not from anger or disagreement, but from comfort. We were comfortable with not speaking. This had been us from the start.

Though this comforting silence was more like a calm before a storm. Appreciating what we had now because we didn't know when it would be gone.

So, what do you want, Paige?

A single tear slid down the corner of my eye and onto Caleb's chest.

I want Alex Connor dead, and if I do it myself, I only hope that, one day, his son will forgive me because I am in love with him.

TWENTY-FOUR

CALEB

It wasn't long after Paige had fallen asleep in my arms that I picked up my vibrating phone from the nightstand. When I unlocked it, a text message from Alex Connor popped up.

> **A.C:** Come to the house at noon.

I looked at the time. It was seven, and it was an hour-and-a-half drive back.

Setting that phone down, I picked up the one next to it and messaged Bailey.

> **Me:** Meeting with Connor at midday. I need to talk to you about Paige. Can we meet at nine thirty?

Bailey confirmed, and I put the phone aside.

I turned to wrap my other arm around Paige, but she jolted awake with a gasp. Kissing her temple, I hushed her. Fuck, I didn't want to leave her. She had this tendency to curl away from me, whenever she fell asleep, and all I wanted was to continue to hold her like this in my cocoon. Nestling her close, I subjected her to a slew of kisses on her cheek until she gave me her lips.

It was probably a bit mental that I didn't want to shower before

I left. And, as I thought about how some of her wetness still sheathed me, my cock twitched. I wanted her scent to stay with me for as long as possible while I went to see Connor. If anything happened, she could stay on me this way. But, as her tongue met mine, magnifying my need for her, I pulled away, worry prickling the back of my mind for how careless I'd been with her earlier.

My wallet was still in the car, and we couldn't have a repeat of what had happened, no matter how fucking incredible it'd felt. Unlike anything I'd ever experienced since I'd always used a condom, but it wasn't even just the way our bodies connected. It was her, a living, breathing drug that seeped into my veins when I was near.

I swung my feet over the edge of the bed and stood. Grabbing my jeans from the floor, I dropped them on the bed and pulled on my boxers. One of her arms stretched out to where I had been lying, and then her eyes closed as she turned her head into the pillow.

A smile pulled at a corner of my lips, and my heart expanded in my chest. Stepping into my jeans, I delayed zipping them up since my erection was in the way, ready to be tucked into something a lot more pliant than jeans.

Fuck. Those thoughts weren't helping.

I walked over to the chair and grabbed my T-shirt, and when my head came through the hole, I found Paige watching me.

"You're leaving," she said, her voice soft.

"Yeah."

I sat on the edge of the bed and brushed her hair back. I traced a finger down her cheek, and her eyes closed again as she turned into my touch, but then she winced.

"What's wrong?"

"My head." Around her eyes wrinkled, and a line formed between her brows as she squeezed her eyes tight. "It hurts."

"Hangover. The alcohol's wearing off. I'll go get you something."

After washing my face and brushing my teeth, I closed the room door behind me and found Rob was already up, sitting on the sofa and drinking coffee.

"You're up early."

He yawned. "Yeah. I couldn't sleep."

I yawned, too, wondering why the fuck yawns were so contagious. "Me neither. Did you happen to see any medicine at all in these cupboards?" I started with the cupboard over the single-serve coffeemaker, but it was filled with cups and plates. Pulling out two plain white mugs, I set one on the counter and the other under the drip before popping a coffee pod into the coffeemaker and hitting brew.

"I don't know. I didn't check. Does she have a hangover?" Rob asked.

"Yeah," I said, frowning when I saw that all the pods were only coffee and no tea.

"I have ibuprofen. I'll get you some."

When Rob returned, he tapped out two huge white pills into my hand from a prescription bottle. I narrowed my eyes at them and then searched the words on the bottle not covered by his finger until I saw a hint of confirmation.

"They're eight hundred milligrams per pill. She only needs one."

After handing one of the pills and a bottle of water to Paige, I bent to remove a tea bag she'd said should be inside the front pocket of her backpack. Only something else came to mind as I felt around and peered inside her bag. Her anxiety meds weren't in there or anywhere.

I went back out to the living room, and as I set her tea to brew, I joined Rob on the couch with my coffee in hand. "I have to leave soon. She might be in bed for a bit longer, but she doesn't drink like that, so can you keep a closer eye on her today? Make sure she's okay?"

Rob nodded.

Bailey and her husband, Agent Langley, sat across from me at the table in a small room, dressed in regular clothes.

Dark circles had taken up permanent residence under Agent Langley's eyes, and he had a small mustache. With that, a dust of black-and-gray stubbles covered his jaw. I glanced back to Bailey's warmer features, though there was a hardness behind her eyes. I couldn't help but wonder if she saw me differently after all the information I'd given. There was no wondering actually. It was a hard yes. The moment I'd slipped into the passenger seat of her car and started talking, I was no longer the victim who'd gone missing with his mother twenty-four years ago.

"I can't wear a wire," I said, my jaw tight.

"It's the only way for us to get evidence," Agent Langley countered.

"Things have shaken up these past weeks, and I need to see what this meeting is about. They already don't trust me. The last thing I need is for them to find a reason not to because then you'll get nothing."

I looked at the sutured skin where a rice-grain-sized GPS chip had been embedded between my thumb and index finger. They should have waited to do that, too, so it would have time to heal, but it wasn't an option after I told them about being carried out into the wilderness to bury bodies. It made me regret giving up so much information so soon when I knew this couldn't be rushed.

"Fine, but at least get something useful while you're there." The chair screeched across the floor as Agent Langley stood. "You're already looking at thirty years, minimum, and depending on how this pans out, you could be looking at life. I would be wearing a wire twenty-four/seven if I were you."

"And then what use would I be to you if I were dead? Connor has held me hostage before when he thought I would report him. So, if he's the least bit suspicious of anything when I get there today, I might not come back for a while." That was putting it nicely. I lifted my hand from the table and waved. "But you'll know where I am. With that said, don't try to get in contact with me because, again, you won't find anything on him."

Yeah, they could charge him with kidnapping, but I didn't have to tell them that would be stupid, considering all he'd done.

I turned my attention to Bailey. "If this happens and Paige contacts you about me, tell her you have me in custody because she'll endanger her life if she thinks otherwise. She's still an innocent victim, and she should have no part in this."

"Why didn't you mention him keeping you at the house before? How long are we talking? Are there other things you're keeping from us?"

A wave of heat and then a chill tore through my body, and something cinched around my throat as my mind delved back ten years ago. A butcher's knife coming down, a hand being dismembered, blood spurting everywhere.

I forced out a clipped, "No," as my throat continued to close up.

I haven't had any symptoms in years.

TWENTY-FIVE

Paige

A few loose rocks rolled down from where Lisa was hiking up ahead. Miller and two of his friends were a few feet ahead of us, and Luke and Rob were a few feet behind. We were an hour deep into the oak-hickory forest surrounding the property. Dried branches and leaves littered the path. A complete contrast to the rich green leaves still attached to the gigantic trees reaching toward the sky. Wrapping my palm around a skinny tree trunk, I stepped onto one of the many dark boulders we'd been climbing over.

Gym shoes weren't appropriate, but I hadn't planned on this being a part of the weekend's activities, and the eerie stillness was starting to get to me. Everyone's excitement had been good when we started, but the talking had wavered and my thoughts had taken over. There wasn't anything to distract me anymore, and all I could do was stare deep into the woods as far as the trees would allow, needing to see anything coming from afar. The feeling of impending doom had been so significant these past few hours that I was surprised I'd been able to contain my anxiety this well. Then again, it had taken everything I had not to stay locked inside that room all day.

A small yelp sounded from behind, and my heart lurched. Swinging my head around, I saw Mickey bent forward, one of her hands grasping on to the same skinny tree I had been holding on to a moment earlier. By the way one of her feet had slid out, it looked as if she'd almost fallen, but Luke was standing behind her, a strong arm secured around her waist. I folded my lips to keep from smiling. She'd barely kept it together this morning when she told me about their long night together, talking by the fire. She would definitely be swooning later.

"Are you okay?" I asked, pushing one of the straps to my backpack off my shoulder and unzipping it to grab a water bottle.

"Yeah." She smiled, her face reddening as she straightened herself. "I was a teenager the last time I ventured this far out here."

A scream rang through the trees and hit me square in the chest, creating a vigorous thump on the left side. With goose bumps spreading over my body, I peered around, my skin crawling. Suddenly, five years didn't seem so long ago.

"What was that?"

Mickey frowned, surveying the land and trees to her left and right. "I don't know."

My eyes fell on Rob and Luke for answers before doing a complete three-sixty again. The rest of the guys ahead of us hadn't even noticed our pause. They kept walking as if they hadn't heard a thing.

"Lisa," I called.

As she turned, another bellow closed in on us, "You stupid dick!"

"What is that?" I asked, pointing a finger in the air, as I couldn't quite grasp which direction it was all coming from.

She swiped a hand against her forehead, letting out a breath of exhaustion. "Somebody got, got. Each year—"

"Shh. Now you've ruined it." Amber set her hands on her hips, her mouth turned down as she stared at Lisa.

Lisa pursed her lips. "Nothing."

I narrowed my eyes as the bad feeling in my belly amplified. I'd been trying to hold on, but I would embarrass myself if I continued to ignore all my symptoms. "I'm going to head back."

"No, no. Don't go. It's stupid really," Lisa said, walking back down to me, the dried twigs crunching beneath her feet.

"No, it's . . ." Shit, I didn't know what to say. It was everything. My anxiety hadn't plagued me this much in weeks, and with Caleb going to see his father and my not knowing what would happen, I couldn't stay here. "I need to head back to the city." I gave Mickey an apologetic look. "I'm sorry. You can stay with Lisa and Amber. I'm sure Luke wouldn't mind staying either." Her eyes bugged, and I cringed. "Sorry . . . uh . . . I'm just going to go."

"I can hike back to the house with you," Lisa offered. "I'm tired of walking anyway, and it's already going to take us an hour to get back. I'm not up to this today. I'm whipped."

"Me, too," Mickey agreed.

"Yeah, I'm done, too. I prefer the pool to these woods," Amber added.

This pulled me into a bind because Rob and Luke didn't look like the kind to bitch out and head back to camp. They looked like they belonged out here and could climb these hills for days. If they followed us back, the girls would recognize how much they were around.

"I can drive you back," Rob said, going ahead of us, Luke following.

I supposed that was the perfect fix then.

After the guys were a stretch ahead of us, Mickey smacked my arm—or more like touched with how soft the contact was. "I can't believe you said that."

"What?"

"About Luke staying with me."

"Oh, I mean, he'd want to. Wouldn't you want him to?" I asked, suddenly confused.

"He doesn't like me like that," Mickey said.

"Why not?"

"Because," she sighed, avoiding a huge rock protruding through the leaves and dirt, "there are so many other girls here who are probably his type."

"Uh, not to eavesdrop, but have you seen that dude?" Lisa asked, pointing at the hulk trampling through the woods with Rob. "Mackenzie, I'm pretty sure he would snap them in two seconds flat. I've seen him try to do just that with his eyes alone, more than a few times. If he gives you even a second of his time, he's into you. Trust me."

Mackenzie blushed as she turned to Lisa and Amber. "Really?"

"Yes." Lisa gave me a wink as I chewed on my lip, listening to her. "I have a good read on these guys, and I saw you two at the fire pit last night. I've never seen those two have an actual conversation with anyone." She waved a hand at Rob and Luke strolling ahead.

I could attest to that. Ryan and Calvin were the only two who engaged with me while they played security.

She placed a finger on her cheek and passed a suspicious glance my way. "Come to think of it, they've been around a lot more since you, Paige."

Shit.

"Not that you mind," Amber said, nudging Lisa. "Now, what's your read on Rob? I'm curious."

Lisa's lips pursed as her eyes widened.

I'd thought she liked Miller. I was so distracted by this revelation, I whisper-yelled, "What? You like Rob?"

"No. Yes. Maybe. It's nothing to even discuss, Amber." Lisa started to walk around us, and when I turned, I realized Rob and Luke had also stopped, patiently waiting for our little discussion to end.

"Crap, did they hear us?" Mickey whispered.

"No, I don't think so," Lisa murmured. "Just act normal."

"Oh my God. Kill me now," Mickey uttered.

"You? I was the one doing all the talking." Lisa raised her voice. "If you guys heard anything, it was all just a test. We didn't mean any of it."

Oh God. I brushed a hand through my hair, my face swelling from holding back a laugh.

I wanted them to keep talking. This was good. Screw the negative feelings tingling along my spine. Caleb would be fine. I would be fine. There was no one here to hurt me.

TWENTY-SIX

CALEB

The multilevel brick building in front of me looked dark and depressing, even in the middle of the day. But my view was skewed. I knew what life in there was like, and because of that, I didn't want to feel anything. And this second, I didn't feel anything. I was the guy I had been before Paige. Calm. Numb. I didn't even need my past doses of anxiety medications to do it this time.

I eased out of the car and glanced down to make sure the small, nude Band-Aid was still in place, covering the three stitches in my hand. Turning my key in the lock, I wasted no time walking in and making a quick turn to the left. My frown deepened when I found Brad lying on the sofa, looking content with life and his choices as he stared into the screen on his phone.

There were so many rooms in this house, and Stacy Lenard could be in one of them.

"Where is she?" I asked, keeping my voice low.

"Well, hello to you, too, brother," he deadpanned.

I wanted to hate him, but I couldn't, and I didn't understand why when he made it so easy.

"Just answer the question, Brad. Whatever you're planning, she doesn't deserve it."

"Oh, I don't know about that, but she does have you to thank for it."

Fuck, he's annoying.

"Is she here?"

All I got was a cocky grin before Alex Connor's office door opened. For the first time, I was seeing him with different eyes. His square jaw, broad shoulders, and buzz-cut, dark hair. My own father.

"Get in here," he said, not aggressive but not nice either.

Suddenly, I was glad I'd removed the security cam from his office a few weeks back. That was one less thing to worry about.

"You too, Brad."

As he moved around his desk, Brad and I took a seat in front of the old desk that looked like it belonged in a principal's office, which was what sitting here in front of him was essentially like. He wasn't our father. He was our manager.

His glare landed on me first. "I know what you've been doing."

My pulse quickened, but I kept a straight face and my mouth shut.

"You know I'm your father and that Brad's your brother. It's nothing you didn't know before."

"I didn't actually." I cast a glance at Brad. "But *he* seemed to have known."

"You didn't want to be a part of the business, and whether you thought you were adopted or my own, what difference does it make? Or does it make a difference? Do you feel more inclined to be a part of what we have going on here?"

With a slow jerk of my head, I muttered, "No." It was a gut instinct, and I shouldn't have said that. I regressed. "Maybe." A way was wide open to get all the evidence Bailey would need. "I wouldn't know because you never trusted me enough to tell me the truth about you and Brad, my own flesh and blood. It doesn't make any sense why you'd even hide that from me."

"Don't try to make sense of it. It was for your own protection and ours."

"So, I'm assuming Brad knows his mother, too."

A muscle twitched in Connor's jaw, and his eyes held a threat I didn't dare question. "Brad, go wait outside." He waited until the door closed. "Your mother is dead."

"How?" I asked, not giving a shit how pissed he wanted to be. She was my mother, and I deserved to know.

"I killed her."

Words evaded me as what he was saying sank in. I'd had a suspicion, but hearing him say it, like it was nothing, like she meant nothing...

Shit.

"See? That look on your face right now is why I kept it from you, so you wouldn't go asking questions you didn't want to know the answers to. But, since you're so desperate to know the kind of person she was, I'll tell you. Your mother was a whore, and she disrespected me," he huffed. "She got what she deserved."

"That's a real fucked-up thing to say about the woman you had a kid with."

"I made her pay, and then you came into the picture. A pity, really. You're fucking weak, just like her. Brad's crackhead mother was a much better payoff." He leaned back in his chair, and that same arrogance that slithered over Brad marred his features.

He'd raped her. My fingers tapped against my jeans before clenching into a fist.

I got up and started for the door.

"Where are you going? I thought you wanted to hear about the family history."

"I did." My jaw tightened as I tried to retain the anger coiling through my veins. With my hand on the doorknob, I twisted to face him. "But you're a fucking liar, so what's the point? First, you told me the Sawyers didn't want me, so you adopted me. Now, you're telling me this. Why should I believe you? Are you planning to stick to your story this time?"

"Watch your mouth. You don't fucking talk to me like that,"

Connor growled, rising from behind his desk, his hands slamming down onto the polished surface. "What, you think she fucking welcomed you with open arms after what I did? Fucking her like the whore she was. It's over with, and unless you want things to change around here, you'd better watch what you do because, the next time you're in this house, we won't be having a conversation."

I jerked the door open as he continued, raising his voice as I walked out, "And, if anything, you should thank me! How many adopted kids do you know who have access to a limitless bank account and have lived in a fucking luxurious suite half of their lives, you ungrateful bastard?"

Brad stepped in front of me with a smug grin. "It just gets better. How does it feel to be the product of unwanted fucking?"

Cocking my elbow, I swung my fist into his face so hard, I could have heard the moment I broke his nose, but I didn't hear it or anything else. I watched the blood gushing as he touched his nose, and then he was on me the next second, pushing and throwing a punch that I blocked. Brad was the same build, and he had been trained, strong and fast, but I was better. He wasn't even a match for me, not when he spent his days getting high. Like I knew he was this second. That was why I wasn't going to fight him. So, I pushed him harder this time, and he landed on the floor and skidded back on his ass.

I continued to the front door as Connor came out.

"What the hell? Caleb, you don't fucking go anywhere. You get back here!"

Two of Connor's men appeared from out of nowhere, blocking my path to the door. With a slow shake of my head, I turned back around, pressing my lips together. Brad was scrambling up from the floor, his white T-shirt covered in blood. I had to admit, that punch wasn't even for his mindless comment. It was calculated. Waiting to happen since the day he'd attacked Paige. I'd never had a solid enough reason to hit him before, but his shit-talking had created the perfect opportunity.

"What, your perfect son can't defend himself in a fight? It's for his own good. You talk about a crackhead delivering better." I bit my lip as I shook my head. "I'm guessing you were talking about her crackhead son. Well, congratulations. Let's see how things work out when he can't get his daily fix."

"You don't come here and make threats in my house. Are you forgetting your place, son?" Connor nodded to the two men standing behind me. "Deal with him. Let me know when you're done."

The last thing I saw was Brad laughing, his teeth red with the blood running down from his nose into his mouth. A fist whacked the side of my head, sending tremors through me, and before I turned, the heel of a boot landed on my back, transporting me to the floor.

I thought about Paige because, if I fought back, I wouldn't get to go home. I needed to go home. I needed to see her again.

TWENTY-SEVEN

Paige

Pacing the living room again, I paused for a second and looked at my phone on the couch where I'd been sitting for hours. I didn't know what to do. What could I do?

In my anxious state, I'd even called Calvin, who pretty much told me what Caleb had—to wait and not do anything rash.

"What's going on, Paige?" Ryan asked, looking up from his phone. "You've been doing this all night. Now you have me on edge."

I stopped and looked at him. His blond waves were cut lower than when I'd last seen him.

"If I asked you to take me somewhere, no questions asked, would you?"

"Depends on where." He narrowed his eyes. "Why? What's this about?"

My hands lifted, and I clutched a few strands of my hair at the root before sliding it through to the ends. I shook my head and gripped my hair again, pulling as I stared at the ceiling.

"And where's Caleb?" Ryan asked as I continued shaking my head.

At the sound of the elevator, I moved, so I could see who was coming through the steel doors. I prayed it was Caleb, but Calvin had said he would check in when his mom got off work, and it felt like it'd been hours since then. The doors slid open, and Caleb stepped out. Tears sprang to my eyes as my heart dropped into my stomach. Blood was all over him—his face, his arms . . .

I moved toward him, wanting to see if he was fine, but stopped, scared I might hurt him if I touched him.

Or is it not his blood? What if he—

"Oh my God."

"What are you doing here?" he asked.

My chest swelled, and my throat clogged. I couldn't speak, and then I realized it was because I wasn't breathing, thinking about what he might have done.

I took in a full breath as I heard Ryan, "Holy shit, dude. What happened?"

Caleb moved around me and kept walking to his room. He hadn't expected to find anyone here since I should have still been at the lake house.

I turned to Ryan. "Thanks for staying with me, but you should probably—"

"Yeah, I know. Call if you need anything."

"Thank you." I swallowed as Ryan departed. Then I stood in place for a few seconds.

Not sure what I would find out, I walked down the short hallway to Caleb's room and placed my knuckles on his door for a moment before I knocked. When I didn't hear anything, I placed my ear to the door and heard the shower spraying and splashing against the tiles. Each of our bathrooms had one of those large rainfall showerheads, so I knew he wouldn't hear me if he was already in the shower.

Twisting the knob, I let myself into his room. The light was off, but the bathroom door was open, and he stood there, his back to me, stripping out of his clothes and dropping them into a pile on the floor. A few obvious pink discolorations were on his back along with the scabbed cat scratches I'd left there. When my eyes lowered, I didn't see any other damage, only a firm ass. And just . . . wow. He was a masterpiece, even from behind.

I stopped behind him and skimmed my fingers over the bruises. He didn't flinch, but when I pressed my cheek to the center of his back and wound my arms around his waist, our eyes locked in the mirror. Caleb was not just naked. He was baring himself to me. And, as confused as I was about what had happened, it was all I needed. Without words, I was letting him know that I would have his back, no matter what.

As I gazed at the dried blood on his face, the steam from the shower started a mist on the mirror. Stepping back, I pulled my T-shirt over my head and removed my leggings and undergarments. Without a word, we stepped into the shower together, and as reddish liquid circled around our feet, I squirted body wash into my hand and massaged it over his skin. First his back and then his front.

Squeezing more soap in one hand, I reached down and rubbed it over the hard length of him. I couldn't believe he was this turned on after the night I could only imagine he'd had. But, with less care than how I'd touched the rest of him, I pumped my hand up and down his shaft until the rainfall above washed away the foam. A sigh came from him, and I continued to watch my hand move over him, steadily but strong. The warm spray from the shower over my skin was no longer soothing. It caressed the nerve endings in my body and sent a teasing trail over my nipples and clit.

The corners of my mouth turned down as I noticed how my hand couldn't close around the girth of him.

Is this even doing anything for him?

I wanted to give him everything, and my hand couldn't even fit. He was his own fortress.

How could I satisfy him? How could I shield him like he shielded me?

I kissed his chest and lowered onto my knees, the size of him even more breathtaking from this position. Guiding him to my mouth, I caught the droplet of water hanging from the crowned tip on my tongue before I lapped around the smooth, delicious head.

As I took more of him between my lips, a ragged breath left him, and when I looked up, he was leaning forward, watching me, one hand braced against the tiles on the wall, which allowed his broad shoulders to shelter me from the spray. My eyes traveled down the taut muscles in his body—his arms, his torso—to the happy trail and hair at the base of his cock. With my own need rising, I remembered how that hair felt against me. The way it teased my clit when he was inside me.

Pumping my hand faster, I matched the rhythm with my mouth as I sucked him hard, and the more I sucked, the more the taste of him became apparent, making me even hungrier for him.

"Oh fuck," he groaned, touching my hair.

My already-hard nipples became tighter, and my sex clenched. This couldn't be normal. We'd had sex early this morning, but I felt like we hadn't had sex in days. I wanted more. So much more. A pop sounded as I withdrew him from my lips, only to take him between them again.

"Oh shit," he mumbled. "Fuck... keep doing that."

I looked up at him. He was biting his lip, his eyes dark and cloudy with desire.

Could he feel how much I wanted him? How much I loved his taste? How much I loved this part when he held my head steady and just fucked my mouth. As I felt the pull when he wrapped my hair around his fist, I pressed my tongue to the thick, velvety flesh thrusting in and out of my mouth and moaned, thinking about how easy it was for him to lose himself in pleasure. So strong and powerful but helpless as he poured himself into my mouth with a gasp. I drank, needing him to release everything down my throat, especially his pain, so I sucked him dry, forcing him to give it to me. All of it.

I knew that was why he hadn't said anything. He was hurting, and all I wanted to do was take it away.

I wanted all of it.

TWENTY-EIGHT

Caleb

I followed Paige into her own bathroom like a lost puppy, afraid if I let her out of my sight for a second, everything would flood back in. With each of us wrapped in a towel and her blow-drying her hair, I brushed my good hand through my hair. My ring finger had been dislocated on my other as a warning about keeping my mouth shut, one they had been so eager in giving that they didn't even notice the Band-Aid between my thumb and index finger.

Paige's eyes caught mine in the mirror, and she licked her lips. I smiled as my cock reacted beneath the towel, needing more of her attention. Needing to ravage her mouth or pussy. At this point, I didn't know which was sweeter.

Distraction.

The moment I'd begun forcing my cock down her willing throat, using her the same way I'd used so many girls before, I'd felt guilty. I'd never intended to do that with her. I hadn't even expected her to be here or for her to want *me*.

I would tell her about the kind guy I could be sometimes. I couldn't *not* tell her. As she ran a comb through her damp strands, I circled an arm around her and tugged her towel loose, hanging it on the chrome rod behind us before I got in between her and the counter.

Fuck, her beautiful tits. I covered one of the mounds with my hand.

The blow-dryer stopped, and I met her sparkling baby blues. "You can keep drying your hair. Don't mind me."

Lowering my head, I sucked on her nipple for a bit before plunging my fingers inside her channel. As she wavered in my arms, the dryer lowered to her side.

"Keep drying," I said, moving down her body.

Seating myself on the plush bathroom rug in my towel, I separated her legs on either side of mine, and then I swatted her ass and pulled her closer. I dove in, tongue first, licking and sucking on her glistening pussy.

Only I have been here. Fuck, it gets me every time that she's all mine.

I dipped in two fingers, working them inside her tightness, as I feasted on her desire. She moaned above me, gripping my head and grinding her pussy on my lips. I flattened my tongue and let her pussy ride over it before I flicked it over her clit. Two seconds later, the blow-dryer clattered on the counter, and she bent over the sink for support. I wound my forearm around her leg as I continued to devour her, moving my finger inside her quivering channel until she collapsed onto my lap, panting.

"God," she sighed into my neck, still squirming.

A huge step up from what I felt like. I would definitely take it.

"I wanted to make you feel good." She drew back, looking into my eyes. "Now, you've disabled me from doing that."

A wry smile spread across my lips. "You're disabled?"

"I don't know. My vagina might be."

"I'm hoping that's good."

"Too good. I don't know if I can come like that again."

Laughing, I leaned my head back on the bathroom vanity. I was worried about using her, and it sounded as if that's exactly what she wanted me to do. "You're worried you might not be able to come again if I fuck you? Were you planning to use your vagina to make me feel good?" My chest jerked. Fuck, I couldn't stop laughing.

She brought her hands to her flushed cheeks. "Stop. Not like that, but maybe. I don't know."

I used my index finger to swipe her hair from her face.

She's so fucking perfect.

"I was worried about using you that way, and you're saying you might be okay with that?"

"Yeah." She frowned. "Is that wrong?"

My gaze dropped to her breast, and I bit my lip as my eyes lowered to her pussy, which was still exposed with the way her thighs straddled my lap. I scratched my jaw and looked up. "I've used a lot of girls that way. Meaningless sex. I used to do it to stop myself from thinking." She dropped her hands between her thighs to cover herself, and I continued, "I try to separate the two, using sex as a distraction versus when I have sex with you, but"—I shook my head—"I don't know. Being with you is just different, and I don't even understand it. I can't explain it."

"So, my sleeping with you to make you feel better should be a bad thing then? But, if it makes you feel good, I don't care."

She seemed unsure, but I smiled as her words clarified what I was trying to get to.

"You make me feel good. That's the difference. Everyone else, I was only disgusted with myself afterward." A chill traveled over my body, and I cursed, my revulsion heavy as I recalled those moments. "It was fucking horrible. I was horrible. But it was the only way I knew how to stop myself from thinking. It was my escape."

I lifted my hand to tweak a taut pink nipple, and she sighed.

Reaching up, she touched the split skin over my eye, and I leaned into her touch, closing my eyes as her soft hand caressed the rough edges of my jaw.

"When you hurt, I hurt, and it makes me wish I could take your pain away."

I opened my eyes to see the worry etched between her brows. "I don't want you to take my pain, Paige. I want you to give me yours." And I meant that in ways she wouldn't understand, ways I didn't even understand.

"I could give it and take it at the same time."

My cock rose beneath the towel. "I'm sure you could."

She persisted in making her point, like I hadn't even spoken. "It isn't a one-way street. You always take care of me, and I want to take care of you, too."

This girl.

"I wish . . ." I silently finished, *I had a mom to introduce you to.*

I thought back on Alex Connor's words and felt heat behind my eyes.

Sighing, I jerked my head to the side. "He killed her. That's why he wanted to see me. Brad had told him about the blood test, and after he told me he'd killed my mom, he said . . ." I pressed a thumb into the ache above my eye and rubbed. "He didn't say it specifically, but I knew it was what he had done. He raped her, and she got pregnant with me."

"I'm sorry." Her hand caught the hand I'd been rubbing my brow with. She pulled it toward her and stared down. Then I saw what she was staring at. My ring finger had ballooned. "Your finger. It's sprained or—"

"It's broken."

"You need to get it fixed. You need to see a—"

"It's fine."

"But—"

I pressed my thumb to her lips. "If you didn't want me to take you to the doctor when you practically had a concussion, then there's no damn way I'm going to the doctor for a stupid, broken finger."

"But you have a Band-Aid on a tiny, stupid cut."

I scrunched my face and evaded her comment with a shallow laugh. That was another story, one that I didn't want to tell her or she'd want in.

Raising her hand, she massaged the same tension-laden spot above my eye. "I hate him."

I ran my hands up the sides of her body. I loved how comfortable she was with being naked. A beautiful distraction. I thumbed the underside of her breast as she leaned in and placed a soothing kiss to my forehead. I'd never had this with anyone, and fuck, maybe I did want her to take my pain. Because that was exactly what she was doing, and I didn't want this moment to end.

"I'm going to get you ice for your finger."

She started to move from my lap, and I secured my arms around her back and pulled her closer, using the heat from my body as a blanket to hers.

"No."

Her hands dropped to my shoulders and slipped to the back of my neck, and with another brief kiss to my forehead, she whispered, "Okay."

TWENTY-NINE

PAIGE

Lying prone on the fabric couch, I stared at the plain ceiling tiles in the room, wondering how many people had lain here like this on this couch.

I wanted to know if they got better and, if they did, how long it took.

This was my fourth session of therapy, and I should feel somewhat better, but I didn't. Sometimes, I felt it could be because I didn't want to get better. Like I was scared to get better.

How stupid.

"The anniversary of the Sawyers' passing is one week away." Marian's voice sounded like the last ten minutes of yoga when the instructor's voice became a tranquil monotone; I knew this from the yoga classes she'd suggested I take. "What do you usually do during this time?"

"Nothing." My arms were folded over my stomach, and my nails scratched the material on my gray sweatshirt. "Usually, I try to forget. A few weeks out, I stop paying attention to the dates. My birthday passes without me realizing." A low feeling slithered around my gut. "But I always remember. I don't have to look at the date to know. I feel it." I shook my head, blinking away the tears before they came.

"And what is that feeling? Can you explain what it feels like?"

The well inside my chest cracked, and I stood at the edge of its rough stone edges in a white gown, peering down into its depths.

"Darkness. Inside and outside of me." I realized my breaths were coming in a quick succession, and I paused, taking a few measured ones. "It feels like a black cloud following me. Everywhere."

"Emotionally, how does that darkness make you feel?"

"Awful. Alone. Scared." I bit my lip, subconsciously drifting away from the girl as she took a seat on the edge of the well, as if waiting for something to happen. "Crazy," I finished.

"Are there thoughts you remember being constant as you get these feelings?"

"No . . . yes," I sighed. "I always wonder why it happened, but I still don't understand, and sometimes, I feel like it would be easier if it had been me and not them."

Marian didn't respond, and in my peripheral, I could see she wasn't taking notes.

I was thankful enough to continue. "I don't have thoughts of hurting myself. I just . . . it really sucks."

Mainly because Alex Connor was still out there, hurting other people . . . hurting his son.

"Have you returned to the house or visited the cemetery since our first session?"

"No." I lowered my feet to the floor and sat up straight. "To both."

The cemetery I couldn't go to, not until Alex Connor and his goons stopped running around; until then, my family couldn't find peace, and neither could I.

"You described revisiting the house as being a bit awful, but sometimes, it is our deepest fears that keep us from moving forward, and in order to liberate ourselves and move past it, we can only accept it. Don't fight it. Don't be afraid of it. Hold hands with it. Talk with it. Find peace with your fear. Your family meant a lot to you, and you meant a lot to them, Paige. It won't be easy. But you will find a way."

I heard her, but I wasn't sure it was time for me to hear this. My reasons for wanting to return to the house had nothing to do with accepting what had happened. But I was banking on it to help me find a way, one that would explain why everything had happened.

Caleb decided not to carry the phone he used to communicate with me and the guys to work, and it was killing me. After what had gone down Saturday night, I wanted to check in with him to make sure he wasn't being dragged away by his father again.

It was Monday, and after spending most of the day in bed with him yesterday, I shouldn't feel this anxious. But something was changing, and I could feel it. His brother had ratted him out. Alex Connor didn't trust him. He'd even told me the reason he wasn't more injured was because of an upcoming deal he had to close for Connor.

So, what will happen after that deal is done?

I was pacing again but stopped as I heard the elevator, and when I looked around the corner, Calvin stepped out.

I ran over and threw my arms around him. "Oh my gosh, you're here."

He returned my hug. "I was gone only for the weekend."

"Yeah, but you said you were coming by, and you never did."

Calvin was still my favorite out of all his friends. Probably because he had to put up with me more, but he was kind and had major points for being a cool roommate.

"Caleb returned my text, so I knew you'd be all right."

"Is everything okay with you? Caleb mentioned you were taking care of your sister."

"I'm sure it'll get better." Seeming distressed with the topic of his sister, he nodded to Rob. "Hey, dude."

He threw his keys on the counter, and a loud clang echoed in the living room. My eyes remained on the keys splayed out from the ring, and it made me think of Caleb's keys. I bet Caleb's keys had access to places I could use to help me find a way into Alex Connor's world where there were answers.

"Shit, Paige. This place is like a fortress, and my boy still has someone here, watching you. It doesn't bother you?"

No, it didn't bother me, but if I went forward with the plan forming in my head, it was going to become a problem.

"It was strange at first, but I don't mind it."

He lifted the cover from his blender and scooped protein powder from the large bottle. "Good, because he's slightly obsessed with your safety. I mean"—he raised his hands to make his point—"not slightly. Obviously."

I smiled. "I like it."

This was proof of how well I'd been hiding my anxiety that only Caleb would know to do this for me. Perching on a barstool around the breakfast bar, I watched Calvin as he added milk to the blender and a few other unknown ingredients to his daily shake.

"Soooo, are any of those steroids?"

He laughed. "All natural, girl." He extended an arm so I could see the cut in his upper arm as the muscles pulled tight. "You can't buy these in a store."

"I don't get it. You have, like, ten different kinds of protein powder in the pantry."

"First of all, one of them is Caleb's."

"Just one?" I shrieked. "Why are you building anyway? Are you planning to compete or something?"

He shrugged. "I like it. It's the only thing I have to do now besides keeping you safe." He flexed a bicep, stretching the already-tight T-shirt around it. "So, don't be surprised if these babies grow another inch in a week."

After a few more minutes of me busting Calvin's balls, Rob took off, and I went back to the sofa and opened up one of the novels Caleb had bought for me while I tried my best to stop my concerns about him.

An hour later, the elevator was called, and Caleb appeared. My chest swelled, and I closed my book. My book boyfriends wouldn't be getting any loving today, not when my real *boyfriend for now* was here. And he was okay. Jogging up to him, I threw myself at him, much like I'd attacked Calvin earlier. Only Caleb got more loving as I tipped on my toes. My hands curved around the back of his neck, and I urged his face down to mine for a kiss. His hands went straight to my ass, squeezing before giving it a gentle slap.

"I just thought of something," I said, my lips next to his jaw as I combed my fingers through his hair. "You're my BFN."

"What's that?"

"My boyfriend-for-now."

"Hmm, I'm your boyfriend?" He kissed my neck.

"Yeah," I muttered, my body arching into him as I melted.

"I have the sexiest girlfriend-for-now then, and I can't wait to fuck her later." He nipped on the skin at the base of my neck, and my knees about gave out. "I'm going to change and get a quick workout in. I'll be back." He looked around, his eyebrows furrowing. "Where's—"

"Calvin's here. He's in his room."

"Oh." He dropped a kiss on my mouth. "I'll see you in an hour then. Unless you want to work out with me?"

My hands slid down to his lapels, and I clasped them, about to accept his invitation even though I'd already worked out today, but something else came to mind. His keys.

Will he leave them here while he's downstairs?

Sometimes, if he knew Calvin and I were up here, he would leave his keys and call us to send the elevator.

"Maybe next time," I uttered, biting my lip.

"Okay."

Calvin came out of his room and turned on the television while Caleb was in his room changing. As we peered at the television screen, Caleb came out, his keys dangling in his shorts pocket.

I cursed under my breath.

Calvin glanced at me before looking at Caleb.

"You two should think of a code for the guys to use when they call for the elevator. It's unlikely Connor can find out where we live, or what floor we're on since I have this condo under someone else's name, but we can never be too sure," Caleb said before walking out.

"What was that for?" Calvin asked.

I shook my head. "Nothing."

He clicked the Guide button on the remote and scrolled through the programs. "Well, whatever it is, you should know, I've got your back. You can trust me."

My ears perked up as my interest rose.

"Ryan told me about the other night when Caleb got back. There's a reason these are my friends, Paige. They're loyal to the very end, and if one of them is stumbling like I know Caleb is, I have to do something. Anyway, if you have a plan, I'm in."

CALEB

It was like we were in a trance.

I would never get tired of fucking her.

Every time I slid inside her, the only things that mattered were the snug muscles gripping my cock and the overwhelming emotions fueling my desire.

She threw her head back, her hands in her hair and breasts moving up and down as she rolled her hips back and forth. I hadn't even had to teach her how to ride me. It was natural for her. She wanted, and she took, turning into my own little vixen. And I fucking loved it. Without lifting my hips off the bed, I worked my cock into her delicious cunt. As she moaned, my fingers dug into her hips, pulling her down so that I could fill her completely.

"Caleb," she sighed, her hands coming down to cover her breasts. She squeezed them before pinching her nipples.

Holy fuck.

The sight alone made me want to release the tension in my balls. My hand moved down to her sensitive nub, and I massaged slowly. Her gaze lowered and met mine, and I knew she was about to come apart so I grabbed her ass and pounded into her, fucking her until she tightened around my cock. Her pussy caressed and coaxed my own pleasure to come free, but I held on, rotating her beneath me and fucking her with everything I had. I couldn't go deep enough, fast enough, and hard enough, but she cried out my name, squirming beneath me once more. I pulled out and flipped her onto her front, slapping her ass and grabbing it as I shoved the weight of my cock into her drenched channel.

Her pussy is mine. Fucking perfect, and all mine.

My name fell from her lips, and as she clenched the sheets into her fists, I pressed my front to her back. Snaking a hand beneath her body and finding her clit, I rubbed. I wanted her to keep coming on my cock. Wetness trickled over my fingers as I quickened my pace, fucking her pliable body until she was stiffening and screaming my name. She almost pushed me off her body with the force of her orgasm, but I didn't budge. I stayed buried, my cock pulsating so hard I trembled. Heat burned between our bodies, and perspiration fought to cool our skin as we panted in sheer exhaustion.

Minutes passed, and she was the first to talk, though it sounded like a hum. "Mmm. What was that?"

I let my tongue lick her skin as I kissed her damp shoulder. "Me being the best boyfriend you've ever had."

I should pull out and dispose of the condom, but I didn't want to. Our connection held a passion I'd never known, and this was the only way I could show her that. So, if it meant fucking her until she couldn't walk, then that was what I would do because words weren't my friend when I'd never felt anything like this.

"Caleb, if you can fuck like that with a broken finger, I think you might go down in history as the best boyfriend *any* girl has ever had. You don't even need to do anything else. Just do that."

I laughed.

Fucking hell. When I should be concerned about a million other things, she makes me laugh.

I didn't know what I would do without her. It wouldn't be long before things would begin to change, and as the clock ticked down, I wanted to make sure my every moment was well spent with her.

"You make me happy," I told her.

"Ditto."

After we cleaned up and settled back into bed, she placed her cheek on my chest. As her fingers skimmed over my collarbone, she said, "Tell me about living at Alex Connor's house. What was it like for you growing up?"

Her question threw me. It was uncharacteristic of her. And I'd never talked about my time at the house, not even with Calvin, who knew about the hell I'd been through. But, with us in the darkness like this, it felt like nothing could touch us. It was just her and me.

Deciding to give her a shred of what she'd asked, I began, "It was shitty. I don't remember much before ten, just being pushed around mostly." By *being pushed around*, I meant, being backhanded, but I couldn't burden her with those details, so I continued, "I was homeschooled, only spent one year in public school when I was ten. Then, I moved into the suite at seventeen, and then I went to college."

"But what was Alex Connor like? Did he treat you like a son? Did he get married? Did you have a stepmother?"

I bit the corner of my lip as I traced circles on her naked back. "No. I had cooks, tutors, maids."

Her question made me curious. I'd never seen Connor with a woman my whole life. Unless he hadn't introduced them to me. Or he had fucked around with the same maids who came to my room from time to time. Even more disturbing.

"I'm sorry," Paige murmured, her hands moving down my torso in a slow caress. "What's the worst he's ever done to you?"

I swallowed and breathed, "Why?"

"I want to know more about you."

"The worst he's ever done is ... let me watch someone else get hurt. Don't ask me to tell you about it because then I'll have to say TTM."

"Okay, I won't. How about Stacy Lenard, the nurse? Do you think he has her at the house?"

"No." I shook my head as I remembered the call Brad had made that night, asking the guys to change locations. Though it could have been a ploy. "I don't know. Fuck, this sucks. I need to do something. I shouldn't have gotten her involved."

There was no point in getting the police to raid the house, with the way Alex Connor's men cleaned and disposed of anything leading back to them.

Paige went quiet for a moment. "When you told me not to come looking for you if you didn't come back, what was that? I know you went away for two days sometime ago when we just met, but what happens? Does he keep you hostage or something and hurt you?"

She was thinking about two nights ago when I had come back here, bloodied with a broken finger. She shouldn't have seen that.

"Uh . . ." I let out a long breath and combed my fingers through her hair. "Yes."

Moving her leg to rest on one of my thighs, she slipped her hand down to cover my flaccid dick, and desire shot through my body, causing it to twitch in her hand.

"What's the longest he's ever kept you there?" she asked.

I pulled my thoughts from her hand casually cupping my balls to answer her question. "I'm not sure. Maybe two months, but my whole time living there, I wasn't allowed out of the building for the most part."

"What is that like? Is it just a room? Why can't you leave? Does he have someone watching you?"

Pain stabbed at my chest. I didn't want to answer her. It wasn't something she needed to worry about. The less she knew, the less likely it would be possible for her to do something impulsive.

"I don't—" Her hand pumped my cock to life, and I tried not to focus on the sensations. "I can't tell you."

"Why not?" Her head moved, and a warm, wet tongue flicked out and slid over my nipple.

Fuck.

"It isn't important." A groan hummed in my throat as she sucked the hardened tip into her mouth and swirled her tongue over the sensitive crest.

Her breath teased my nipple as she spoke, "Tell me what it was like."

"Paige, I—"

Her hand tightened around my cock as she bit down on my nipple, and my hips lifted off the bed.

"Ah, fuck."

That felt fucking amazing and as my ass settled back onto the bed, I wondered if she could tell by the way I was throbbing in her hand.

"Tell me."

I wanted to be stubborn so she would bite me again.

What the fuck is wrong with me?

Paige was turning me into her little bitch, and I fucking wanted.

"Why do you want to know?"

"I'm curious. I want to see what it was like through your eyes."

Her tongue teased my nipple again, and like a horny animal, I thrust into her hand like we hadn't just fucked.

"It was dark, always dark, except for when someone brought me food." The first few days, I would be limited to one small meal a day, but I couldn't tell her that. "I couldn't get out. The door was always locked. I would try it every day. There was only a bathroom and mattress inside the room. I masturbated a lot to keep my mind off the pain and other things."

My body stilled as my mind went back. "I never ran out of things to think about. Mostly, I'd fantasize about what life would have been like if my parents had loved me enough to keep me instead of giving me to Connor. Then when I was older, and had overheard his men saying that they couldn't believe Connor had taken out my whole family. I wanted to be thankful because they hadn't wanted me anyway, but it sucked. And when I asked him about it . . . that was the fourth time he locked me in that room. At least when that was happening, I thought I'd been adopted. Because knowing what I know now, I would have had to think about how much more fucked up it all was."

"Was it the same room you had while growing up? And wasn't

there a window you could climb through or something?"

"No, it's on the highest floor. There was no getting out, and the windows were all sealed with a grill inside. It felt like I wasn't even in the house at all. Sometime I wouldn't hear anyone talk for months. I thought I was going to go fucking crazy. But, sometimes, I could hear cars driving by at peak times of the day. I didn't know if it was morning, when people were heading to work, or evening, when they were returning, but I looked forward to it after a while. It was the only thing keeping me connected to what was outside those walls."

"How many times has he done this to you?"

"Four."

She resumed massaging my cock that had gone soft. "Did he come to see you in there?"

"Once or twice close to the end. Just to threaten me or other people I knew, to see where my head was at, to see if I would be compliant."

"I want to ask what you did that would put you in jail, too, but, Caleb, I don't want to know."

She sounded upset, and with the pain lacing her voice, my initial curiosity about why she was so interested in knowing about my time at the house faded. She was hurting for me because she'd reached inside me and taken the pain I hadn't wanted to give to her, and fuck if I didn't regret it.

THIRTY-ONE

PAIGE

With my hand in Caleb's, I walked up the driveway to the mansion, to the perfect life I'd once known. It looked the same as it had when I visited a few weeks ago. Overgrown bushes and untrimmed trees surrounded the building. Dried and fresh vines ran up the sides. I stopped and stared for a moment, trying to picture the way it used to be.

Turning around, I looked at the moss- and dirt-covered stone fountain that used to be the center of a beautiful garden. I could almost see Reese, Alaina, and I lying in that garden, staring at the clouds as they traversed the sky or when we would use our hands to scoop water from the fountain and splash each other.

Climbing the three steps to the door, I pushed the key into the lock. Caleb released my hand and stepped inside first, and I followed, stopping at the first whiff of fresh paint and sawdust. Someone else had been here or was here.

Caleb turned to me for directions.

Should we stay, or should we go?

I swallowed and inhaled as I called out in the foyer, "Is anyone here?"

I moved farther inside, noticing that the pieces of furniture that white sheets had been covering were no longer present. The flooring had been redone with new wooden panels, and a section of the wall separating the dining from the living room had been eliminated.

What? No. Why?

Caleb's fingers combed my hair back, and his lips touched my temple. Placing my hand on his lower back, I leaned my head on his chest and inhaled, needing to breathe in a bit of his strength. When I exhaled my peace with the disappearance of everything I'd wanted to go through in the house, my hand drifted down his back, and I felt a familiar hard metal tucked against the small of his back. I hadn't known he was carrying, but it settled me, knowing he was prepared.

"I just can't believe it's all gone. Why would they take everything away after all this time? When I'm finally ready to deal with it. It was supposed to be mine to deal with." Turning away from him, I started up the grand staircase, needing to see that everything *was* all gone. I walked from room to room, pausing in the rooms that had belonged to my parents, my sisters, or me. But there was nothing.

"Who do you think did this?" Caleb asked as I gazed through my old bedroom's window.

He had stayed in his business suit, except for the tie, and the hem of his white dress shirt hung outside of his pants. One of his shoulders leaned onto the wall as he casually slipped a hand into his pants pocket. There was that dominance again that I often overlooked due to my own strong nature.

My eyes traveled up his physique as I answered his question, "Your grandparents, I hope. It's been vacant for five years. Who else would have access to it?" I looked back out the window, and the question I'd wanted to ask since my last therapy session came to mind. I turned my head. "Why do you think he wanted them dead?"

With a slow shake of his head, Caleb replied, "My best guess is that they knew something they shouldn't have."

"Like you and your mom being taken?"

"Maybe, but that was years before they came to this place, looking for you guys. How about you? You've been here since you were a baby, so how did that happen?"

I thought about that and sighed. The only person who had the answers to these questions was the man himself. Maybe that was what I should ask in my last letter to Alex Connor. I had written it earlier today, inspired by what Caleb had shared with me last night.

My thoughts sobered with what we needed to do next. It was risky, but if we wanted more answers, it had to be done.

A male voice echoed down the corridor, and my heart jolted the same time chills broke out over my skin. My ears perked up, and by the time I looked at Caleb, his gun was out, gripped in his hand at the side of his thigh.

The rented car we used to come here was in the driveway, so whoever was out there knew someone else was here. Putting a finger on his lips, Caleb pointed for me to go to the closet.

Does he not know me by now?

I shook my head. There was no way I would let him put himself in danger to protect me, which was pathetic to think about since he was already doing it every day he was with me.

With three long strides, his body closed in on my stubborn stance while I listened for activity outside the room.

"Please," he whispered.

I wanted to defy him, but he was the only one with a weapon, so I nodded.

He moved to the doorway, peeped out, and then disappeared into the corridor.

I walked to the window and peered outside, my heart thumping. I would not die here. Not like this. And Caleb . . .

What if he gets shot?

I couldn't deal, knowing I'd waited behind.

As I was about to exit, I heard footsteps, and I slid into the small space behind the door, peeking through the long slit the door hinges allowed. A tall figure entered and then another. Surprise would be my greatest form of defense, but as I edged out, silver-gray hair caught my eyes. Before I could make a run for it, his head turned, and he jumped, holding his chest.

Grandpa.

My eyes darted to the man next to him, assessing. He was bald-headed and bulky and looked like he was in his mid-forties.

"Paige," Grandpa mumbled, his bright blue eyes becoming glassy. "It's really you?"

I nodded. Scared. Excited. Confused. Worried.

This was going to be my next move. Talking to my alleged kidnappers' parents, Caleb's real grandparents. There had to be something they knew that would get us closer to the truth about what had happened. Since I hadn't gotten a chance to mention it to Caleb, I didn't know if he was ready to meet them. He didn't want to put them at risk by contacting them, and neither did I, but it was a little too late for that.

"Hi," I said, not sure what else to say. There was too much to say, but I wouldn't say a word. At least not while the man next to him kept staring at me like he'd seen a ghost. "I was just leaving."

Shit, I shouldn't have said that.

God, I'm an asshole.

"Dan, could you give us a moment?" Grandpa asked the man, who hurried out like he couldn't wait to leave.

I don't trust him.

I looked into the hallway to make sure Dan was walking away and not hovering to eavesdrop.

Where did Caleb go?

My next thought answered that question. *He doesn't want them to know he's here.*

Whatever had happened in the past, Caleb's grandparents couldn't have known anything about it. If they did, they would have been hunted, too. Yet here I was, creating that risk for them. Shit, maybe Caleb was right, but it was too late. That Dan guy, whoever he was, had seen me. He could be a normal guy, or he could be linked to Connor.

I rubbed my palms on my tights. "I'm sorry I didn't get in touch."

I was confused, suspicious, and even now, it isn't safe. Is Grandma here, too?"

"Yes. She's in the car. We weren't sure who we'd find in here."

"You shouldn't come here. It isn't safe until those guys get caught. They're still out there, and they're looking for me. So, I can't trust anyone, and I really have to go, but ... I have questions, a lot of them."

"I figured." He cleared his throat. "My son wouldn't have kidnapped you, Paige. You know that, right?"

I nodded as he confirmed what I'd always known, that the Sawyers hadn't kidnapped me. "Is there somewhere private we can meet? You, me, and Grandma?"

Caleb and I walked by the front desk at the hotel without stopping. We made a right, as instructed, and found the elevator on our left. As soon as I pressed the arrow pointing up, the doors opened. Caleb used a knuckle to press the button for the sixteenth floor. I wondered if he did that as a habit to avoid leaving fingerprints.

Circling my arms around him, I looked up, needing to know he was okay with this.

When I'd asked Grandpa to call that Dan dude and Grandma inside the mansion, Caleb had managed to slip out, unnoticed. We couldn't be spotted together by anyone who knew about me and what had happened.

Resting his hand on my shoulder, he looked down at me. Still seeing the worry etched in his face, I brought my hand up and rubbed a thumb between his brows. Even though his grandparents had been hoping to find him for years, Caleb thought they wouldn't care to see him, especially when they found out what his dad had done to their daughter—his mom, Olivia Sawyer. But they didn't need to know that, and it had taken me twenty minutes to convince him of that.

"Still worried?" I asked.

The only family he'd known were the evil ones, not the

kind, loving grandparents I remembered spending time with—his grandparents—and there was nothing I wanted more than for him to meet them, so he could see that for himself.

Squinting one eye, he lifted his hand, bringing his index and thumb close together to show me *a little*.

I frowned at the duct tape wrapped around his broken finger. The sound of his guitar used to drift through the condo almost every day, and I hadn't heard it since his finger was injured, reminding me once again of how much I hated Alex Connor.

I pressed my cheek to his chest and tightened my arms around him until the elevator came to a stop.

Room 1612 was only a few doors down the empty hallway on the right, and before I could knock, Caleb dragged me up against him, crushing his lips to mine. The pure intensity of it made my legs wobble. His tongue glided between my lips to toy with mine, and the taste of his lust ignited mine. Raw need peppered the nerve endings all over my body, and when my back hit the wall behind me with an *oomph*, his lips left mine.

"Shit," he whispered, pulling my hips from the wall.

I whipped around to face the door. 1612. "Shit." That hadn't been the wall. Swallowing, I took a few deep breaths, but soon, my body was shaking with stifled giggles. *Oops*.

Caleb's hand slid around and pinched my nipple through my blouse, effectively shutting down my fit of giggles as he turned my laughter into hunger.

"Okay, okay," I uttered.

The lock clicked, and my breath caught.

God, this is embarrassing.

I brought my hands up and fanned my face, quickly dropping them to my sides as the lock clicked.

They had no idea I was bringing Caleb.

Grandpa opened the door, and his eyes spent only a split second on me before they focused on Caleb. He hesitated and then said, "I didn't know you were bringing company. Come in."

Grandma stood behind Grandpa, both of them looking as fancy as any wealthy person who spent lavishly on themselves. It made me wonder if Grandpa still had that old noisy truck that never did fit into their lifestyle. They looked the same as five years ago. And Grandma might be sixty-five, but she looked fifty with her hair pinned back and makeup flawless, and if I remembered her correctly—

She came forward and threw her arms around me, and the memory of this softness, her smell, the familiarity was almost overwhelming.

"God, Paige, I've missed you so much. I can't believe it's really you."

"I've missed you, too." I released her and hugged Grandpa, too, since earlier, I'd been too anxious to do anything other than rush out of that mansion.

After what felt like minutes, I pulled back. "I have a surprise." I looked at Caleb, and when my glance passed back to them, they were staring at him. "I don't know if you want to sit down for this."

"We knew you'd be dating by now, Paige. Don't be silly," Grandma encouraged. "I think we can handle it." A warm smile spread on her thin lips, and her eyes drifted to my stomach before coming back up with stars. "We can handle anything. Even if you were pregnant with quadruplets."

Maybe I should ask Caleb to sit down, because clearly she's trying to give him a heart attack.

My hand went to my neck. "Not quite. This is your grandson." Pride swelled in my chest as the words left my lips. "Your real grandson. Caleb Sawyer."

Grandma's hand flew to her mouth as she mumbled, "Oh my God," shaking her head. "No. It can't be. Is it?" Her eyes filled with tears, and they immediately streamed down her blush-covered cheeks.

Grandpa had a hand to his chest. "Young lady, this is the second time today you've nearly given me a heart attack."

My own eyes welled with tears.

"Nice to meet you," Caleb said. He sounded so uncertain.

THIRTY-TWO

CALEB

I didn't know what to feel or how to act. These people were more Paige's grandparents than they were mine.

"I'm Harry."

Gray stubbles covered the tall, slender man's jaw, and he had a full head of silver hair. He extended his hand, and I took it, expecting a feeble handshake, but it was strong, welcoming, as he covered the back of my hand with his other hand. I nodded as he released my hand, only to be squeezed into a hug by the blonde-haired, older woman as she secured her arms around me. I wasn't as thrown off as I would have been if Paige hadn't briefed me on what to expect. Still, I'd never felt this awkward in my life.

"I'm Lydia." She stepped back and brushed a tear from her face, and Harry circled an arm around her shoulders. "Today has been the best day I've had in a really long time. Thank you for coming."

"Dinner should be here in a few minutes. We brought the photo albums Paige asked us to." Harry stepped away from his wife and lifted five large albums off the dining table and deposited them in my hand.

Paige's description was so accurate that I wanted to smile.

Mrs. Let's Be Best Friends and Mr. Let's Get Straight to the Point.

I sneaked a peek at her, and she folded her lips, smiling.

Mrs. Sawyer walked us to the sitting area and sat next to me on the sofa. "So, how did you find each other, and how long ago?"

"We met at a coffee shop about two months ago," Paige replied. "We didn't know we were connected at first, but, Grandma, no one can know you've seen us."

I leaned back, so Mrs. Sawyer could watch Paige explain what we'd talked about before coming here, repeating some of what we already know, whilst keeping out any mention of their daughter, Olivia Sawyer.

"I wasn't planning to bring this up until later, but as I briefly mentioned to Grandpa, the people who broke into our home that night are still out there, and they're searching for me. It's so bad that Caleb and I shouldn't even be here right now. With that being said, you both need to be really careful about whom you trust or talk to. Even the police officers. Some of them have been working with those monsters."

I cringed at her reference.

"Right now, we're looking for answers to things we can't find without some help. But, after tonight, we can't see you again until this is over because we don't want anything to happen to you, too. You're the only ones we have left. Please understand," Paige begged.

Mr. Sawyer nodded, and then so did Mrs. Sawyer after a long inhale.

But then she asked, "Can I ask about Olivia? Do you know where she is or what happened to her?"

I swallowed. *Fuck.* This was what I hadn't wanted.

I fidgeted with an edge of the photo album, letting my eyes travel between the two Sawyers. "I was also taken at a young age. I never met her."

"Oh, honey. I'm sorry." She patted my thigh.

"Besides the foggy old picture from the missing person file, he's never seen her. So, I think these should really help."

Paige's hand rested on my forearm, and I had a feeling she'd asked for these photo albums for me. She wanted me to get to know the other side of my family, even the ones my own father had sent to their graves, including my mom. But as the gravity of the situation hit me, I would rather keep the album closed.

Paige squeezed my arm. "We can look at these after dinner."

I gathered it would be just as hard for her to see these photos. She looked from her grandmother next to me to her grandfather standing a few feet before us. "Who did Olivia date before she went missing? Do you have any idea?"

Mrs. Sawyer shook her head. "Your grandpa and I were traveling when she got pregnant. We didn't know until she was six months along." Her eyes met mine. "Your mom was a very private person. I think she took that from your grandpa—both her and your uncle, David. It's why he had a studio at home and wrote instead of performed."

"So, how did you know when she went missing?" Paige asked.

"David's wife. Those two were best friends. Leanne told me she had gone to visit Olivia's condo a few days after Caleb was born because she wasn't getting Olivia by phone. Since she had a key to the apartment, she went right inside. Everything except for her car was left behind. The police said she ran away, but Olivia had no reason to do something like that. She would never have left Leanne without saying anything."

If that were the case and the two were that close as friends, maybe Olivia did say something to Leanne. And if Leanne knew about Alex Connor, that he was the one who might have taken Olivia, she would have mentioned it to her husband. That had to be why Alex Connor had gone after the Sawyers—to keep them from talking. But why would he have waited for so many years?

"What about Paige?" I asked. "You didn't know about her either? Like where she came from or how?"

"Leanne was pregnant. Everyone knew, and all of us thought Paige was hers. She loved and took care of you like her own," Mrs. Sawyer said, her attention turning to Paige. "So, there was no other reason to think otherwise."

"Your hair color, it changed," Mr. Sawyer said. "Tell her, Lydia."

"Uh, well, it wasn't by much." Mrs. Sawyer shook her head. "It was just something I noticed when I had visited Leanne and David at the mansion. At the hospital, the little hair you had was more like a light brown, but it changed to a lighter blonde when we visited a few weeks later. I didn't think too much of it because you had grown so much, and babies' hairs change all the time."

"How did Leanne seem when you visited her those few weeks later? Was she happy? Was there anything you noticed that was different with her?" I asked, chewing over the fact that Leanne had a baby girl who wasn't Paige, which meant I had a cousin who was out there.

Lydia looked at her husband before she spoke. "She went through a really bad postpartum depression. That pregnancy changed her. She was a social butterfly, but after she became pregnant, she started to stay home more, and stayed home altogether after she gave birth. Her doing that hadn't been strange, it was just that she hadn't done that after Reese. It wasn't until she became pregnant with Alaina that she started to become more like herself again."

"The FBI told us that Leanne had an STD testing done about two weeks before she went in for a pregnancy test." Mr. Sawyer said. "They wanted to know if we had any reason to believe that there were any marital problems between our son and Leanne, or if either of them might have been involved with anyone else."

A knock came from the front door.

"That must be the food," Mr. Sawyer said, heading to the door.

Paige and I bolted up off of the sofa.

"We're going to wait in the bedroom while it's delivered," Paige explained.

I agreed with her. After everything, I wasn't willing to take any more chances.

When we walked into the room, Paige wrapped her arms around me and I held her close.

"Leanne was sad because I wasn't hers," Paige murmured, squeezing me. "Every time she cried, she wasn't only crying about Olivia being gone." Her voice hitched. "She was crying because her daughter was gone too."

"But what happened to her baby that she needed to replace her with you?"

A strong feeling told me that Alex Connor had happened, but I still didn't see how those dots could connect.

Did he kidnap Leanne's child out of spite? Maybe as a warning because she knew he had taken my mother. But, if that were the case, what happened to Leanne's real daughter?

"What if Connor did to her the same thing that he did to your mother?"

"You think he would have raped Leanne, too?"

"I don't know, Caleb. I don't know." She sighed. "But with the STD test thing and . . . if he did, you might have a sister."

I swallowed, then cupped her head as I kissed her forehead and closed my eyes. I couldn't think about her speculations, because then, I would have to think about the worst-case scenario if that had been the case.

The conversation over dinner was lighter than the heavier stuff we'd started the night with, but the whole time, all I thought about was Leanne's pregnancy.

"We started some work on the mansion about a month ago," Mrs. Sawyer was saying to Paige. "Since we hadn't heard from you and we were back in town, we wanted to do something to help make it ready for you in case you wanted to sell it or whatever you decided to do with it. It's still yours."

"But why?" Paige's mouth turned down as she forked the last broccoli on her plate, leaving the rice and chicken breast for last. "I'm not your real granddaughter. If anyone should have it, it should be Caleb."

"What?" She couldn't possibly think I wanted anything to do with that place. "No, it's yours. Please, you know I don't need it." I also wouldn't be able to use it if I was in jail.

"What happened to all the stuff that was inside?" Paige asked. "The furniture and everything."

"Most of the furniture was donated, some tossed," Mr. Sawyer said. "The personal stuff was placed in storage until you're ready to go through it. We weren't sure what to do with them just yet, especially without hearing from you first."

THIRTY-THREE

PAIGE

Caleb and I settled on the couch after dinner, and I was sure his brain was overflowing with as many questions as mine. As we flipped through the thick sheets of the album, I leaned onto his chest, and one of his arms draped around my shoulders. It was strange, staring at the wealthy, carefree life I'd once had in comparison to how I'd been living my life since then. And, even though it made me sad, I couldn't keep my eyes from looking. I wanted more of the smiles and happy faces staring back at us.

I slid my arm between Caleb's back and the cushion, and I tucked my face closer to his chest. He was so warm and cozy; I could fall asleep here. He ran his thumb over a picture of his mom. She looked like the rest of the family I'd known with blonde hair and blue eyes, but her hair was cut into a bob. In the picture, she was laughing with my dad in his studio, and the neck of a guitar hung from her hand, the body of it touching the floor at her feet. I closed my eyes, listening to Caleb's heartbeat against my ear.

"Do you think the Sawyers would let me have this picture?" Caleb asked.

Grandma and Grandpa had retreated to their room to give us some privacy as we went through the album.

"Yeah, take it." I didn't have to look to know it was the picture where his mom had the guitar. I knew he was starting to see what he shared with the other side of his family.

"Are you sure?"

"Yes."

He waited before sliding it out of the clear pocket. When I heard a click from the room door, I started to ease away from him, but he kept me secured to his chest.

"They know."

"No, they don't," I whispered.

"Let's see how surprised they act, and then you can tell me if I'm wrong."

Silence dragged on as we waited for an interruption until I got impatient and turned to see Grandma leaning against Grandpa, a hand over her chest and hearts and stars exploding in her eyes. She didn't look surprised, just delighted. He wasn't wrong. They knew.

Grandma smiled. "We wish you two could stay with us. Please know, our door is always open whenever you're able to see us again."

I nodded.

"We're falling asleep, but you're welcome to stay," Grandpa said.

"No, it's okay. You've really helped us a lot, and we should get going," I responded.

Caleb held up the picture he'd removed from the album. "Paige said I could take this picture. I hope it's okay."

"Yes, of course, sweetie. Take whatever you need." Grandma okayed it, and I swore, I felt as Caleb's heart stuttered in his chest.

"Thank you."

As Caleb skimmed through the albums one last time, I sat up straight and stood, hugging Grandma and Grandpa. A quiet sadness still lingered in their eyes, but for the most part, they seemed to have moved on.

When Caleb stood, Grandma embraced him. "You can take the albums and return them when we see you again," I heard her tell him.

Grandma was still casting her hooks. Smiling, I waited for

Caleb to bite.

"I can't do that," he said, not biting.

"No, it's no problem at all. I promise. You should take them. It's the least I can do," she encouraged, a huge smile on her face as she pulled back and stared up at Caleb, so much love in her eyes even though she'd just met him.

"Okay," Caleb accepted.

I was glad. He might be scared of our grandparents learning the truth about his mother and what his father had done, but he'd had nothing to do with what that evil asshole did.

"Take care of her," Grandpa told Caleb with a firm handshake.

"I will."

"He's your grandson," I said. "I think you should be telling me to be gentle with him."

"I know, but first and foremost, I need to make sure my grandson's a gentleman."

I grinned, wrapping my arms around Caleb. "He is."

That was another characteristic Caleb had gotten from the Sawyers. I didn't know much about the Connor side of his family, but I was starting to see how much more like the Sawyers he was and less like the man he'd been around his whole life.

Alternative music played softly in the background while light rain sprinkled on the windshield on the ride home. Both of us were deep in thought, a habit we still needed to break. His hand reached over and touched my thigh, and warmth flowed through my body. He was signaling his need for some kind of connection, but my fingers were laced together. His hand drifted up and down my forearm before it slipped between my hands.

"I'm proud of you," he said. "For today at the mansion and for looking through those albums, looking into your past. You did good."

I looked at him, the streetlights and darkness casting shadows over him. Even though I'd had an ulterior motive to find anything that could bring us answers and take Alex Connor down for good, he was right. I didn't feel the world caving in on me like I had the last time.

"I'm proud of you, too. Thank you for going with me." I waited a moment before I told him, "You shouldn't listen to Alex Connor. Your mom wanted you. Think about it. What does your birth certificate say? What name is on it?"

"Caleb Sawyer, but that doesn't say much. He could have coerced her to do that in order to keep his name off the records. That would keep him out of the spotlight when things went awry."

"You're right. But I want you, and so does Grandma and Grandpa. And don't say it's because they don't know the truth." I smiled. "I know them. I know the truth, and I still want you. You're not him."

He looked somber as he said, "It's crazy."

"What's crazy?"

"Music and how it just called to me. I didn't know about the Sawyers until I was nineteen. I started playing when I was eighteen. But, before that, I used to listen to acoustic versions of songs on the radio or live performances on TV. By the time I had some freedom, I was itching to get my hands on any instrument, so I took music my first semester in college. The same week, I signed up for private lessons from a guitarist, but I caught on to it so fast, the sessions only lasted for a month. It was just weird because I couldn't understand how I'd learned it so fast or where the passion for it was coming from. So, when I found out about the Sawyers, it made some sense. Then I hated it as much as I loved it every time I thought about what Connor had told me, about them not wanting me. It was stupid, but each time I picked up the guitar, I felt like I was sharing something special with the people who didn't want me. But I couldn't stop playing." His head jerked. "I tried."

"Well, I'm glad you didn't stop. I watch you play at the bar or hear you sometimes practicing at the condo, and I don't think you realize how talented you are."

"Yeah?" He squeezed my hand. "You're just saying that because you're my girlfriend-for-now."

A smile tugged at my lips.

The whole bar quieted when he played, but I had a feeling it wasn't what he wanted to hear. I was also sure he didn't want to hear what'd been on my mind lately, about how my feelings for him had increased and how my stupid, juvenile heart hadn't gotten the *just temporary* memo.

"But I love when you play, and I love your voice, so you should totally sing to me sometime."

He glanced at me. "It won't make you cry?"

"You've noticed?"

A corner of his lip tipped up. "A little bit."

"I don't think I will next time, but I'm not promising anything."

He chuckled. "Okay."

Pulling his hand from mine, he clicked a few buttons on the dashboard until "Push" by Matchbox Twenty came on. He'd done a cover on this one at the bar a few times, and it was one of my favorites, but I hadn't expected him to sing it this second.

Oh my God! I mouthed, unable to contain the emotions bursting inside me.

I felt like a starstruck teen backstage with a lead singer. And, with the rain on the windshield and Caleb's raspy voice reaching over Matchbox Twenty's vocals in the background, I'd never experienced anything this perfect. The ache in my cheeks from the wide grin on my face could attest to that.

When the last note from the song left his lips, I said, "Caleb, you love this. You love playing. Get an X-ray done on your finger. It would be stupid not to. It could heal wrong and bother you for the rest of your life and keep you from playing. You *have* to play."

He was too incredible not to.

He reached across the console and took my hand. Lifting it to his lips, he whispered, "Okay."

THIRTY-FOUR

CALEB

I wasn't looking forward to today. Not like I looked forward to any day I had to go to work for Alex Connor, but today, I would have to see him in person with documents he needed to sign before I could close on a unit in New York tomorrow. These past few days, I'd been considering not showing up, but I was involved with a criminal, the cops, and the FBI. It reminded me of how things weren't and would never be that simple. But I would do my best to make it simpler for her.

Speaking of her, she wasn't in the bed where I'd left her while I showered, and even the bed was made.

Tossing my towel onto the bed, I walked to my dresser, removed a pair of black boxers, and pulled them on. When I went to the closet to grab one of my dry-cleaned suits, I smiled. Paige had removed the plastic from all of them. I was guessing she didn't know I left them in the plastic because I didn't have a lint roller.

After donning my pants and dress shirt, I brought my suit jacket out to the living room and hung it on one of the barstools. Calvin was in the kitchen with a cup of coffee, and I glimpsed Paige on the area rug in front of the sofa. I grabbed a cup and poured myself some of the hazelnut coffee that had been taunting my senses for the last half hour. When I turned around, I stopped, almost spilling the coffee. Paige was in a full split on the floor in front of the couch. Not one of those side splits, but a full-on fucking split. My head tilted to the side as she leaned forward.

Holy shit. I hadn't known she could do *that*.

"Hot damn, dude. I know we're like brothers, but—"

My hand whipped out, smacking Calvin in the chest.

"*Ooomph.* Asshole, that was my sternum."

"Yeah, well, finish that sentence, and I'll knock you out."

"Whatever. I'm only fucking with you. You're the only one who could handle her. She could chew up and spit out any other motherfucker, including me."

"It's the other way around. She's the only one who can handle me."

"Clearly," he quipped, staring at what I was guessing was the scratch Paige had left on my neck. "Is that why you're all dressed from top to bottom when you come out now? She's handling you in there? Dude, you can talk to me. I know she can be aggressive, but—"

I narrowed my eyes. "You're trying to get hit, aren't you?"

"Nah. Just you got balls, dude. Sometimes, she looks at me like she has the keys to the gates of hell, waiting to toss my ass in if I say the wrong thing. You're good with each other though." He lowered his voice, his mouth forming a thin as he jerked his head. "But you've already gone to the cops. And for what? You're going to lose the closest thing you've had to normalcy, happiness even." He shook his head again. "I don't get it. I really fucking don't, man."

With that, he went to his room.

I wasn't about to talk about it in front of Paige, not knowing if she could hear us. There wasn't anything to talk about anyway. Calvin might not like my plan, but he wouldn't understand the amount of guilt and confusion I'd struggled with over the years.

And, since I'd started to see Alex Connor for who he was, the things he was capable of doing to get what he wanted, I had to do what was necessary to stop him before anyone else got hurt. That thought made me wonder how many friends Connor had who worked in law enforcement because, with those connections, it could take years before the FBI could pin him down for any wrongdoing. But I would be patient. I would be his little pawn, like I'd been my whole life, even if it meant being locked away in that dark room again for months. This was my life, and I would live through it all over again if it meant no one else would get hurt.

The loud music thumping in Calvin's room pulled me out of my head.

Coffee in hand, I walked over to the couch, my mood shifting as I drew closer to her, my axis. Her hair was bunched on top of her head, and she was in tights and a T-shirt. She acknowledged me with a smile but kept the small white earphones in her ears. This yoga thing must be a part of her therapy, but that kind of flexibility had to have come from back when she had been a cheerleader in high school. I watched her for a few minutes before I took a seat.

"Hey, do me a favor," she said.

Setting her hands on the floor between her legs, she crawled forward on her hands until her butt lifted, and her feet flattened on the fluffy gray rug. Her firm bubble butt was in the air for my viewing. I licked my lips, my hand unconsciously drifting to my crotch.

She pulled an earbud out. "Can you tell me if my leggings are see-through?"

I cocked my head. "What?"

"My leggings," she said, impatiently wiggling her butt. My eyes widened, not wanting to miss a thing as she explained, "After too much use, they start to become see-through. Are they?"

"Hmm . . ." As my thoughts drifted to peeling away her tights, my palms twitched, wanting to touch, caress, and spank those tender cheeks. I glanced at Calvin's closed door. Setting my cup on the floor at the side of the couch, I said, "Come closer."

She stood and moved back a couple of inches before bending over again, and I smiled.

"Closer. I think the lighting's kind of bad or something."

She stood as she moved back, and I reached out, taking her

wrist and tugging her to where I wanted her.

"Right here. I want to make sure." My hands slid over her tiny waist to the heart-shaped curve of her ass, and my dick swelled. Placing a hand at the small of her back, I pressed for her to go ahead and bend over. "Hmm, let's see."

She bent, and my lips parted.

The only thing I saw was how the material clung to her like a second skin. My words came out husky as I told her, "It's fine. But maybe you shouldn't wear these in public."

"No one else gets *this* close, so I think they're okay if *you* can't see through them."

"I know, but . . ." I palmed the glorious cheeks, desperate to take a bite. My fingers caught the waistband of the stretchy fabric, and I began to peel it away. She tried to move, but I maintained my tight grip on the material, whispering, "Shh."

"Calvin might—" she started before we both froze at the sound of the lock.

I dragged her onto my lap, extending my injured finger out of the way of her fall.

"Hey, I'm going to get you dirty," she protested, trying to get up, but I enclosed my arms around her.

Calvin walked out, dressed in jeans and a black shirt like he was going somewhere, but he was staying here with Paige. At least, that was what he'd told me last night when I thought Luke was the one coming over.

My phone buzzed in my pocket, and I shifted on the couch to retrieve it from where it was buried. I sighed upon seeing Brad's name on the screen with a text.

Brad: Where are you? You are needed at the hotel. Now!

"Shit," I whispered. "I have to go. What time do you get off work later?"

"Not until three thirty. I'm downtown tonight." Her head lolled back onto my shoulder.

"Damn it, I should have woken you this morning."

She turned her face into my neck. "We could have a quickie."

Holding her head to my neck, I moved my lips close to her ear, hoping the music would drown out my words before they reached Calvin, who'd gone into the kitchen, ignoring us for once. "I can't have a quickie. I've just witnessed how flexible you are, and because of that, I'm already thinking of about ten different ways to fuck you."

"Don't tell me that unless you're ready to follow through." The tip of her tongue traced a short path on my neck, and as my nipples tingled, a low groan rumbled from my chest.

"You're killing me." I looked at my watch and then at Calvin, who was sitting around the breakfast bar, his back to us and his head down. "Are you and Calvin going somewhere?"

"We're low on groceries." She lifted her head and twisted to me, nibbling on her lip as she adjusted my tie. Her eyes met mine, and she looked at me like she either wanted to kiss me or slap me.

Deciding for her, I brought my hand to the back of her head and kissed her soft lips until their sweet bubblegum flavor infused my mouth. One of the things I liked about her was her directness. I paid attention and could read her well when she wanted me to. So, the fact that she'd looked at me the way she just had meant she was struggling. My lips prodded hers apart, and fully acquainted, our tongues tangled, seeking the connection our bodies demanded.

With a rough, final kiss, I pulled back and looked into her eyes. I never knew what to expect when she hid from me. I was letting her see me, so why was her guard up?

THIRTY-FIVE

PAIGE

The elevator doors closed, and Calvin wrapped a turkey sandwich inside a piece of foil. "Ready?"

"You already texted Luke?" I asked as I walked to my room to grab my backpack. It was packed with my work clothes for tonight along with a few other essentials in case I couldn't make it back in time to change.

"Yeah. He'll let us know when Caleb rolls out," I heard him say while I was in my room.

With my backpack on, I braided my hair to the side and twisted a rubber band at the end, and as I entered the living room, I pulled a fitted black cap over my head.

"Wow, I almost didn't recognize you," Calvin said, sarcasm oozing from his playful voice.

My lips pressed together, and I showed him my middle finger. "I bet you couldn't hide your big head anywhere."

He snickered. "Wow. Okay, I deserved that."

As he tossed his keys into the air, I opened the fridge and removed the container of filtered water. Setting it on the counter, I unscrewed the top of my water bottle and poured water inside until it was about to spill over, my thoughts on Caleb. I hadn't lied to him this morning. All I'd said was that we were low on groceries; that's all. But guilt still gouged a hole in my gut.

My forehead crinkled. *Ugh.*

It had been three days since Calvin told me he wanted in and two days since Luke and Rob had been watching Caleb. The terms Caleb had initiated with Calvin and his friends had changed without him knowing, though it pained me that I had to keep it from him. But if anything happened, I needed to know how to find him. A small part of me was also curious about what he did for Connor. Things that didn't relate to hotel or property management. Because how bad could it be? Caleb was good. So good, I had a hard time believing there was any bad in him.

But, since he didn't care to elaborate on his plan B, I was going with plan A to use myself as a target when the time was right. Besides, Calvin had said Caleb would never agree to it. I didn't know what made him so sure, but he was Caleb's best friend, so I trusted his opinion.

Calvin stopped at a nearby gas station to fill up the tank and grab some snacks before our unofficial stakeout began.

Yesterday, the first day of our watch, I hadn't even thought about the fact that I would need to urinate at some point, but Calvin had already thought of it when he showed me a portable toilet at a construction site two blocks away. He even had a set of binoculars we could use to spy from a safe distance. They were so nifty, only I also realized it was how they'd kept an eye on me before I met them.

He pulled into a parallel-parking spot on the road behind a car, a couple hundred feet from Alex Connor's property. We were in Luke's SUV today. In some weird way, I also enjoyed doing this. I got a slight rush at knowing that I held the upper hand on Connor this time. Because, through these binoculars, I was right in his yard, standing on his doorstep and walking around his driveway.

A few hours went by without any activity, but I kept the binoculars to my eyes as I asked, "Why did you warn me to stay away from here before?" I could smell the beef jerky he'd been nibbling on for the past fifteen minutes. I'd been contemplating having a bite myself just so I could ignore the scent. The bag crumbled, and I glanced at him. "Those smell like crap."

"But they're so good. Have one." He popped the bag open for me, and I reached in because we'd already been here for so long, but we still had ways to go before the scent would vanish. "You should ask Caleb. He knows more than I could tell you. He was the one living here."

I squinted. "You waited a whole two minutes to tell me that?"

He shrugged. "Caleb never talked about it, but I just remember when we were kids . . . I think we were about eleven. I didn't really know much about him then, but we were inseparable at school for that year. So, while I was out one day riding my bike, I figured I would stop by his place after school. After that day, I didn't see him again for years. He found me, and the only thing he told me was that he'd gotten homeschooled. But I knew it had been much more than that, and I also knew it was my fault that he hadn't gotten as much freedom as he could have. If I hadn't gone to his house that day, he wouldn't have been homeschooled."

Holy crap.

"I know you didn't tell me that, so I could tell you this, but I'm telling you anyway. It wasn't your fault, and Caleb wouldn't want you to believe that it was. Also, if he held it against you, you wouldn't have been the first person he sought out when he was able."

He bit off a piece of the beef jerky in his hand and chewed. "Either way, it's time I did something for him. Even if it means acquiring a couple of blocks of C-4 and blowing up that fucking building, Alex Connor included."

I winked and clicked my tongue. "Now you're talking." I moved the binoculars back to my eyes while I laughed. "Can you imagine? That would be awesome. Seriously, we should look into that."

Calvin chuckled. "So, how's therapy going for you?"

My mouth fell open. *He did not just go there.* Though I had made fun of his big head this morning.

"That was dickish. Very dickish." I gave him a tight smile.

"Damn it, Paige. Stop doing that. I was just telling Caleb about your crazy-ass eyes this morning."

"What?"

Calvin and I goofed off a lot when no one else was around. Our tendency to speak our minds had helped our friendship evolve into this cool, sarcastic kind. So, I was curious about what he'd been telling Caleb about our weird moments together. Caleb only knew about some of my crazy, and I was almost self-conscious about him finding out more.

"You get this look in your eye, and it intimidates the shit out of me," Calvin admitted.

Well, that explained why he'd been so honest since we met. *And that does not sound like a problem. I like it.*

"You're doing it again."

Oh.

"Sorry, I can't help it. But you know I'm not evil."

"We're laughing about blowing up Alex Connor." He smirked.

"Okay, so a little evil then."

He shook his head and sighed.

"Hey, you brought it up," I accused. "You're just as evil."

"I know I'm evil." He grinned. "But, unlike you and how you make it apparent, no one knows I am until it's time to light the match."

He was serious, and I'd be shaking in my boots if I didn't know him better. This was Calvin we were talking about. Though I had a sick suspicion he was up to something.

"Noted. Evil partners in crime then?" I held up a hand for him to high five, and as the slap of our palms echoed in the SUV, a light bulb went off in my head. "Evil Partners In Crime. E-P-I-C. Epic." My mouth opened. "Whoa."

"Whoa." Calvin's head tilted. "I was going to say your knack for coming up with these stupid acronyms was a little tired but"—he shook his head—"that was pretty epic."

"I am awesome. Just say it. *Paige, you are awesome.*"

"Uh, no," Calvin said at the same time he pointed ahead.

I brought my binoculars back to my eyes to see someone heading out of the building.

Only one person had walked out of there yesterday and gotten in one of the vehicles parked on the side of the road, and it had been someone I didn't recognize. This someone I recognized. It was Caleb's brother, Brad.

That asshole.

Caleb didn't talk about Brad, but I knew enough to gather that he was a douche. Especially for snitching on his own brother. I might not hate him as much as his stupid father, but for the way he'd set up an attack on me that night after my shift at the gym, it was reaching pretty close.

With his brisk walk down the driveway, I only caught a glimpse of his screwed-up face. Like he was pissed about something. He trekked down the sidewalk toward us but on the opposite side of where we were parked. A tree blocked him from view before he branched out onto the street, next to a bright blue Ford Mustang. As he folded himself inside, my eyes dropped to the spiderweb tattoo on his elbow.

His black workout shorts and red T-shirt made me wonder if he was still working out at my gym. Maybe awaiting my return. If only I could go and strangle him until he told me everything.

What is his motive? And why doesn't he care about Caleb?

I could only imagine how hurt Caleb must have been to find out Brad had known they were related all along, only for it not to have made a difference.

No wonder he didn't want me to give him hope.

The hair on my skin bristled as a strong need to be with Caleb swept over me. I needed to feel his warmth. I needed to hug him, kiss him, make love to him, and maybe one day tell him how I really felt about him. I wanted him to be more than just my boyfriend for now. I didn't care about the worst thing he'd ever done or that he might go to jail. I loved him. And maybe I could help him. Maybe I could talk to Bailey, and she and Agent Langley could help him with legal immunity if he talked to them. There had to be a way.

The Mustang roared to life and eased out of the parking spot before zipping forward and out of sight. My stomach cramped, and I realized I'd been holding my pee for some time.

"How does no one know what Alex Connor looks like?" I asked. "He owns the most luxurious hotel downtown. Shouldn't his picture be up on the website, or some other corporate crap at least?"

"I'm guessing he doesn't want anyone's attention on him, whether it's good or bad."

"Or maybe the good could lead to the bad," I mused.

Calvin's expression turned pensive.

"I'm going to go pee. I'll be back."

Putting my sunglasses on, I got out of the car and walked down the quiet street. With the clear blue sky today, the day was scorching even though the sun was beginning to fall in the sky. The days without a cloud in sight were strange. Like something was malfunctioning in the universe because I was so used to a cloud hanging over my head.

Ten minutes later, I got back to the vehicle, and before I could close the door, Calvin said, "Caleb's here. He just walked inside."

A slow ache eased into my chest. I'd wanted to see when he got here.

Calvin set his binoculars between his seat and the center console and took up his bottle of water. "It's five thirty. We should head back to the condo. It won't take him long to put two and two together if he heads there next and finds out we aren't there."

He was right, but I wanted to wait.

Picking up my binoculars, I looked to where Caleb had parked in the driveway. "Why did Brad leave in such a hurry right before Caleb showed up?"

THIRTY-SIX

CALEB

While Connor skimmed through the documents I'd given to him a few minutes ago, I paced the large space in his office where the old carpet below my feet hid the vault I couldn't stop thinking about.

My gaze passed over the silent clock on the wall. It had been over ten minutes.

Why is he taking this long?

He usually signed whatever I gave him without bothering to read it through.

As the air reduced in the room, my hand itched to loosen the tie around my neck, but I couldn't give him any signs of discomfort. He needed to think I was still his obedient son. It was the only way any of this would work. I walked to his desk, and as I was about to sit, a piece of notebook paper caught my eye. It looked like a handwritten letter and was half a page long. It hadn't been there when I handed him the folder with the contracts. That led me to believe it was what he was reading with how it was positioned next to his forearm. I didn't know why he wore suits all the time; it wasn't as if anyone saw him outside of these walls. I was guessing it made him feel important.

I sat, leaning back to appear as relaxed as possible while I stared at the man, my father, who'd destroyed my entire family.

How could he possibly think I'd ever be okay with everything he had done?

"Keeping love letters from the maids now? Who'd have thought you had a soft spot?" I muttered.

He looked up, his features tense. "Why don't you read it? I heard you might personally know this one. Maybe you could finally be of use to me."

"Doubt it. I haven't fucked a maid since I was eighteen. You might want to check with Brad though."

What the fuck? Who would tell Connor I knew this person?

None of his guys knew about my personal life. Unless it was Brad. Though, the only person I'd tried to introduce him to was Amber, and he hadn't even shown up. Amber had no reason to write a letter to Connor, and the only other woman I could think of was Paige, but it couldn't be her.

There's no fucking way.

He picked up the letter and dropped it onto the desk before me. As I watched it fold over into its creases, a sense of foreboding edged up my gut, and I swallowed.

Forming an exaggerated sigh for effect, I picked up the letter, and as I unfolded it, I could feel him watching me. My stomach churned, sending acid to the corners of my jaw, but I tried not to react. The familiarity of her handwriting smacked me in the face, altering my vision. Her name appeared in one or two places, but it was all I saw on the paper.

Paige.
Paige.
Paige.
Paige.

Fuck, I was going to pass out if I didn't clench my jaw or swallow or fucking something. Adjusting and leaning forward, so he wouldn't catch my reaction, I laid the paper out on the desk and lowered my hands between my thighs.

CASEY DIAM

Thoughts of Paige kept popping up as my mind neglected to read what was in front of me. Not wanting to believe it. If I didn't read it, it couldn't be real. She couldn't have written this. She'd seemed okay. Everything had seemed okay.

Fuck, I'm stalling.

Alex Connor,

Paige here.

I hope you've been enjoying my letters. It's been quite an interesting experience to write them. I could describe it as whispers from the graveyard, your victims telling me what you hadn't given them a chance to tell. Like the last letter I sent you. The spirits of everyone you killed know what's coming to you. I know what's coming to you. It's what happens to evil, sick bastards like you. You don't get to live in peace and be happy. Evil gets to follow you now because darkness awaits you.

I wish I could be there as you read this letter because I'd gladly send you there myself. Unfortunately, timing is everything, as you know very well, considering the way you intricately killed my parents, covered it up, and then kidnapped me before placing me in the Sawyers' household, only to kill them all. And for what?

Obviously, you're hiding something much bigger. Something you think I know. At one point, I even wanted to forget about all of this, but not anymore. I want to watch you pay for every single life you've taken, and I hope you die a thousand deaths in hell. So, yeah, congratulations, you sick fuck. You've twisted my morals, and I will make you pay.

P.S. All of your men are fucking idiots.

Oh fuck.

Mustering the strength to appear unfazed and clueless, I eased back into the chair. "So, I'm guessing she's connected to the Sawyers, my family. Who is she?"

"It isn't who she is; it's what. And she's fucking dead; that's what." My heart fell through the cavities in my chest.

This was so fucking reckless. Why would she have done this?

My mouth formed a thin line. "So, you want to kill her because she wrote you a stupid letter? Shocking."

Anger hardened his face as he pushed the contracts into a pile and held them out to me. "Scan these and send them to me when you get back to the office." When I took them, he pulled open a drawer and dropped a small black cell phone on the desk. "Give this to your brother and fix whatever the fuck is going on between you two, or I will."

A distended vein was starting to form in his forehead, and I got up, not bothering to grab the folder I'd brought the documents in. I needed to get the fuck out of here.

When I stepped out of the elevator and into our unit, the lights were on, but Paige or Calvin wasn't in sight. I could almost feel the blood rushing through my veins and the heat pitching off my body as I seethed. My feet ate up the floor to her room, and a second later, I was banging on her closed door.

I'd skipped going back to Luxe first just so I could catch her before she left for work, which shouldn't be for another hour. So, if she wasn't here, I was going to be fucking furious. I twisted the lock just as it gave, and I came face-to-face with her. Her hair was down, and she was dressed for work in a tight-fitted black T-shirt and jeans.

My jaw tightened. "What did you do?"

"What?"

"Don't play dumb with me. What. Did. You. Do?"

She folded her arms across her chest in defiance, which only meant there was a lot more she wasn't telling me.

"You've been sending letters? How did you know where Connor lived?"

Her eyes widened enough for me to catch it before she looked to the side, her throat moving as she swallowed. "How—"

"I read it," I bit out as the calm I had been trying to exude fell apart. "Now, how the fuck did you know where Connor lived?"

Self-conscious, she combed a hand through her hair. "You weren't supposed to see that."

"Well, I did."

Why isn't she answering my goddamn question?

I cocked my head as something struck me. Calvin knew where I had grown up.

Nostrils flaring, I marched from Paige's room and found Calvin already in the living room, heading to our side.

"What's going on out here?" he asked, stopping short when he saw I was coming for him.

"You fucking told her."

"What?"

"You told her where Connor lived." As soon as I recognized his tell—his hand moving to the back of his neck to scratch—I shoved him. "I fucking trusted you to protect her."

"Leave him alone. It isn't his fault," Paige said from somewhere behind me.

"Really? Well, explain. Because it's like I've done all of this for fucking nothing." I turned to the couch and kicked it. "All of it just so you could fucking put yourself in danger. For what, Paige? For what?"

"You weren't doing anything, and I couldn't just sit back and do nothing while that asshole continued to live like everything was fucking fine," Paige argued.

"That wasn't your call to make. I *am* doing something. Something that doesn't include you putting yourself in danger." My finger stabbed the air as I pointed at Calvin. "He fucking knew that." A death glare followed my finger because, in all the years we'd known each other, I would never have thought Calvin was disloyal. He was the only fucking family I knew before Paige. The only one I truly trusted with her. "Dude, I can't even." Distrust and disappointment clear in my eyes, I shook my head. "I guess your loyalty lies with her now. And you"—I turned my attention on Paige—"talking to me, asking me for answers that I'd never fucking told anyone. That wasn't about me, was it? You've been planning something and fucking using me." I let out a breath, my head still shaking.

"It isn't like that," she said, pain glistening in her eyes, but I willed my eyes away.

"I trust her judgment," Calvin exclaimed. "We were only looking out for you."

"No. That isn't what I pay you for. I pay you to protect her. I don't need you endangering her life to protect me. I don't need protecting."

"Why? Because you're planning to get yourself locked up for fucking life? You don't deserve that shit, dude. And, if Connor's out of the picture, you won't have to worry about that."

He'd said that so fucking casually that I knew for a fact that the two of them had been working together.

"What?" Paige asked.

"Dude, are you even fucking hearing yourself? She's going to get herself killed, and you're putting yourself in line to be next. You don't know the fucking half of it. You don't know what I do or don't fucking deserve."

"Seriously, what the fuck?" Paige hissed. "What plan? What are you two talking about? Caleb, what did you do?"

Swiveling my head to Paige, I said, "I've already told you. But *you* didn't want to talk about it. TTM, remember?" I'd had no intention of telling her at the time, but for some reason, I wanted to place the blame on her for what she'd been doing behind my back when, in actuality, it was all my fault. I sighed. "I turned myself in. And, after I help secure some information that could be used against Connor, well, I'm going to go to jail for a long time."

"What? Why would you do that?"

"Because, for twenty-four years, I've been weak; that's why. But you guys wouldn't know that. If you had, you would have stayed out of this and not put yourselves in danger for nothing." I brushed a hand through my hair as I looked at Paige.

I couldn't push, or she'd push back. There was only one thing I could do.

"I need to talk to you alone." As I walked to my room, I expected her to follow, and she did though hesitantly. "I'm going to sleep at the hotel from now on." I gestured my hand between us. "Because this, this is what I didn't want. You putting yourself in danger and . . ." I paused before more suspicions about her manipulating me to get to Connor fell from my lips. "We both knew it would come to this, and it's better I leave now."

"Caleb, please, you don't have to leave."

She hugged herself, and I couldn't look at her because, if I did, I would go to her. I wouldn't be able to walk away.

Looking at the wall behind her, I told her, "I have to."

I'd been seeing it little by little. She would put her life in danger for anyone.

I could only imagine what she'd do for the person she was closest to. Me. I couldn't let her do that.

"Please," she whispered.

Grabbing the doorknob, I pulled the door open enough to let myself out, but not before I brought the hammer down, smashing my own heart as I told her, "I might be pissed at him, but he's good. He'll be good to you if you guys ever, uh . . . you know, whatever."

She needed to know that I would be okay with whatever happened between her and Calvin because she and I didn't have a future, and I needed to set her free.

Walking through the door, I felt like I was leaving my entire world behind. She was no longer my axis. She'd become my fucking world. And, fuck, I almost faltered at the pull to go back to her, but I couldn't stay. It was either I did this or lost the only two people I cared about. If I went willingly, then there would be no point in them doing something they shouldn't have been thinking about doing in the first place—going after Alex Connor. They were good in this world, and Alex Connor might deserve to die after all he'd done, but I couldn't

RISKING HOPE

fathom one of these two being responsible.
I might not love him, but he was still my fucking father.

THIRTY-SEVEN

PAIGE

H*e doesn't know he's breaking your heart.* Caleb's name was a whisper beneath my breath as he left the room, left me.

I inhaled, blinking and holding the emotions at bay as my chest tightened. I had done this. But he'd come back. He had to. He just needed time to cool down; that was all.

I looked at the bed I'd made this morning, knowing he probably wouldn't be here with me tonight. The crisp gray comforter taunted a sense of loss in me, and I wanted to run out to him, beg him to stay, but that would be too desperate, and I was stronger than that.

Damn it. I need him to come back.

Would he still have left if he knew I was in love with him? Should I have told him?

I took a seat at the edge of the bed, a small part of me regretting those letters. But a larger part of me was glad they'd made it to Alex Connor. But not Caleb.

I can't believe he read it.

Calvin tapped on the door and walked in, a frown on his face. "Are you still going to work or ..."

"Yeah." Swallowing, I nodded my head as I stood. "I'll grab my bag."

"Lisa texted me earlier. They're hanging out at Stilts tonight." He looked concerned. "Will you be okay seeing them?"

Caleb's words came back to me about Calvin being *good*. *Does he really think I could be with Calvin after him?* Calvin *was* good, but he wasn't Caleb.

"Fuck," I cursed as tears welled in my eyes.

"Should I—" Calvin began.

I waved a hand. "No, it isn't that. It's fine," I managed, my voice breaking at the end.

The first part of the night at work went by fast. My sworn nemesis, Chelsey, hadn't been much of a pain in the ass as of recently. I didn't know if she'd finally seen Ian for the douche he was for forcing himself on me or if she still believed I'd made out with her boyfriend, but whatever she'd decided, I didn't care. It was still disappointing to know she had believed I would do something like that as her friend, although, if she had been my friend, she would have known I wouldn't have. In fact, the only thing thinking about Ian or Chelsey made me want to do was vomit in my mouth.

I moved around the wooden tables and crowd in the bar, grabbing empty glasses as I went and tuning out the drunken madness escalating around me.

"Paige!"

I turned with the glasses in my hand and saw Mickey, Amber, Lisa, and Calvin, all dressed up for the night, looking pretty and lively with wide grins plastered on all their faces. For the first time tonight, a real smile stretched across my lips. They'd definitely started drinking at home.

As they got close enough to hear me over the music and the loud conversations circulating, I said, "I can't hang out, but I can take a quick break in twenty minutes. Where can I find you?"

Calvin pointed to the back. "Or we'll be outside for a smoke. Not me, you know. Them."

"Whatever." Lisa stuck her tongue out at him and made a silly face. The dark curls behind her shoulders glimmered in the lighting. She was dressed in a tight deep blue dress with spaghetti straps.

Amber stood behind her, also in a dress, only hers was striped with pink, black, and white. Mickey was in a trendy black top with tights, matching Calvin, who was also in all black.

No Caleb.

I'll see him later. He'll come back.

I refilled all the napkin trays with napkins, the ice bin with ice, and washed all the glasses I could manage before taking out the trash. I made another round, sweeping all the empty glasses sitting on top of the tables as well as the bar tops positioned against the brick wall in the room.

I was glad I was working here tonight. It kept me on my feet and busy. If I was busy, I couldn't think, which was also why it took me an hour before I remembered to take my break.

I'd passed by my friends a few times while cleaning up, so it didn't take me long to spot them in the back, but Luke was here, which was interesting. His man bun was up, as usual, and he wore a white shirt that made his full arms of tattoos stand out even more. I followed his eyes that were set on Mickey as she was talking about something. It'd completely slipped my mind to ask Calvin about Luke's love life. But, from where I was standing, I was pretty sure Lisa was right, he was more than interested in Mickey.

"Paige, you're here. Oh my gosh! It's been, like, hours." Mickey slid off her stool, throwing her hands up to give me a hug.

Eek, I'm dirty. Too late.

She flung her arms around me.

"Luke, how come you never let your hair down?" I asked, punching him in his side, which, for a guy his size, I was sure it felt more like a little tap from a kitten's paw.

"No!" Amber interrupted. "Wait for Ryan to tell you. It's soooo much better."

"Okay. Uh, never mind then."

"Where's your lover boy?" Lisa asked, making kissy faces.

I glanced at Calvin before replying, "He isn't feeling up to it."

"Oh." Lisa wagged her eyebrows. "At least you live with him."

"Yeah," I agreed, a streak of optimism hitting me upside the head. *He's probably at home, waiting for me right now.*

"Now," Lisa sang, "we get you all to ourselves. So?" Her smoky eyelids glittered with silver as they jerked up. "What is Mr. Broody Rock Star like in bed? I need to know."

My eyes caught Amber's before she looked to the pinkish fluid in the martini glass before her. I hated the image in my head of her and Caleb in bed together. I'd kept my mind from going there. But since he'd walked out on me, my mind had been open to all sorts of reflections.

What if I was another distraction for him? Why do I think he feels about me the way I feel about him?

Love could be given, but it didn't have to be returned.

"He's okay, I guess," I finally said.

"Okay!" Lisa shrieked, shaking a finger at me. "Don't make me have to tell him he needs to step it up."

"Lisa, drop it." Calvin's voice came out firm. His Amber voice. He never talked to anyone else that way.

I understood why my seeing the girls tonight would be a problem. He had known Caleb's name would come up in conversation. Maybe I had, too, but I was the master of disguise when I wanted to be, but for the first time ever, I didn't want to be. But I had to be, so I squashed the tiny doubts creeping in and smiled.

"Calvin gets enough of Caleb and me at home. I'm sure we're the last thing he wants to talk about when he's out, trying to have a drink. But how about you, Calvin? You promised I'd be seeing girls waltzing in and out of your bedroom, but I haven't seen any. What happened with that?"

"Well!" Lisa twirled a finger in the air as drunken words

tumbled out without a thought behind them. "I would say, by the way that bartender almost spit in his drink, you haven't been paying much attention, Paige. This one's sneaky. You have to watch him."

"What?" I looked toward the bar in time to see Chelsey passing a dirty look our way, and as I swung my head to Calvin, I saw his *oh shit* look.

He slept with Chelsey?

My eyes must have conveyed the question without me having to voice it because I saw his answer loud and clear.

Later.

Although, "That's old news," was what he actually said to everyone else.

THIRTY-EIGHT

Caleb

The lawyer who was at the closing with me on the New York condominium sat in front of me inside a coffee shop. We were a few blocks from the real estate office where we'd closed an hour ago.

My fingers caught the handle on the cup, and I brought it to my mouth while I read through the new deed to my Quincy condo, which had initially been bought under my power of attorney. I signed in the appropriate places that would make the property officially owned by Madelyn Wells a.k.a Paige, and Calvin, though they would also get to use the same method I had used to protect my identity. They could schedule a meeting with this lawyer once I mailed them these documents. I didn't know what would happen once I returned to Boston, but I felt the need to finalize these documents before I found out.

My accounts in the States had already been turned over to the FBI on the case as well as all of Alex Connor's accounts that I knew about. I'd already reached out to my bank overseas to grant the only two people I could call family access to my legitimate accounts. The accounts the FBI didn't know about. Those were my authentic accounts, including the condo I was gifting to Paige and Calvin, but the FBI wouldn't see it that way. They would see everything I had as connecting to illegal activities. But, since I hadn't ever had to pay for rent or for anything until recently, all the money I'd made from my position at the hotel and property management were deposited overseas. That account, along with my investments in Bitcoin some years ago, was still worth at least ten million.

I didn't know why I'd isolated my accounts. One would think pussy was the only thing on my mind at eighteen, but I guessed I hadn't been as distracted as I wanted to be—or maybe I'd just known this day would come.

"I was fourteen at the time, and Brad, my brother, was eleven." I positioned my arms before me on the metal desk as I looked into the camera. "I heard a scream that day. A woman. She was screaming for someone to stop, like she was being raped or abused. Maybe both. I wanted to help, so I tried to get out of the house, but I was caught by one of my father's men. I got upset and told him I was going to tell someone and that they couldn't keep me indoors forever." My throat echoed in the still room as I cleared it.

"After that outburst, one of his men escorted me to a room in the building, and I was left there for a few days until one of them came to get me. He covered my head with a black cloth, and I was put inside a vehicle. I remember the drive taking a while, and when the cover was removed from my head, I was standing inside some room, could have been a basement. There weren't any windows, and the floor was just concrete, covered in a clear plastic.

"Brad was there with me. He looked just as confused as I was. A man was standing in front of us, against the wall. A rope hanging down from some wooden planks in the ceiling was looped around his neck, and duct tape covered his mouth. I don't know who he was. I'd never seen him before, but he looked to be maybe in his thirties, Caucasian."

I sighed, trying to keep my mind in focus. I needed to verbalize enough without sorting through all the explicit details stowed at the back of my mind.

"Three of my father's men came in with some huge fucking knives. I don't know what kind, but they could have been butcher's knives or something." In my mind, I saw the blades glinting in the light from the ceiling. "Then, my father came in."

"Would you be able to identify any of those other men today?" the attorney sitting across from me asked. He had salt and pepper hair, and the crow's-feet around his sunken eyes indicated he was in his mid-fifties at least.

I shook my head. "They looked the same. Each of them had on a helmet with long, thick black gloves almost reaching up to their elbows." Their outfits had made a lot more sense with what happened after.

The attorney's head dipped and lifted in a quick nod. "Continue."

I looked at the camera again, keeping Bailey's and Langley's doubtful glares at the other end of the table out of my periphery. "My father came in and handed me a gun. Told me it was my fault that this man was about to die."

"If you'd minded your own business and kept your mouth shut, this wouldn't be happening. So, now that you're old enough, I'll paint the picture for you. It's becoming clearer every day. You'll never be good enough to be a part of this family, but this might be your chance to change that. I've upgraded your paper targets. Let's see you practice," Alex Connor spit, pointing to the man against the wall.

My hand trembled at my side with the heavy weapon as I shook my head, my heart sinking as I stared into my father's eyes. "I can't."

"But you will. Look at him."

The hunger I'd felt with the little food I'd had over the past couple of days evaporated as I saw the fear in the man's eyes.

"Each time you so much as think about snooping into things that aren't specifically told to you, someone gets to die. Each time you get the urge to disagree and question anything I do, this will happen. You tell anyone about this, and we will come back here to do this again and again until you

learn. Shoot him."

"He directed his men to dismember the man until I shot." Fuck, I didn't want to get into the details. "Now that I'm older and think about it, I think the man had passed out from shock after both his hands were"—I swallowed—"chopped off, but I didn't shoot. I kept telling my father the guy was already dead. When he saw I really wasn't going to shoot, he took Brad out of the room and sent back one of the guys with a chainsaw. Left me to watch them finish dismembering the body. He told me that I would be back in that room, watching someone else die, if I disobeyed him or said anything to anyone about what went on at the house. After that night, they brought me back to the house and locked me inside the room again as a part of my punishment, and that was where they left me for the next two months."

"Did it happen again?"

"No." *Not like that,* I finished in my head, *but just as fucking ruthless.*

"We can stop here if you two are okay with this," the lawyer said to Bailey and Langley.

"Yeah. That's good for now. He needs to get back. We'll pick this up next time," Langley answered.

I left the building and headed to my car, feeling a weird prickling at the back of my neck. I'd been feeling it all day. Ignoring it, I hurried to my next stop at the post office. Since I'd left the condo yesterday, I'd been itching to check in on Paige, though I was still fucking pissed at her and Calvin. I mean, fuck, they were the only two I trusted not to use me as a pawn in their games, the way my father had.

My phone vibrated in my pocket, and when I pulled it out, I saw *AC* lighting up the screen. I pressed the Answer key to see what the hell Alex Connor wanted this time.

"Come to the house. We have some things to talk about."

My jaws tensed and I swallowed.

Fuck.

THIRTY-NINE

Paige

Snuggling myself tighter into Caleb's sheets, I stared at the wall from his bed.

Twenty-six hours.

That was how long it'd been since I saw or heard from him. He'd been so angry with me when he left that each second that he didn't return, my hope lessened.

I just wanted to tell him I was sorry.

But what if this was really it? Where the road ended, where we each walked in our separate directions? He would go to jail, and I would . . . I would, what? Be pathetic?

I'd had a life before Caleb, yet here I was, wearing his T-shirt and moping in his bed. I'd even called in sick so I wouldn't have to work at the bar tonight.

This was stupid. I didn't need him.

Though every part of me was fighting that lie.

He shouldn't have turned himself in and not told me. How fucked up was that? Like what we'd had and what we'd shared in this bed was nothing.

God, he's such an asshole.

A few tears fell from my eyes, and I wiped them away, inhaling a breath as I brought his shirt to my nose.

Sometime later, a knock came at the door, and I sighed. "Come in."

Calvin peered inside. "So, you're going to spend all day and night in bed?"

"No, just until I figure out what I'm doing with my life."

"Well, I hate to break it to you, but I'm five years older, and I still don't know what the fuck I'm doing with my life, which means you might be lying there for a while."

"Thanks." My eyebrows furrowed, but my lips twitched, wanting to smile. I couldn't believe he'd admitted to sleeping with Chelsey. "Don't make me smile. You're a douche, and you're sleeping with the enemy. Now, go away, so I can mope."

"It was one time, and she was being a bitch to you. No one messes with the family."

I narrowed my eyes. "You slept with her out of spite?"

He shrugged. "More like flirted with her until she broke up with Ian. Then I fucked her and quit."

"Calvin!" I scolded. "I don't even know you anymore."

He crossed his arms over his broad chest and leaned against the wall. "I know. It was horrible, but I needed to get laid anyway. But, I will grant you your moping wish before I leave."

The solemn expression taking over his nonchalance was telling enough, but I waited for him to speak.

The rest of the guys hadn't stopped following Caleb. So, even though he had left for New York this morning, Rob had been watching Connor's house all day, and Luke had been at Luxe, waiting for Caleb to return.

"Caleb returned to Connor's house five hours ago, and we don't know if he's left."

"What do you mean?"

Calvin jerked his head around as he gathered his thoughts. "Luke said, after Caleb arrived, a guy came out and pulled his car into the garage. About an hour later, his car pulled out, but you know with the tint, it's impossible to know if it was really Caleb driving. Also, the car never made it back to the hotel."

I grimaced, pulling myself up into a sitting position in the middle of the bed. "It wasn't him. That's why they pulled his car into the garage. Because, if his car was in the garage, then whoever might be watching wouldn't know who drove that car away. That means—"

"They know someone is watching."

"Yep."

"Shit."

We stared at each other for a moment before I let out a breath and shook my head. "If it's the cops, if Alex Connor knows Caleb has been talking to the cops . . ." I didn't have to finish that sentence.

"Shit," he said again, inhaling.

"Yeah."

Suddenly, I wished I hadn't voiced my thoughts. I didn't want to involve Calvin any further because Caleb had been right about that. There was no need to put a target on Calvin's back. Connor wanted me. He would get me and hopefully one of my bullets in the process. I didn't care. It was ridiculous how he kept getting away with this, and I'd be damned if he kept Caleb locked away in his freaking little world again. And, if he hurt him . . .

My fist curled into the sheets, and I looked at Calvin.

"Damn it, Paige. Your eyes are doing that thing again," Calvin complained.

"Shut up. Ugh! I'm not killing you with my eyes . . . yet." I scrambled out of the bed while I plotted inside my head. I needed to call Bailey. Find Caleb's brother. He was probably at the gym, or if he wasn't, maybe Alex Connor's men were still there watching, waiting for me to show back up. And I would, tonight.

I threw on my disguise as I told Calvin, "I need you to drop me off at the gym."

"What?"

I punched him in the gut with no force behind it as I headed to my room. "I don't want you involved beyond driving me to places,

Calvin, and that's only because I don't know how to drive."

"Wait, you don't know how to drive? What the hell?"

"Good. We're on the same page."

"Paige, what? Don't do anything stupid. Just because Caleb isn't here doesn't mean I'm going to—"

"Calvin," I said, calm, as I entered my room. Turning to him, I forced a smile on my face as I looked at him with the eyes he was so scared of. "Whatever I plan to do, you were on board with it before. I just didn't give you all the details, which I'm still not planning to do because you won't like it. A week from now, it will be exactly five years since that bastard came into my life and killed everyone I loved. Twenty years, if we're counting my real parents. A month and a half ago, I found out who *he* was. That *he* wasn't dead. *He* didn't get caught, and most importantly, *he* wasn't just a figment of my imagination. Alex Connor was still living, breathing, and ruining lives. He is still out to get me, and I have no freaking idea why." A tear streaked down my cheek. "I'm done. You can't stop me. Bailey can't stop me. I can't sit in fear, looking over my shoulder, waking up in the middle of the night, crying for no fucking reason, or being scared awake by a stupid fucking dream. And, *now*, I have to wonder what the fuck he's doing to Caleb. I can't do it, Calvin. I can't. So, I'm done. I'm done sitting, and I'm done freaking waiting."

"At least wait until tomorrow. Maybe he'll come back. We're still not sure they took him. With Caleb disappearing tonight and then you showing up at that gym, it's too simultaneous. They could have caught sight of us or the FBI tracking Caleb. We don't know anything, and it goes without saying that he still wants you safe, no matter what. So, let's wait it out for tonight and then—"

"Don't tell me what to do!" I bit out. "It makes me want to do the opposite."

"Fine. Fuck! How did he do it? Jesus, bless his heart." He squeezed his eyes shut, and then he caught my glare. "Fine. Sorry. Just cool it with the eyes, Evil Partner In Crime. Whatever you—"

"Stop. Just stop."

He was trying to make light of the situation, but I couldn't, not when Caleb was in harm's way.

"Okay."

I inhaled a long breath and paced as I let it out. "I won't be able to sleep tonight. He left the phone he used to call or text us on in his room. I need two of the guys to keep an eye on Brad. He's the only way I'll be able to get to Caleb. But, fine. For tonight, what do you want to do?"

"Stakeout?"

Doubtful I'd be able to sit still for long with all the thoughts running through my head, I nodded. Anything was better than sitting around here, waiting.

Caleb

A set of fingertips grasped my chin and turned my face from side to side. My back was lying flat on the cold floor, and I didn't want to wake up. Every time I did, it got worse.

But, as the fingers left my chin, I heard Alex Connor's voice, "Have you figured out a way to fix this yet?"

My eyes squinted open to the room they had placed me in. Not even a chair was in here. The only thing besides Connor and me were the ropes binding my wrists behind me and the piece tying my ankles together because blocking the hits was not allowed. But at least I wasn't in the dark room. It'd been so long that I couldn't remember which was better. Darkness or pain?

I closed my eyes to remember.

A fist connected with my jaw, snapping my head to the side and smacking a side of my skull onto the floor. Sucking in air, I opened my mouth, tasting blood as I tried to work out the pain and the muscles that had tensed on impact.

This was the first time I'd seen Alex Connor since I walked through the front door today. This wasn't the first time he'd taken the time out of his day to hit me on his own, though it'd been years since he had done it. I hadn't expected it. I must have really fucked up to have this privilege. I still didn't know how much he knew, so I wasn't about to say shit. I'd been there, done that, and I didn't care what they did to me. Being mute and keeping him uninformed was the only way I could be of help to the FBI, and with that, he could go where he needed to be—behind bars where he couldn't hurt anyone else.

"Fix what?" I uttered, my voice hoarse and the metallic taste of my own blood for the past few hours sickening. I needed water.

"You're a fucking disgrace to this family," he roared. "Thirty fucking years, I've been running this operation, only to get sold out by my own."

The tip of his shoe landed into my side, close to my already-bruised ribs, and I rolled away onto my side, bringing my knees to my chest.

"I should have eliminated you a long time ago, like I did your mother and her pathetic family. I should have fucking killed you before you were born, but I thought, *Why not have someone who can take over my legacy one day?* What a fucking mistake. I'd let you choke on your own blood before I let you bring me down, you son of a bitch, so I suggest you think real fucking hard. Just in case you need encouragement to help you think about how to fix what you've done, we still have your little nurse friend. Don't think I've forgotten any of my promises to you over the years."

A low tapping sounded from his dress shoes on the tiled floor as he headed for the door.

"Fix what?" I grumbled, but the door slammed shut.

Fuck.

With his rant about ruining his operation, I knew it couldn't be about Paige, which left one other option—the cops. He knew.

I was sitting and leaning against the wall with my head toward the door when Brad walked in. Could have been an hour, but having a grasp on time only made being here worse, so I tried not to think about it because then I would think about food, water, and how badly I wanted to piss while my hands were tied behind my back.

"My brother. Tsk-tsk. What have you done?"

I'd expected nothing less than his sardonic voice, but as a wide, telling smile twitched across his mouth, I knew he'd had everything to do with Connor finding out about what I'd been up to. That led me to wonder how much he did know and how. I'd been so careful, especially with Paige. Fuck, I hoped he didn't know about her.

Hope.

I shook my head with a low sniff.

After all these years.

Keeping my mouth shut and my stare hard, I watched him pace the room, his phone in hand.

"Payback's a bitch, isn't it? The nurse should be here any second. I'm just here for the show. Though her pussy must be done for, the way they've been fucking it. I think she gets about five dicks a day, dude. I don't even want to fuck it anymore."

I swallowed my disgust as spit diluted the blood in my mouth. He was just trying to piss me off, but I couldn't react. It was what he wanted. But, fuck, I couldn't help but wonder if it was true. Because, if it was, it was happening because of me.

The door opened again, and my chest caved in. Stacy Lenard came in with two of Connor's men behind her. She was naked, her brown hair about her shoulders and her eyes on me. According to Bailey, she was forty-one and had a son in college. I looked to the floor as she tried to shrug out of Dee's hold. He was one of Alex Connor's largest fucking men, so the only thing her struggle earned her was a harder shove into the room.

What the fuck does Connor expect me to do? If he knows he is now on the cops' radar, there is nothing I can do to make that go away.

Brad clapped his hands together. "Finally! Something to get my dick hard while I wait to get my hands on that pretty little blonde. I'm starting to think she might be worth the trouble after all. A new *page* in my book." He snickered.

My fists clenched so hard the ropes bit into my skin, no doubt drawing a small trickle of blood behind me.

"Now, that, *that* I definitely want to fuck," he continued. "Yo, Dee. Make sure you fuck her in the ass first. I want to watch this bitch bleed." He turned his head to me. "How about you, bro? Any requests?"

I drew in a long, steady breath. "Stop calling me brother, bro, family. You don't mean shit to me. You're a dick, just like Connor, and this is stupid. What is watching this woman getting fucked by this disgusting asshole supposed to do?"

Except make me feel as if my soul is being sucked through a flaming, barbed wire tunnel into hell.

"Nothing." He walked over and sat a few feet away from me, keeping his eyes on Dee and the nurse. "Just live entertainment, brother." His mouth stretched into a smug smile as he twisted his head to me. "Might as well have Dee enjoy her before you watch her die, right?"

I blinked, the muscles in my body tensing the same time a yelp came from the nurse. "Please don't."

"Bringing back any memories?" he taunted, the smile never leaving his face. When he realized I wasn't going to say anything, he cleared his throat. "Since you might be here for a while, I might as well give you something else to think about. I know you know Paige. I also know you won't admit it. But I saw you, and I've been trying to pin you down ever since. I have to hand it to you, you've been pretty fucking good about staying out of sight. I couldn't even figure out where the fuck you've been sleeping."

I wanted to ask how he knew, but I also didn't want to clarify what he thought he knew.

Dragging the heels of his boots to his ass, he rested his arms on his knees and sighed with a slight shake of his head. "I was waiting for this girl to show up. All of Dad's men were *so fucking* obsessed with finding her. Then after hours of sitting in my car, waiting, guess what happened? Your car stopped right smack dab in the middle of the road that night, and guess who hopped out? Paige. The one and only."

That had to have happened before the car accident, which meant it could have easily been the first week I'd met her.

"Oh, man." He laughed. "You had no idea. Shit, what I was thinking?" He stood. "I shouldn't be here. If you're here, it's only a matter of time before she comes out of hiding. Enjoy the show. The next time you watch one, your little princess is going to be the star. I hope you already fucked her because when we're done with her . . ."

FORTY-ONE

Paige

Pushing Calvin's car door closed, I strolled through the park and toward the river with doubt tiptoeing up my spine. My period had started an hour ago, and even though I'd taken four ibuprofens, a low cramp lingered in my stomach. My legs were weak, and I felt like shit. The morning's humidity was making my skin feel sticky, and it wasn't even 9:00 a.m. yet. On top of it all, I hadn't slept in about fifty hours, and the last time I had seen Caleb was thirty-eight hours ago. He didn't know I wasn't manipulating him to get to his father, and I needed to tell him that. He needed to know I was sorry for making him even feel as if I'd betrayed him. Feeling like shit was an understatement.

I regarded the few people jogging and cycling down the paved path until I spotted the person who'd summoned me here. He was sitting alone on the park bench facing the Charles River, a baseball cap on his head.

I took a seat next to him, leaving my sunglasses on. "Where's Bailey?"

"She couldn't be here," Agent Langley replied, keeping his focus on the river.

"Right." I swallowed. "So, why am I here?"

His face was hard but weary. Like someone who'd seen too much, been through too much. But I still didn't trust him.

"I heard her on the phone with you last night . . ."

I recalled my brief rant to Bailey from the night before.

"You'd rather not sacrifice the life of one girl, so a mass murderer could continue to run around and kill other innocent people! He isn't going to stop, and he has Caleb."

I cleared my head as a few errant strands from my messy ponytail tickled my neck. I used a hand to sweep them back into place as I listened to Agent Langley.

"You could help us. We were planning to go about this in a different way, but a lot of details are coming to light that have changed things, so to speak. This has been flying under the radar, and we haven't had anyone who could get us this close. But you, they seem to be obsessed with you."

"What do you want me to do?"

I didn't have to think about it. Every second that went by, Caleb was getting hurt, and all I could envision was him in that dark room again, thinking about how I'd deceived him. I was ready to do anything.

"Get him to talk to you."

"Who?"

"Anyone."

A few hours after meeting with Agent Langley, it took everything to quiet my mind enough for a thirty-minute power nap. Anything over, and I would risk falling into a deep sleep. A deep sleep would mean a potential nightmare or an anxiety attack, and I couldn't be on edge at all for this.

I checked my reflection in the visor inside Calvin's car, and then I checked the mini microphone taped to the underside of the sleeveless black cardigan I'd thrown over my black camisole.

The sun would be setting soon. Nerves tingled all over my skin, and a low feeling settled in my stomach. I didn't know how this would turn out.

Am I helping Caleb or putting him in danger?

"Be careful," Calvin warned, a stern look in his eyes.

"I will."

He shook his head. "I can't believe I'm letting you do this shit. Caleb would have never—"

"Trust me," I said, my voice calm. "And you're not letting me do anything. I'm doing it on my own."

He blew out a breath. "Fine."

While I waited to hear from the agent sitting inside the gentlemen's club, I turned my attention to the sidewalk and the few pedestrians walking by. My eyes stopped on a homeless man sitting on the pavement against a store on the strip, his clothes soiled and his head bowed to his chest. I used to wonder how it could reach that point in one's life where you had nowhere to go. No possessions. No money. No food. But that could have easily been me if Caleb hadn't taken me under his wings. I still didn't have much. My grandparents might have gifted me a mansion, but it didn't belong to me. It felt more like a burden if anything. So I still didn't want to accept it, but suddenly, I knew what I wanted to do with it. A charity foundation for the homeless. I could have my grandparents sell it and use the money for that, and I knew Mackenzie would help me. She had been good at stuff like that in high school.

An agent's voice came through my phone's speaker. I hadn't met him, but he sounded young. "He's heading out."

Hitting the unmute on my phone, I responded, "Got it."

I quickly dug out the twenty-dollar bill I'd stashed inside my backpack.

As I cranked the door open, Calvin said, "Say '*Copy that*' next time, okay? You sound amateurish."

I rolled my eyes. "Shut up."

I hurried over to the homeless man to hand him the twenty,

and then I made my way toward the entrance of the gentlemen's club. There was a dramatic pause in my steps the same time Brad's dark eyes landed on me. My mouth formed a tiny O as I feigned shock. He was dressed in a blue shirt with black pants, and he looked five years older than the last time I'd seen him, which was just over a month ago. I reminded myself that the agent had said he'd been drinking, so there was no better time to get him talking.

Starting forward, I stopped in front of him, and with my face impassive, I taunted, "Not in the mood to attack me in broad daylight? Are you scared I might kick your ass again?"

His lips curved up, and his eyes grew mysterious, dangerous. "I would apologize and offer you my hand, but my favorite stripper's pussy is all over it."

Ew. What the hell am I supposed to say to that?

"What a shame." I stepped forward as I attempted to walk away in hopes of furthering his interest.

"Wait." Though a bit sluggish, he moved into my path. "Have dinner with me."

"And why would I have dinner with a guy who tried to kidnap me?"

Admit to it, I mentally pleaded.

"Because, Paige, you know who I am, and I'm sure you have questions. So, we can talk over dinner."

"Oh, I do have questions."

He smiled.

"But not for you." I decided the FBI wasn't the only one who needed answers. I needed answers, too. "Take me to Alex Connor. I have questions for him."

This wasn't a part of the plan, but Caleb was my priority. There was no way I would let him spend another night in that house with this kind of opportunity. And, in order to get to Caleb, Alex Connor needed to be taken out of the picture—tonight. Actually, Alex Connor *and* his men were going down tonight. I would make sure of it.

He cocked his head, and a slow grin extended. "It would be my pleasure. Let me call my driver."

"It will be just you, your driver, and me in that vehicle. Needless to say, I don't trust you. But, while you're at it, call Alex Connor's men too. I want them present when I get there." I smiled, though it was so forced, my whole face became tense. "It's been too long, Brad, and I'm done. So, I don't care what happens to me after. The only thing I want is to look every one of the bastards who had something to do with what happened to my family in the face. Show me proof that they're all at the house, waiting, and then I will go with you."

He looked at me, eyes squinting as he read my face, probably seeing the blatant honesty and wondering how stupid I must be. But this was my one shot. The one night I had to rescue Caleb and destroy the only life he'd ever known.

Tonight, darkness would find Alex Connor, and I was the one who'd take him there.

This would be for everyone he had wrapped around his finger.

This would be for Alaina. Reese. Leanne. David. Olivia and ... *Caleb.*

FORTY-TWO

Caleb

The darkness was better.
I had memories.
I had Paige. I regretted not getting the chance to tell her I was sorry for blaming her and for leaving her the way I had. I'd let my fears get in the way of letting her know how much I cared for her. But, still, my recollections of her, of us together, were doing a great job of keeping me company and making me forget I hadn't eaten in a while.

It had to have been over a day since they had taken me. I'd been moved into the dark room. It was still so familiar. Like in the past, I'd merely woken up to find myself here with my arms and legs no longer bound.

I had water at my disposal in the small bathroom. It had been my saving grace when hunger stabbed at my insides years ago, and it would be my saving grace again.

I inhaled, rubbing at the itch the rope burns had left on my wrists, as I lay on the tiled floor and stared into the blackness. It was better if my eyes were closed because it helped to make this place illusive.

The nurse might not be safe, and they would kill her soon, probably in front of me as a lesson, but it was a relief knowing that

Paige was safe. Calvin would look out for her. She wouldn't have to suffer through what Stacy Lenard had today or worse.

A low beep sounded as someone entered the code that unlocked the door, and I looked over. This was the only time light spilled into the room, and I needed to see it, to feel . . . hope, ever the preamble to sorrow in my life.

The light came on as Alex Connor walked in, and I closed my eyes from the temporary pain the brightness incited. I hadn't expected to see him this soon.

Ignoring the pain spiraling through my body, I moved up against the wall and stretched my legs out as I sat.

He paced the room without looking at me as he spoke. "Since you haven't come up with your own plan to fix this, I've been working on it for you. In fact, the only thing left is for you to turn yourself in. You will take the fall for the murder and disappearance of all the people you were so gracious to have had a part in. You will leave out any knowledge of my guys, your brother, and me as being a part of it."

Like I was going to leave them to hunt down Paige. In his fucking dreams. "I'm not going to jail without you and Brad right next to me."

"But you are."

I sniffed. "Keep thinking that."

He stopped a few feet away from me, and I stared at his shoes, shining like they were freshly polished.

"I see. So, you're opting to be the reason more people die."

He was trying to reach me at the spot he knew hurt me the most. My breaking point.

But it's been too long, and I'm fucking over the games he is still trying to play.

I was older, and I'd like to think I'd grown wiser after discovering all the things he'd kept from me all these years.

"Yeah. I guess I am. Because, now, I know it doesn't matter what I do. I'm still just a pawn in your world. I could be obedient, or I could tell someone about the kind of monster you are and try to stop you. But it all leads to one thing—people getting hurt. So, why wouldn't I want to do the right thing and make sure you ended up in jail where you couldn't hurt anyone else?"

He inhaled, and I looked up into the hatred leaking out of his eyes.

"Because your mother's alive, and you have a sister, too. I'll leave you in here until you heal. Then you'll go to the cops and tell them this was all a mistake and that you are the one they're looking for. If you fail to do that, I will bring your mother and your sister here, and eviscerate them in front of you."

"Yeah, try again. Like I'm going to believe that, or anything you say. What are you going to do? Raise Olivia from the dead?"

I shook my head. He'd do whatever it took to get me to do what he wanted. I didn't believe him for a second.

He pulled his phone from his pocket and clicked on a few buttons. Then he turned it to me. It was a camera feed from a room. With the size of the room and how luxurious it seemed, it had to be the inside of a large house. A woman was curled on a chair, a book in her hand. She had long blonde hair, but I couldn't make out her face.

I shrugged. "That could be anyone."

He pressed another button on the phone and waited.

"Hello?" a rough voice said through the phone's speaker.

"Let me talk to Olivia."

He turned the phone to me, so I could watch as a muscular man walked toward the woman on the chair.

"Your husband's on the phone."

My heartbeat sped up as the woman didn't even turn to the man. She ignored him as if he hadn't even spoken.

"Grab her by the hair and slap the shit out of her until she gets on the fucking phone," Alex Connor barked.

My throat dried, and my chest tightened as I watched the man do to the woman as he'd been instructed until her sobs filled the phone line.

"Yes," she answered, visibly shaken.

Connor brought the phone to his mouth as he hissed, "Is that how you answer the fucking phone?"

"No ... hello, sweetheart." The woman's voice trembled through the speaker.

"That's what I thought, but you still haven't fucking learned," he snarled.

I cracked my knuckles, causing a pain to shoot through the finger that was still healing from the fracture.

"Now, what is the name of your son? And I won't ask you twice."

"Caleb," she whispered.

"Last name."

"Sawyer."

"And where is he now?"

"I don't know."

He pressed down on a key on his phone so hard, the phone about snapped before he shoved the phone back into his pocket. "I don't need to show you your sister. I'll save that for the grand meeting where you either get to watch them die or meet them from behind bars. Your choice."

"That still doesn't prove anything," I managed.

"Then, you get to live with watching them die for the rest of your life, however long I decide that is. I've had your mother suffering all these years. Don't think I won't do the same to you. Just remember this, son, anything happens to me—they each get a bullet in their head. Olivia is the one who caused all these fucking problems in the first place. So think about that for the next few days while you contemplate which road you will wander for the rest of your life. You should have kept your mouth shut. Running straight to the cops when you got back from New York. You think I wouldn't have my guys watching you after all the suspicious shit Brad told me had been going on with you? You're just like your goddamn mother."

The door slammed, and I swallowed.

She's alive. She's alive.

A few hours later, I stood at the sink in the darkness, scooping and drinking water from the pipe to curb the pangs of hunger.

Everything Connor had disclosed barely registered.

My mother was alive, and I had a sister.

Am I willing to call his bluff and watch them die in order to put him in jail?

Of course not.

He'd kept me prisoner in this house before, so what would have stopped him from holding *my* mother prisoner for all these years? Nothing, if he knew he could get away with it.

I could take the easy way out and believe it was all a lie, but the way he'd talked to that woman, how scared she'd been of him, and how he'd wanted her to call him *sweetheart*, there was no lie in the way she'd reacted. So, whether that woman was my mother or not, someone else was his captive, someone else who needed saving.

If it was my mother—my chest tightened—he was still raping her.

But where has he been keeping her all these years? And a sister?

FORTY-THREE

Paige

It had taken two hours of walking around and then getting a bite to eat inside a café before Brad sent me a message to meet him outside.

Dusk had fallen, and I knew Calvin was pissed at me. Not only had I turned off my phone after the fifth time he'd tried to call me, but also the only message I'd sent him was to tell him to go home.

Right after, I'd sent a similar message to Agent Langley.

Me: Don't interfere until you get what you need. I don't know if any one of Connor's men has been watching me since I talked with Brad.

I disposed of my half-eaten sandwich inside a trashcan by the door before stepping outside. The air was less muggy than earlier, and I was glad. With the temperature dropping, my cardigan, though sleeveless, was less conspicuous.

Brad hopped out of a dark-tinted SUV with his phone out. There was a video call on the screen with five men inside a living room; one held the phone and moved it around, so I could see everyone else there, waiting. All unmasked and chilling on the sofas like this was nothing to them. Just another day on the job.

"Okay." I nodded, the naked feeling of not having my weapon somewhere on my person sweeping over me.

He held the phone to his mouth. "Keep this from Connor until I get there. I want it to be a surprise." He grinned at me and opened the back door of the SUV. "Shall we?"

I should have thought this through. It was clear I wasn't carrying a weapon in my simple tights and cardigan, which was why Brad might have been so quick to do as I'd asked. But knowing that I had my knife tucked into one of my combat boots gave me peace of mind because, if Caleb's brother or any of those other fuckers touched me, their balls would be coming off.

Looking around the inside of the SUV to make sure it was only the driver inside, I stepped one foot in and turned my head to Brad, who seemed elated.

"If you touch me before we get to the house or make any detours, this is off. And don't test me either because I will show you what I did to you outside that gym when you attacked me wasn't just luck." Evilness dripped from the smile I gave him that would make anyone else tremble, but his grin only grew wider.

"Don't you worry. I'm taking you right where you want to go."

A peace of mind also came from knowing the FBI could hear everything going on, and with that, I hoped they would get to me before anything *too* dreadful happened.

I hoped this wasn't all for nothing.

And I really hoped whatever Caleb had done wasn't bad enough that I would be sending him to jail with everyone else.

The SUV pulled into the garage on Alex Connor's building, and Brad escorted me inside through a side door. He stayed behind me with the angry-looking driver. And as I stepped inside, a thick cloud of apprehension hovered overhead before draping itself around me. My eyes traveled down the old, almost antique foyer. Burgundy rugs covered parts of the hardwood flooring in the hallway, and two large golden-framed paintings hung on the walls.

There was a wide archway across from me that led into a wide-open space, and a half-cracked door to my right. I peeked through the small opening into that room.

I recognized the brunette from my curious search online after Caleb had told me about the nurse he had bribed.

What the hell?

Stacy Lenard was sitting on some giant dude's lap and rubbing her hands over his chest so affectionately that my mouth fell open and almost hit the floor.

Stacy's voice came out low and raspy as she said, "God, I wish I didn't have to go back to work. That place is a drag and—"

Brad blocked my view and yelled into the room, "Dee, get out here and send your woman on her way. And don't forget to take the back way, hot stuff, or the FBI will be on your tail." He pulled the door shut.

Your woman?

Hot stuff?

What the fuck?

As I edged toward the open arch for the other room, a hand grabbed my ass. I reached back, caught it, and twisted it to the point a subtle move would snap it.

"Fuck," Brad cursed. "You're in my territory now, darling. Do anything stupid, and I'll have every motherfucker in here fuck you at the same time I shove my dick in your throat."

I inhaled.

This is it.

There is no running now.

He hadn't given much of anything during the drive over, but that, what he'd just said, was something. Although, if getting information out of him on the way here while he was intoxicated hadn't worked, I had no idea how I would manage with these other men who were skilled beyond my years.

Both physically and mentally.

Shit, maybe jumping the gun like this was a stupid idea.

I made a note to keep a lookout for where these men carried their weapons on their person as well as for any that might be carelessly lying around.

I released his hand. "Put your hand on me again, and I'll break it. That's a promise."

"Yo, I'm going to go talk to Connor," Brad said, walking into the room. "She doesn't go anywhere." He turned so I could see the dark threat in his eyes. "You know what to do if she tries anything." He nodded to one of the men settled in a chair. "Get Caleb." A malicious grin skirted across his face. "I can't wait for this fucking show to start."

One of the men jogged up the stairs, and I swallowed. Caleb was fine, but I couldn't see him yet. He was going to be pissed that I was here, and I needed to focus. I stepped into the large living room, and before I could get a good look at all the men inside, a door swung open on the far wall. A tall man about the same height as Caleb with a buzz-cut and no beard came through the door, and everything stilled around me. As if the air had been sucked out of the room.

Brad, seemingly unaware of the tension, gushed, "I have to get a bonus for this. Look who got the job done—again."

"Where did you find her?" the man hissed through clenched teeth.

I had no doubt this was Alex Connor. I could tell by how everyone's attention remained on him, unmoving, waiting for a command.

"I ran into her downtown, and now, here she is."

"So, she was just walking, and you took her?"

I sensed his suspicion, and that was the last thing I needed. If he knew Caleb was working with the cops, he might be quick to suggest it was why I was here. And, even though that was one of my reasons for being here, he couldn't know that. It would ruin everything.

Before Brad could make him question the coincidence, I said,

"He didn't take me. I came here. I wasn't too excited about running into this asshole either, but I thought, *you know what? I'm done running.* I'm taking it you've received my letters, so now, I'm here for answers." I gestured to the men around me, who had begun to stand from their chairs. Ignoring them, I pushed on. "I'm guessing these men killed my family, but I don't need to hear it from them. I just need to hear why you ordered them to kill my family and why you're trying to kill me. Is that too much to ask? Because I'm fucking tired of running."

His face remained impassive before he fixed his gaze on Brad. "How long ago did you run into her?"

"Almost three hours, but I wanted to gather everyone, so you could see that I'm still capable of doing this. Caleb was the one getting in the way."

Connor's hand came up and smacked Brad across the face. "Why am I just hearing about this?"

I found myself feeling sorry for Brad even though he was an asshole because no child should be treated that way. Just like Caleb, Brad was merely a player in whatever fucked-up shit their father had set out to do. He had a motive, but it needed to end tonight. The sooner I got him to talk, the sooner the FBI would get here.

"Are you making the calls now?" Connor yelled. "You have any idea the trouble you've caused by withholding this information from me?"

When I glanced at the other men in the room, one of their shirts had hitched on a gun at the side of his waistband. And, as I looked back to Connor, the clear sign of another weapon was tucked in the back of Brad's jeans. He was standing only a few feet from his father.

I was here, and my main goal was getting information, but to get out of here, knowing I could snatch a weapon from one of these guys eased my disquiet.

FORTY-FOUR

CALEB

As I walked down the stairs, light-headed, Connor's yelling distracted me from my gut trying to eat itself.

"You've just fucked up everything I worked all these years to cover up. I used the last straw I had to save you, all of you, and you kept this from me?"

What the fuck is going on?

As I rounded the corner, I stopped and blinked. Then I closed my eyes and opened them again. Maybe it was the lack of sleep and food. I was hallucinating. That had to be the answer because there was no way in hell that could be who I thought it was. But that hair, that body . . . my heart swelled and collapsed in my chest.

Fucking hell. How did she get here? What the fuck is she doing here?

As I stood by the door dumbfounded, the man who had come to get me found his spot in the room.

Paige's back was still facing me, but not even a second later, her head turned, and our eyes locked. The pain was evident on her face as her gaze lingered on the bruises on mine. My pain was no longer physical, though. I was hurt but because *she* was fucking here, in the last damn place I wanted her to be.

She must have seen the anger burning behind my eyes because

she turned her head and spoke just as fast, getting Alex Connor's attention, "Can you yell at him later about this *last straw* crap and answer my fucking questions? Why did you kill my family? David, Leanne, Alaina, and Reese. And don't think I don't know you killed my real parents, too. Why?"

Connor's eyes lifted and landed on me. "What the fuck is he doing down here? Who let him out?"

"Damn it!" Paige marched up to Connor, fists clenched at her sides while my heart just about dove through my chest.

Fuck. This is not going to end well.

"Why did you kill them? What had they ever done to you?"

What is she doing? Paige, you need to stop.

Connor's eyes narrowed on her.

Weapon. I need a weapon.

I moved across the room at an easy pace so as not to draw attention, and then I stopped by two of Connor's guys standing close together. They'd been waiting for the next move. Almost anxious for it.

"I don't care what you do to me. Just tell me why," Paige begged.

"They knew too much, and they wouldn't leave it alone," Connor said, a bite in his tone.

His words made a connection in my head. If my mother was alive, the Sawyers must have known. Either that, or they had known who had taken her. They had known it was him.

"Well, that's stupid because I don't know anything, yet you've been hunting me."

"There's a lot a kid can overhear and shed light on, unless you're too stupid to remember. But you're here now, so that does explain a lot. Dee, can I trust you to finally finish what should have been done that night, or do I need to take care of her myself?"

"She fell off the side of the building. How was I supposed to know she wasn't dead?" Dee defended.

Connor's jaw tensed. "By doing what I fucking instructed. You shouldn't have left the property until everyone had a fucking bullet. How much clearer could I have been? Months of planning, and you still fucked it up."

Dee hung his head, and I saw the moment Paige fixed her eyes on Brad's weapon tucked into the back of his jeans.

Shit, if she kills Connor, I will never find my mother or my sister, if I have one.

"How could you live with yourself going around kidnapping innocent babies and fucking up their lives? What did you do with Leanne's child? You had to have taken her, too. That's the only thing that makes sense. So where is she?" Paige pressed.

"Watch your fucking mouth. That was my child, and I could have done whatever I goddamn pleased with it." Connor looked at his five men scattered around the room. "Take her to one of the rooms and do whatever you want with her for the next few hours. I'm tired of hearing her fucking mouth. This ends tonight." His eyes stopped on me. "And, since my son claims he doesn't know her, I want to test out Brad's theory. Do your worst to her until Caleb agrees to do what needs to be done. Three lives are in your hands now, Caleb, your call."

"I'll do it," I said.

"What?" he asked.

"I said, I'll do it."

"In that case, we'll keep this one for leverage until then."

Paige grabbed Brad's gun from the back of his jeans just as he was turning to face her. I snatched the weapon from one of the guys next to me before he could grab it. And, as he turned, I pressed the weapon to his heart at the same time I heard Brad let out a loud grunt across the room.

"Don't move." Energy rose from somewhere deep even though I still felt weak and shaky from the lack of food in my system. "Get down on your knees."

When I glanced at Paige, she had the weapon pointed at Alex Connor, and Brad was curled on the floor, cupping his balls a few feet away from her.

"Paige, no," I said the same time about four different guns cocked in the room. She was surrounded, and if she fired, she would die, too. "Paige."

She didn't even look at me. It was like I wasn't even there. She was on a mission, and nothing would stop her. I should have known the moment I had seen her here. She wouldn't have come on a suicide mission unless she was planning to do this. He was the one thing keeping her from moving forward, and she wanted him dead.

Connor moved forward and grabbed the top of the weapon in her hands, whirling around and out of the weapon's danger zone. I had known he would do that even before she pointed the weapon at him. He had been trained, just like the rest of us.

Stepping back, I shot the man in front of me first. As I shifted back some more, I turned to everyone else in the room, squinting and lining up the weapon's front and back sight on the rest of the men in the room, taking out the one closest to Paige first. They wouldn't shoot me unless Connor gave them an order, and in my peripheral vision, Connor was still trying to wrestle the weapon from Paige.

Each bullet that left the weapon in my hand penetrated someone until all five of the men who'd been inside the room were on the floor, groaning.

Brad made a move to get up, and I aimed the weapon at him.

"Don't even think about it," I warned, looking to see the headlock Connor had Paige in, her back to his front. "Let her go."

"Not until she drops her weapon, or maybe I'll just kill her right now."

"You kill her, and you'll be right fucking behind her," I threatened. My voice calmed as I spoke to Paige. "Paige, just drop it."

"Okay."

Connor must have loosened his hold on her when she pretended she was giving in because she used it to her advantage to dip and rotate out of his hold. Only the second she brought her weapon up to point at Connor again, a shot fired. She jerked and glanced at me. It wasn't mine, and it wasn't hers.

Was it hers?

Connor was still standing. With my weapon still raised, my

eyes darted around the room and stopped on Dee's weapon pointed at her.

Shit.

I fired two rounds, and his arm dropped to the floor as he went limp. When I looked back at Paige, her weapon was still pointed at Connor. Dee's shot must have missed her. I didn't see any blood on her, and she was still standing her ground.

"Paige, don't. My mom is still alive. I need him to—"

Her weapon lowered, and she slowly turned to me as I started forward. She inhaled, her breath shaky. "I'm sorry."

"What?"

The weapon fell from her hand.

Is she . . .

She was in all black, so I couldn't tell if there was any blood on her. A hand went to her stomach the same time I heard a loud banging on the door.

"FBI! Open up!"

"You bitch!" Connor spit, backing into his office. "Brad, get in here."

Then I saw it—the blood trickling over the fingers pressed to her stomach. Her knees began to give out, but I caught her in time, and as I dipped, lowering her onto the floor, tears welled in my eyes.

"I'm sorry," she whispered once more.

Setting the weapon down, I pulled the tight tank up over her stomach. She let out a whimper the same time I saw the pool of blood spilling out below her rib cage. Pressing my palm to the wound, I blinked back tears as a huge glob formed in my throat.

"Paige." I shook my head.

"Caleb, I'm sorry," she cried. "I'm so sorry." Her body trembled from her tears.

"It's okay." I swallowed. "We're going to get you to the hospital. You'll be okay."

Her head jerked from side to side as her breaths shortened, face pinched in pain as nonstop tears leaked into her hairline.

"No . . ." I used my other hand to tilt her body up from the floor and saw what I feared. The shot had gone straight through, and a huge pool of blood had already gathered beneath her body. "Shit. Fuck. No." I pressed one hand up to stop the flow from coming out beneath her while pressing down with my other hand on top.

My vision blurred as I looked at her face. "I'm sorry," I told her. "I'm so sorry. This is all my fault."

Tears ran down my face as I tried to think, but all I could think about was how I couldn't let go. If I let go, she would bleed. She couldn't lose any more blood. I had to stop it.

"Caleb, I love you."

My throat closed as I squeezed my eyes shut. Fuck, I couldn't breathe. She was the one dying, but I couldn't fucking breathe.

"I love you," she murmured again.

I opened my mouth, but words evaded me.

A yell came from somewhere behind me. "Sir, put your hands where I can see them. Put your hands above your head."

I shook my head.

"Hands above your head and slowly move away from the body."

I shook my head as Paige nodded.

"Do it. It's okay."

"No," I blubbered, lips trembling. "I can't. I can't."

"Hands above your head."

"I can't!" I yelled. "She needs help."

A hand grabbed my shoulder and yanked me backward, and I watched as my hands involuntarily fell away from her. A hard device pressed into my back and a crippling shock spiraled through my body. A second later, I was flat on the ground. A knee jammed into my back, and my hands were yanked behind me and cuffed.

Fuck. No, no, no. I need to stop the bleeding. She can't die. She can't die.

I tried to look at her and saw the blood flooding down her side. She wasn't being helped . . .

Why isn't anyone helping her?

"Please, she needs help. Someone! Paige . . ."

"You're under arrest for the murder and disappearance of Sophia Cruz. You have the right to remain silent. Anything you say or do . . ."

Chills broke out over my body.

Brad killed Sophia Cruz. She'd been inside his suite that night. But I was sure that wouldn't be what the evidence would say. Sophia Cruz had been wearing the same outfit the night she knocked on my door looking for Brad. I had a drug test done days later after being drugged. It had been a trap for me like I'd known, and I'd walked right into it. But that didn't matter, because as I was dragged outside into the night where about five police cars and three SUVs surrounded the building, my head hung. I was an empty shell. I was walking, but I wasn't here. I was still inside with Paige.

A few radios squawked into the night. "We need an ambulance. Two dead. Three in critical condition . . ."

The door to the backseat of the cop car opened, and I was shoved inside.

She loves me?

Before the door closed, I shivered as wind blew across the hairs on my nape, and her words passed over me.

"Caleb, I love you."

"You love this. You love playing . . . It could heal wrong and bother you for the rest of your life."

"I love you."

"I can't have a quickie. I've just witnessed how flexible you are."

"Don't tell me that unless you're ready to follow through."

"Caleb, I love you."

I felt her leaving me, and I wanted her to stay. She needed to stay.

Please, don't leave me. Please, I can't . . .

I tasted the tears streaming down my cheeks as I pulled my lips into my mouth.

I'm sorry I got mad at you. I'm so sorry.

FORTY-FIVE

Paige

I sat on the edge of the stone well, my legs swinging and the heels of my bare feet hitting the wall as they came back before I kicked them out again. I was in my quiet place. I came here when I was sad, but I couldn't remember why I'd come.

I stared at the gravel path before me that didn't lead anywhere.

Turning around, I looked at the bucket hanging from the gray-dusted wooden beams over the well swaying back and forth. Suddenly, I felt parched.

Why am I here?

The surrounding trees seemed older, and some of the branches were broken and hanging by a thread, ready to fall to the ground with the slightest breeze.

"It's time," a voice said inside my head.

"Time for what?" I asked without uttering a word.

"You're dreaming."

What? I'm not dreaming.

I came here when I wanted to, didn't I?

I stood and watched the leaves swaying back and forth on the trees nearby. A branch snapped and fell to the ground from a breeze I couldn't feel. I looked down at the white frock I was dressed in, soaking wet and sticking to my skin.

What?

I remember this.

Why is this so familiar?

"Hey," a deep voice uttered.

I ignored it, remembering the train wreck I'd felt like the last time I opened my eyes. My body had been heavy, and I couldn't move, couldn't think.

Confused, I walked a few feet ahead before sitting in the middle of the gravel path. Resting my palms against the small stones behind me, I leaned back and tilted my head to the darkened sky.

"Wakey, wakey. I can see your fingers moving."

Calvin.

Calvin?

Where are you?

I stood and moved down the path, but the next step I took forward, I was free-falling.

No, no, no. I inhaled. *No. Not again.*

My eyes flew open as I inhaled. I glanced around the room I was in, and my eyes quickly found Calvin sitting in a chair next to the bed.

"There she is."

My throat was excessively dry, and I felt sick to my stomach. The hospital. I was still here. The first time I'd opened my eyes, I had been alone. That was why I had gone to the well. But it had been a dream.

"You okay?" he asked.

I gave him a blank stare as my mind tried to piece together my reality.

Caleb.

I tried to swallow, but my throat was too dry, and when I spoke, my voice came out hoarse. "Caleb. What happened?" I coughed and winced at the pain ripping into my gut. My hand immediately rose from my side to cover the tender area.

Calvin stood and handed me a cup. "Here's some water. Sip slowly and don't move."

I removed my hand from beneath the blanket. With the back of the bed slightly raised, I could drink without moving, but I coughed again, almost spilling the water over myself. I cringed, handing him the cup as my insides tore apart. "Ah."

He placed it on a white stand nearby and grabbed a pillow that had been resting at the foot of the bed. Placing it on my stomach, he explained, "The nurse said it would ease the pain when you needed to cough or move. Just hold it to your stomach when you need to do either."

I looked up at him, my eyes pleading.

"He's in jail . . . without bond."

My chest grew heavy, and my breath shortened. "He shot all those guys. It's my fault."

"Hey. Don't go there."

"But, Calvin, I shouldn't have . . . if I hadn't . . . I'm sorry."

"Shh. There are officers outside, waiting to get a statement from you. Two guards are standing by as well." He took a seat again and leaned forward.

"He shot them to protect me," I said, closing my eyes. "He can't go to jail for that. I'll tell them it was me. I'll tell them I'm the one who did it."

"You can't do that." Calvin pressed the heel of his palm to his forehead. "He already admitted to shooting them. Also, that isn't even what he was charged with." He sighed. "He's being charged with the murder of some Sophia Cruz."

"What? Who is that?"

Calvin shook his head. "Some girl who disappeared sometime ago. They have hard evidence that Caleb was responsible. Not only that, but"—his Adam's apple bobbed as he swallowed—"he also confessed to burying her."

"What?" My eyes widened, and my heart stopped. I had no words, but when I was finally able to speak, I said, "I don't believe it."

Calvin nodded, but his expression remained neutral. I thought about the last few weeks and how hurt Caleb had been that the nurse had been caught by his father.

"Connor probably forced him to. He wouldn't have killed anyone," I confirmed, frowning. *Except Alex Connor's men.* "How about Alex Connor? Did they get him?"

He shook his head.

"What?" A cough sidled up my throat again, and I swallowed, trying to relax.

"They raided the whole house, and they couldn't find him or Brad."

"That's impossible. They were there. How long has it been?"

"You've been here for a day. And you've been out for a few hours. It's eleven in the morning right now."

I shook my head and swallowed the nausea rising from my stomach to the base of my throat. "I can't stay here. I need to go somewhere safe. After what I've done, Calvin, he's coming for me. I can't stay here."

"Okay, we'll figure this out. Caleb mailed a package to us. It seems you won't have to worry about your medical bills. He also signed over the condo to you and me."

I frowned as I continued to listen.

"He called me yesterday. He didn't even ask for a lawyer, but I've been trying to find one. I figure we can use the money he's given us for that. He sounded lost. Like he'd given up. He asked about you, and I told him you were in the ICU. It was all I knew at the time. But he knows Brad and Connor are still out here, and . . . he said to tell you he's sorry. He also said Alex Connor had told him his mom and sister were alive and locked away somewhere."

My mouth fell open. "His sister . . . his mom is alive? Oh my God . . . Leanne was pregnant." I turned my head to him as my brain searched through the scraps I'd gotten out of Connor. "He said it was his baby. That was who they replaced me with, Calvin. Leanne was pregnant. Leanne was Olivia's best friend. If Connor had raped

Olivia. Olivia must have told Leanne, so he probably did the same to Leanne as a warning and kidnapped her baby when it was born. She's still alive." I shook my head. "When I was young . . . I remember my dad and mom having a small disagreement in the studio. I think he had hired a private investigator. That meant my mom must have told my dad what had happened to her. Maybe that was why there was a P.I. involved. My parents were trying to find their real daughter. I think that was why they were killed. It has to be. Shit. Caleb's sister and mom are alive." I sighed, bringing my hand to my head at the onset of a headache. "Shit, Calvin. I screwed everything up."

"It sounds like you're solving it to me."

"No." I shook my head. "Alex Connor got away. He knows the cops are after him now. I don't think he's going to be showing his face anywhere anytime soon. And, if Caleb has reason to believe his sister and mom are hidden somewhere, how are we ever going to find them?" I took a few painful deep breaths as I got worked up.

Lowering my voice, I admitted, "I almost killed Alex Connor. I was so close. I don't know what stopped me." I paused to think about it. "Caleb was watching me. That was why. That was the only reason I didn't kill him. Is that horrible?"

"No. He's a criminal, and he ruined your life, Paige. You have every right to want that bastard dead." His lips twitched. "And right now, Bailey told me that with all the shit you got Connor to confess to, you're kind of heroic and crazy. You remember that copy of Caleb's keys you had me make?"

I nodded.

"It's what the FBI used to get inside the building. It's probably what saved your life. Everything I know, I heard from Bailey, by the way. She was here all night, too. She left not too long ago."

I bit my lip and looked down. "You know, I barely felt when it happened. I mean . . . there was a burn or something. But I was just shocked, not wanting to believe it *had* happened. Then I looked at Caleb. His gun was pointed in my direction, and for a split second, I thought he was the one who had done it to stop me from killing his father. I thought Caleb had shot me when he was searching for the person who had." I shook my head as tears filled my eyes. "It feels so shitty. Why would I have thought that? I love him, Calvin, but dammit, I don't deserve him." I swallowed before taking a deep breath. "He doesn't deserve to be in jail either, and I'm going to do whatever it takes to get him out. I owe him that."

"He's never had that, you know," Calvin said.

"What?" I asked as my queasiness worsened.

"What he has with you."

"Don't say that." I shook my head and closed my eyes for a second. "You're not helping." I inhaled slowly, trying not to aggravate the pain and nausea in my stomach. "Do you know how long my recovery will be?"

"I don't know. I'll get the nurse."

"Thank you, and, Calvin, my grandparents. I know they'll find us a good lawyer for Caleb."

His lips pursed. He nodded before turning and ambling out the door, the top of his head barely missing the top of the frame as he walked out.

Stacy Lenard walked into the room a few seconds later, and the quick breath I sucked in tightened the muscles in my sore abs. I winced, holding the pillow firm against my stomach. Caleb had sworn they'd taken her, but I highly freaking doubted it, not after seeing her looking so at home in Alex Connor's house. I needed to get out of here. As the last of the heavy breaths I'd inhaled aired from my lungs, I smiled.

"How are you feeling?" she asked.

"Good," I said with a small shake of my head, the smile never leaving my face. "Better."

Calvin stood behind her, his forehead furrowing.

I sent him a message with my eyes. *Don't ask.*

"Well, good. You're one lucky girl. Since the bullet went straight through, there weren't any significant damage. The surgeons took care of everything while you were under. But, now that you're awake, I'll let the doctor know as soon as he's done with his current patient. For now, I can tell you that there is an estimated recovery time noted in your chart for two months if you heal well and no other problems arise, such as infections."

As she walked up to the IV stand to check the fluid, I peered up in caution, checking out her perfect manicure and relaxed expression.

What the fuck is she doing here?

"That's good," I said. It wasn't good.

That's a really long time. Will I be able to work out? How am I going to do anything? I can barely breathe without pain right now.

"Are you sure you aren't in any pain?" she asked.

"Nope, I'm good."

"Okay, well, I'll go find your doctor."

As she went through the doorway, I peered at the IV cords leading into my veins at the crook of my elbow, wanting to drag them out. I didn't trust that woman. Drugs or anything could be seeping into my veins. "Calvin, I'm not spending another night in this place."

"I don't think you have a choice in that, Miss Wells."

I looked up to see Superintendent Rodriguez, who I remembered all too well from the highway and the station.

She stood in the doorway for a second longer before she moved forward. "I have a few questions for you."

"Funny, so do I. Did you help Alex Connor kill my parents? Did you watch him kill them, or did you show up after to help hide evidence, like a good little helper? How about when I was kidnapped?"

She glanced over her shoulder at Calvin. "Sir, I need you to leave the room while I get a statement."

My unblinking eyes remained fixed on her screwed-up face. "He isn't going anywhere. Ask me your damn questions."

I bet Stacy Lenard was also on Alex Connor's payroll. It had to be why she'd taken a vacation—to make it seem like she was missing or being abused so they could fuck with Caleb's head.

"He can either walk out of here on his own, or I'll have my officers escort him out." Rodriguez rested one of her hands on the weapon at her hip.

I didn't know if she meant it as a threat, but she didn't get to see my weakness. She deserved every bit of my crazy.

So, I mumbled, "No, you won't. You're screwed. Just like Connor. You sit back and watch innocent people die. Help cover it up when it's your job to unveil it. What are you going to do next? Try to make sure *I* go away?" I made a small chuckle in my throat without wincing at the pain it'd instigated. Then I looked her dead in the eyes. "I'm not going away, Rodriguez. I'm going to be your worst fucking nightmare."

Olivia Sawyer was out there somewhere.

The real Paige Sawyer was out there somewhere. I'd involuntarily stolen her life, her identity, and I just hoped life hadn't been too hard on her, but I would find her. I would help her.

I would help them.

Madelyn Wells never had a chance, and I couldn't be her when I'd been Paige Sawyer my whole life. But I was alive for a reason, and I wasn't going to waste it. But I also wasn't going to stop until everyone was okay. Until Caleb was okay. Until I was okay.

Will I ever be okay? Will we?

TO BE CONTINUED . . .

ALSO BY CASEY DIAM

Romantic Suspense

Danger & Attraction Trilogy
Risking Trust
Risking Hope
Risking Love

Contemporary

Alpen Springs Series
Can You Hear It
Bad Choices and Heartaches
Heat and Summer Love

ABOUT THE AUTHOR

Some years ago, Casey rediscovered her passion for writing and hasn't stopped writing since. She writes sexy, funny, steamy, and emotional stories that are a bit more in depth, but so much fun to read.

Casey is an Army Veteran who loves to travel. She has a ridiculously short attention span and loves coffee and tea. She was born and raised in Jamaica, and apart from reading and writing, she loves to snowboard.

For questions or news about
Casey and her books, connect with her.
She loves to hear from her readers!

Casey's Reader Group
www.facebook.com/groups/CaseyDiam

Newsletter
www.caseydiam.com/newsletter

Website
caseydiam.com

CPSIA information can be obtained
at www.ICGtesting.com
Printed in the USA
BVHW071340100521
606942BV00006B/1001